Jack Batten, after a brief and unhappy career as a lawyer, has been a very happy Toronto freelance writer for many years. He has written thirty-five books, including four crime novels featuring Crang, the unorthodox criminal lawyer who has a bad habit of stumbling on murders that need his personal attention. Batten reviewed jazz for the *Globe and Mail* for several years, reviewed movies on CBC Radio for twenty-five-years, and now reviews crime novels for the *Toronto Star*. Not surprisingly, jazz, movies, and crime turn up frequently in Crang's life.

Books of Merit

TAKE FIVE

JACK BATTEN

TAKE FIVE

A CRANG MYSTERY

THOMAS ALLEN PUBLISHERS
TORONTO

Library and Archives Canada Cataloguing in Publication

Batten, Jack, 1932–
Take five / Jack Batten.
(A Crang mystery)

Issued also in electronic formats.
ISBN 978-1-77102-273-6

I. Title. II. Series: Batten, Jack, 1932– . Crang mystery.

PS8553.A833T33 2013   C813'.54   C2012-907834-4

Editor: Janice Zawerbny
Cover design: Michel Vrana
Cover image: design56/istockphoto.com

Published by Thomas Allen Publishers,
a division of Thomas Allen & Son Limited,
390 Steelcase Road East,
Markham, Ontario L3R 1G2 Canada

www.thomasallen.ca

ONTARIO ARTS COUNCIL
CONSEIL DES ARTS DE L'ONTARIO

Canada Council   Conseil des Arts
for the Arts   du Canada

The publisher gratefully acknowledges the support of
The Ontario Arts Council for its publishing program.

We acknowledge the support of the Canada Council for the Arts, which
last year invested $20.1 million in writing and publishing throughout Canada.

We acknowledge the Government of Ontario through the
Ontario Media Development Corporation's Ontario Book Initiative.

We acknowledge the financial support of the Government of Canada
through the Canada Book Fund for our publishing activities.

13 14 15 16 17 5 4 3 2 1

Text printed on a 100% PCW recycled stock

Printed and bound in Canada

For Victor

1

Judge Harry Keough was tearing a strip off me.

"For crissake, Crang," Keough said, "how could you lose a client? A guy who's been around the criminal courts as long as you? Your woman's supposed to be in court for sentencing this morning, and you lose her? I mean, come on, Crang, this is embarrassing for everybody concerned. Me included."

"If you don't mind, Judge," I said, "could we think about rephrasing the situation?"

"Like how?"

"More nuanced, along the lines of my client keeping me in the dark about her plan not to show up today?"

"It all comes down to the same damn thing."

"Maybe we're just debating emphasis," I said. "Mine's on the client giving me the slip."

"You're not convincing me, Crang," Keough said.

"That's odd," I said. "It happens to be true she gave me the slip."

It was ten-thirty on a June Monday morning. The judge and I were sitting in his chambers on the third floor of Osgoode Hall. We still wore our courtroom costumes, black gown and vest for me with a stiff white collar and a dickey. Keough's gown came with a slash of scarlet. It made him look like Ruritanian nobility.

The judge stayed on his rant.

"All you counsel agreed on the plea, unanimous with every-body," he said. "Your woman and the guy, her co-accused, the two of them admitted guilt. The Crown lawyers agreed. So no trial's necessary. Nothing to do in court today except the sentencing, and we're wrapped up before lunchtime. Everybody signed off on it. What could be simpler? And you can't keep your end of the bargain."

Keough was a tough old bird, more than thirty years on the bench. He had an erect build and a full head of wiry white hair. The lines on his face looked as deep and permanent as the Grand Canyon.

"With respect, Judge," I said, though what I was feeling was more like irritation, "my client may have a convincing reason for staying out of touch. Maybe a third party's responsible in ways we don't know about. Got her in his clutches."

"Damn case is making me grumpier than usual."

"Even her cell's turned off."

"Does she have a real phone?" Keough asked. "A land line's what I'm talking about. Can't get used to that phrase. Land line, what a ridiculous thing to call an ordinary telephone."

"Hers isn't in service."

Keough made a sighing sound and shifted in his chair to face out the window to his right. The view was west over Osgoode's green and perfect lawns to University Avenue, which wasn't perfect unless you liked traffic twenty-four hours a day.

The judge turned back to his desk and shuffled through a stack of court documents. "When did you last see . . . uh . . . what's her name again? Never laid eyes on the woman myself."

"This would have been her first appearance in anything except bail court," I said. "No reason for you to have seen her before. Anyway, the answer's Nguyen, Judge. My client's Grace Nguyen. Her co-accused is George Wu."

"Yeah," he said, checking the names against a court paper in front of him. He looked up, an expression on his face I'd call petulant. "Woman probably just got cold feet. What'd she seem like the last time you talked to her?"

"Unreadable, same as usual," I said. "Saw her yesterday afternoon in my office for a preview of today's events. What was going to happen when she got walked from the courtroom to the clink. Went over all that with her. The prospect didn't fill her with dread. Nothing seems to."

"That's the Chinese for you. Inscrutable."

"Your Honour," I said, "a lot of people might think what you just said is racist. Besides, she's Vietnamese. Came here as a little girl."

"Boat people, right?"

"Wrong," I said. "Grace reached Canada years after that."

Keough grinned. "You think I'm getting myself in deep with the political correctness monitors?"

"I'm not going to rat you out, Judge, if that's what's on your mind."

Keough flapped his hand in my direction. "My problem," he said, "it's how do I wrap this case up when one of the two players is somewhere in the wind? Biggest marijuana grow op in Canadian history is what I heard."

"Those are police numbers, Your Honour," I said. "Exaggerated without a doubt."

My objection was what we criminal lawyers call pro forma. Defence counsel were expected to complain. It was our role in the legal fandango. But this time, my heart wasn't in the moan about the figures. The cops had nailed Nguyen and Wu for running grow op houses across Metro Toronto that produced forty thousand marijuana plants. That was enough dope to bring in thirty million bucks on the drug market. The numbers were too solid for me to make a dent in. They were the reason for the guilty pleas.

I glanced around the judge's chambers. A golf putter was leaning against the wall near the door. On the floor, at the far end of a Persian rug, there was a little plastic contraption with a hole in the middle. I hadn't swung a golf club in years, but I knew the contraption was for the judge to practice his putting.

"Got a foursome later this afternoon," Keough said, noticing me noticing the golf paraphernalia. "But before I leave, we'll all go back to court first thing after lunch, and set a new sentencing date."

"And in the meantime," I said, "between now and whatever new date you set, you expect me to find my client? Am I reading our little exchange the right way, Judge?"

"The law doesn't make a counsel responsible for producing a missing accused person. But in this case, I'd appreciate it."

"I'll put my best efforts to it, Judge."

"You know I'm retiring in five months? Seventy-five my next birthday. It's mandatory."

"And you don't want to leave any messes behind you?"

The judge nodded. "Not a big deal to most people, but it is to me."

"One hot bulletin for you, Judge," I said, "I've already got my investigator beating the bushes for Grace."

The judge raised his eyebrows, which were as thick and silvery as his hair. "Get you, Crang. Now you've got an investigator." He stretched each syllable in in-ves-ti-ga-tor.

"Part-time," I said. "But he's a pretty sharp cookie."

"What'd this investigator of yours work at before he started investigating?"

I hesitated before I answered. "A related field."

Keough gave me a long look. "What's this, Crang? Now you're playing your cards close to the vest? Like you said, we're just having a little exchange here. What's your guy's name?"

I shrugged. "Maury Samuels. That mean anything to you?"

"Should it?"

"Thought it might."

"Off the top of my head, the name doesn't register," Keough said. He stood up from his swivel chair. "You want coffee, Crang?

Got a pretty slick steward looks after this part of the building. He says he gets his coffee in a deal with a foreign outfit. Unique to us judges. You aware of a coffee from Kenya?"

"Only every time I pass the coffee section in Loblaws."

"Loblaws?" The judge looked baffled. "It doesn't come directly from Nairobi?"

"Not unless you're talking about Nairobi Avenue out in the east end."

"You're joking me, Crang."

"I am about Nairobi Avenue."

"But not about Loblaws?"

I shook my head. "The steward's running his little game on you, Judge."

"Well, hell," Keough said. "But it still tastes damn fine."

While Keough and I were talking, I'd felt the cell in my pocket vibrate. After the judge left the room, I pulled the cell out, and scrolled down till I found a text timed a few minutes earlier. It was from Maury, telling me to meet him outside Grace Nguyen's condo building at eleven-fifty. Why was he so specific about the time? A bigger mystery was the last line in the text. Wear your gown. Then he repeated the same thing in capital letters. WEAR YOUR GON. The misspelling must have meant Maury was in a rush. Was the rush a favourable sign? Could be.

The judge came back into his chambers carrying a small silver tray holding two china cups and saucers in an elegant-looking blue-and-white pattern. Both cups were filled close to the brim.

I sipped some of the coffee from Kenya. The stuff had a nice hit to it.

"Your guy the steward makes a powerful cup," I said. "No wonder you judges don't nod off on the bench the way some used to."

Keough frowned at me.

"I heard from Maury," I said, rushing before the judge got more freaked over my crack. "Maybe nothing to be excited about, but I'm meeting him at my client's condo later this morning."

"Results count, Crang," the judge said. He went at his coffee with big slurps. "Keep that in mind."

I said I would. I sipped some more Kenyan and resolved to buy a package from Loblaws on my next shopping trip.

"Let me ask you something," Keough said.

The judge put down his coffee cup, stood up and walked over to the putter leaning against the wall. He waggled it three or four times, loosening his wrists.

"This morning," Keough said, "my wife dropped me off down here close to nine-thirty. That's awfully damn late for me. So I took a shortcut through the courthouse instead of going all the way around to the Osgoode entrance. Happened to see you over by that snack counter on the first floor where they serve the watery coffee. You were talking to a tall man in a very nice tweed sports coat."

He took a golf ball out of his pants pocket and dropped it on the rug about four feet from the plastic contraption.

"You with me so far?" the judge asked.

"If you're wondering about the guy in the very nice tweed jacket, yeah, it was Maury."

Keough lined up his ball and stroked it. The ball went in the contraption's hole.

"Nice putt, Judge," I said. "Ms. Nguyen was supposed to meet me at the snack counter at eight forty-five. When she didn't show by nine-fifteen, I called Maury. Got him to go looking for the lady."

"I've seen Mr. Samuels someplace before," the judge said. "Terrible at names, but I don't forget a face."

"Even twenty years back, give or take?"

"Twenty years is nothing at my age."

The judge lined up his ball for another putt. This one was from about eight feet.

"A longish putt there, Your Honour," I said.

"It's a game I play against myself. Double the length of the putt until I miss. Then I have to start over."

The judge putted. His eight-footer fell into the cup.

"So tell me where I saw Maury Samuels twenty years ago, give or take," he said. "I'm thinking it must have been in court."

"The jury had convicted Maury," I said. "You were handing out the sentence."

"Aha."

"Aha?"

The judge's aha sounded more triumphant than mine.

"What'd I give Mr. Samuels?" he asked me.

"Two and a half years."

The judge stood over the ball for his next putt, a sixteen-footer.

"Two and a half?" he said. "That meant penitentiary time, but not too much of it."

He stepped away from his putt but kept his back to me. I was still sipping the Kenyan.

"I can't imagine you acted for Mr. Samuels at the trial," the judge said. "You're not that old."

"Didn't get my call until a couple of years after that," I said. "So, no, I didn't act for Maury. Never have. He's just a guy I got to know pretty well around the courthouse."

"What did I give him the two and a half for?"

I let a beat go by before I answered. "Break and enter, Your Honour."

The judge's back stiffened just a little. If he was bothered about Maury's past and his current role in the Nguyen case, and I felt sure he was, the stiffened back was the only giveaway he allowed himself. He moved away from the ball again.

"Can I assume Mr. Samuels isn't currently in difficulties?" Keough asked me. "With the law, I'm talking about? Not still doing break and enters?"

"The time you put Maury away," I said, "it's the only sentence he ever served, the only time he went through a trial. His record's clean as a whistle since then."

Keough concentrated again on his sixteen-foot putt. The damn putting was getting on my nerves, but I wasn't about to tell him to knock it off. The guy was a judge. He could give me the time to find Grace before the cops got into the hunt or he could cut me off at the pass. He stroked the sixteen-footer. It went in the hole. He set up his next putt. This one was in the neighbourhood of thirty-two feet.

Still with his back to me, the judge said, "I need to make one thing clear."

"Name it, Judge."

"If Mr. Samuels is successful in his search for Ms. Nguyen, there's no need in law for you to inform the court how he carried out his responsibilities."

I couldn't blame Keough for his caution. The man was about to retire, and he didn't want somebody like Maury smudging his lifetime reputation as a straight shooter when he was so close to stepping down.

"Rest assured, Judge," I said.

"You know, Mr. Crang," the judge said, tilting his head in my direction, "you're somewhat known for impetuous action."

"Not really warranted, if I may say so, Your Honour," I said. "I only have the interests of my clients at heart."

Jesus, I thought, where had the homilies come from? If I wasn't careful, the next words out of my mouth would be something about calling them like I see them.

"Okay, Mr. Crang," Keough said, his attention back over the golf ball, "I'll delay sentencing for three weeks. I'll even continue her bail, and you see what you can do about bringing Ms. Nguyen to court."

"We're in business, Judge."

Keough tapped the thirty-two-footer. It lipped out to the right.

"Hell and damnation," he said.

2

Toronto's early summer was out in full force. Clear blue sky, brilliant sun, young women wearing bright dresses with sandals revealing toenails painted in colours not known to nature. In this summer parade, I played the role of the horse's ass in the lawyer's gown. Gowns weren't meant for wearing beyond the doors of courtrooms. On the street, I felt like a kid decked out in a Halloween costume on a day that wasn't October 31.

I was walking east on Queen, aimed for Grace Nguyen's condo on Lombard Street. No more than fifteen minutes from Osgoode Hall. Passing City Hall, I detoured to one of the long benches next to the ornamental pool on Nathan Phillips Square. I took off the gown and folded it into my briefcase, careful to minimize the wrinkle factor. Gownlessness liberated me, and I sat on the bench to ponder an approach to the Grace Nguyen crisis.

In no time at all, my mind wandered to questions of a more abstract nature. Why did City Hall's council chamber look so dorky? Was it the shape? Like an unopened clam? Across Bay Street to my right, Old City Hall seemed as always to be hunching in the shade of the newer building. More than just metaphorically. Did anybody ever call the old one dorky? Probably, but now it just looked ancient, distinguished and lovable.

My cell trilled. Cheri Havlat, the screen read. Did I really want to speak to her? Cheri was one of the *Sun*'s crime reporters, a perky person a couple of years out of Ryerson journalism school. If crime reporters got any younger, I'd be dandling them on my knee. Cheri had been in the courtroom that morning, and I'd given her a quick interview about the fiasco over my absentee client. I told her Grace's present whereabouts were a mystery to me. Talk about clichés, those were my actual words. "A mystery to me." If I were Cheri, I'd be phoning me back too. Asking if I could produce something a smidge less lame than what I'd said. All right, I owed Cheri a livelier quote. I'd talk to her. Besides, I liked any chance at getting my name in the papers.

"What can I do for you, Cheri?" I said into my cell.

"Hey, Crang, good news." Cheri was bubbly when she wanted a favour. "And I know you like to see your name in the paper."

Oh dear, was I that obvious?

"My editors want me to go in depth on the story of Nguyen and Wu's grow op," Cheri said. "Tell the readers the nitty-gritty about the drug scheme, especially Nguyen's part in it all. Which is where you come in."

"How deep in depth?"

"Well, you know, juicy but not too many words. This is for *Sun* readers, remember."

"The lips-moving crowd."

"We don't say that around here."

Were people who worked for employers of low accomplishment aware that their outfit stunk? Maybe they were, and just put a brave face on it. Or maybe they knew more than I did about the wonders they wrought. I never read the *Sun* except the crime news when I thought a case of mine might get a mention. Did that qualify me as an expert in *Sun* matters? Not even close.

"What do you know about the case already?" I said to Cheri. "Wouldn't want to repeat old news."

"Nguyen was in real estate sales, and so was Wu."

I got myself settled on the bench.

"That was in their legitimate lives," I said. "Wu bought and sold commercial properties, Grace did houses. That gave her an edge, her knowing the home-rental market, in the way they organized their grow op business."

"What's she like, this Grace?" Cheri asked. "I've only seen pictures of her."

"Beautiful. First thing you notice is her good looks. Beyond that, she's not what you'd call giving of herself in the social sense. Driven, ambitious to make big bucks any way she can. Tends to be abrupt. Shirty even. But when it comes to her line of business patter, she can be pretty much irresistible. Butter wouldn't melt in her mouth, that kind of thing. Charm the birds out of the trees."

"This is awesome, Crang. Now tell me how she used her talents for, like, illegal purposes."

I felt as if puffs of smoke were coming out of my ears. Jesus, I hated the way kids tossed around that word. Duke Ellington was awesome in every sense. The Eiffel Tower. Caravaggio. But nothing I'd said so far about the grow op case came near to awesome. And it never would. Had I already given Cheri my lecture on the subject? Would it be worth beating my gums again? It wouldn't. That was my snap decision.

"The process, Cheri," I said, "began with Grace approaching people she heard of who wanted to rent their homes for two, three years, unfurnished. The way Grace put it to each of the homeowners, she had just the right tenants for their house. She'd say her people were a couple with good jobs. Their kids were honours students, behaved themselves, no drugs. All that, the perfect family."

"What was the catch?" Cheri asked.

"There were no families, perfect or otherwise," I said. "Grace made them up. She invented the families, and forged signatures for these phantom people on the leasing documents. She got her hands on seventy-three houses that way."

"Those were the houses where the grow ops got started?" Cheri asked.

"Yeah, marijuana farms. That was Wu's side of the enterprise."

I told Cheri about Wu putting a couple of guys in each house to grow marijuana. Everybody called these guys farmers. Wu supplied the farmers with marijuana seedlings and all the grow equipment. Humidifiers, coolers, planters, ventilating systems, lights with super-high-wattage bulbs to grow the crops in the planters. Explaining all of this to Cheri, I had to slow down to fill her in on the role of each piece of equipment. It was background stuff, as detailed as I could make it. I told Cheri how the farmers did other things around the houses like mowing the lawns to keep each place looking respectable. Whatever they could do to make it less likely the neighbours would get nosy or complain.

"Awesome scheme," Cheri said.

"I bet you don't put that word in any of your stories," I said. "Awesome."

"Of course not," Cheri said. "This one old guy on the copy desk just edits it out anyway."

I was thinking of asking the age of the geezer editor. But the air all of a sudden got very noisy around me. A class of kids had arrived at the ornamental pool. Eight-year-olds by their looks. Three teachers acted as shepherds. One wore a hijab. The kids were screaming and yelling.

"Crang," Cheri said on the phone, "are you still there?"

"Talk louder, Cheri," I said.

"Just tell me how Grace and Wu got caught," Cheri shouted.

"Their own people's bungles mostly," I said. "A couple of farmers in one house let the condensation from the high temperatures inside build on the windows. That bothered a neighbour, and he phoned the cops. Another house, a guy at Toronto Hydro noticed the hydro bill was way up. Growing pot uses a lot of power. So the cops raided the two houses, and that was when a pretty sharp drug detective picked up something that broke the case open."

The kids playing around the ornamental swimming pool in front of me had taken off their shoes and were paddling in the water. That brought a robust woman security guard to the scene. She told the kids the pool was for looking at, not playing in. The hijabed teacher said the guard was ruining the kids' fun. Voices were raised.

"Crang, you hearing me?" Cheri said. "What'd the sharp detective come up with?"

"What he noticed," I said, "was Grace's name on both leases, the one for the house with the condensation and the other with the sky-high hydro bill. Cops put wiretaps on Grace's phone, then on Wu's."

The security guard and the teacher with the hijab were getting into it at the pool. An obscenity flew through the air. I was pretty sure it came from the teacher. The guys at her mosque would go ballistic if they knew about this.

Cheri was still on the phone. "It was a pretty clever scheme Grace and the other guy thought up."

"Clever but doomed," I said. "Four years after the wiretaps, we were in court."

Cheri thanked me, and before another awesome could pass her lips, I clicked off. As soon as I did, the cell chirped again. I checked the screen and answered.

"Maury," I said, "I'm on my way."

"From the sound of wherever the hell you are," Maury said, "you're coming by way of a friggin' war zone."

"It's a debate over water rights," I said. "I'm thinking of offering my lawyerly wisdom."

"I need you here," Maury said. "You're gonna love what I got."

3

Maury was pissed off.

"Goddammit, Crang, you didn't get my message about the gown?" he said. "You're sabotaging my strategy."

We were standing in a delivery alley across Lombard Street from Grace's condo. Not exactly skulking, but not making ourselves obvious either.

"A strategy is always good, Maury," I said, "but you didn't mention one on the phone."

"The gown, man. Where's the gown?"

"In my briefcase."

"Well, put the thing on. It's what'll make the plan work."

The very nice Harris tweed sports coat Maury wore was in many shades of brown. He had on dark grey flannels with discreet pleats. He wore a light brown shirt and a darker brown wool tie with a Windsor knot. People think of criminals as guys in black suits, white shirts and big cufflinks. But those were mob guys. Maury was never mob. When I met him, he was just a big, good-looking man with a lot of wavy hair who liked to watch trials in his spare time. Maury introduced himself to me back then, saying, "I'm a member of the subculture." It was a significant distinction from mob person. Though, as I told Judge Keough, I never acted for Maury himself, my practice tended to run to subculture people. I shied away from mob guys, and they from me.

Certainly no gangster kingpins had beaten down my door begging me to represent them in major prosecutions. Not my thing.

Before his retirement, Maury was an independent burglar, the kind who went into rooms in luxury hotels late at night when the customers were sound asleep, their baubles and valuables strewn on tables and bureaus. Maury had been caught at his labours only the one time when Keough sentenced him. He put in decades more of successful B and E work, not quitting until he got older and less adroit, apt to awaken the dozing schmoes in the beds. Maury turned sixty-five a year or two ago.

"Here's the picture, Crang," Maury said. "The condo's manager with the French title says Grace hasn't been around for five, six months that he remembers."

"The concierge?"

"Yeah, that guy. He says Grace and her boyfriend both moved out."

"Boyfriend?" I said. "Grace never mentioned one of those."

"The concierge says her bills still get paid every month, condo fees, taxes, so on, so forth. And somebody picks up the mail."

"Meaning she hasn't vanished altogether."

"The strategy I'm talking about," Maury said, "we want to have a look through her apartment, am I right?"

"It's all we've got to work with at the moment."

"Maybe we pick up a clue, correct?"

"Clues are helpful."

Maury looked to either side as if he was checking the neighbourhood for eavesdroppers. There was nobody within thirty feet. He lowered his voice anyway.

"Crang, they guard this place like Fort Knox."

"Isn't there a Canadian version of that simile? The place where we keep our gold?"

"Just a goddamn figure of speech," Maury said. "Anyway, to get into the condo building, the concierge needs to give everybody the okay. You know, let people past security and through to the elevators."

"Do I really want to know where my gown fits into your plan?"

"You're going too fast. I got more analysis here."

"Analyze away, Maury."

Maury rubbed his hands together. "The concierge, the guy I been talking to about Nguyen, we can't pull the gown idea on him. He'd be suspicious after me asking him the Nguyen questions."

"When's he go off duty?"

"That's the point. Noon he leaves, and a guy named Kevin takes over." Maury looked at his watch. "We got fifteen minutes to wait for Kevin."

"Now tell me what the thing you call the gown idea adds up to."

"This is the beauty part, Crang," Maury said. "We go in, you wearing your gown, and I tell Kevin you're a judge, I'm your clerk, and we're here for a meeting with the broad in apartment 1409. We're gonna explain to her, at her request, what happens next week when you marry her and her boyfriend, you being a judge."

Was Maury crazy? Me pretending I was a judge? What kind of wacko idea was that? On the other hand, I needed to find Grace, the sooner the better, and this might be as good an opening gambit as any.

"I spent the last hour setting it up," Maury was saying. "Got the broad's name in 1409. Emily Drake. I know where she goes every day, where she works it must be. She happens to be there at this minute, miles away in York Mills. Everything's breaking just right, Crang. This Emily woman's out of the way."

"Nice to know that part's taken care of," I said.

"Crang, listen to me," he said, speaking with great enthusiasm. "All you have to do is look superior the way a judge does. I'll take care of the chatter with Kevin. Get him to let us past security.

We ride all the way up to the fourteenth floor in case Kevin happens to be watching the elevator indicator, him making sure we're going where we said. Unlikely he'd do that, but you never know. Then we take the stairs down to Nguyen's floor, number 808."

I let a couple of beats go by. "Maury," I said, "it's a cockamamie plan."

"I know it is, for crissake," Maury said. "But are you in?"

"I'm in," I said. "Now I'm going to tell you why."

Maury looked at his watch. "This gonna take long?"

"Edited version," I said. "I just want you to know the whole story. I don't want to be holding anything out on you."

I waited while a gaggle of chatty middle-aged ladies passed us coming from the health club farther along Lombard.

"This entire pain-in-the-ass situation about Grace," I said, "goes back to the deal I made with her four years ago. When I took her case, we agreed she would pay me a big advance out front."

"The advance is the problem we're working on?"

I shook my head. "She paid it without a whimper."

"So what're we sweating about?"

"From the time Grace came to me, her head was set on pleading guilty. It was the same with George Wu and his lawyer. But first, before I signed on to the guilty pleas, I looked at the case from all the angles, spent months on the thing, fine-tooth combed it, and there was no doubt the cops had her and Wu cold. No wiggle room for the defence, not a reasonable doubt to be found. So, from the start, Grace and Wu resigned themselves to doing the time. Maybe both of them've got some of the drug money stashed away in the Bahamas, Liechtenstein, some dodgy place like that. I don't know. Don't care. Got nothing to do with my job."

"What's the part that went wrong?"

"I spent the past four years negotiating with the Crown about Grace's plea, the sentence, the whole deal. Felt like I took a thousand meetings. At the end of all this, according to our agreement from the beginning, Grace would pay me the balance of my fee before she went behind bars."

"I was right? It is all about the money?"

"Which she agreed to bring me this morning," I said.

"It's always the money in deals like this."

"Maury, how do I know?" I said. "I've never been in a deal like this before."

"How much?"

"Seventy-five big ones," I said.

"Seventy-five grand?"

"In round numbers."

"She owes you this money, and we need to find her?"

"In a nutshell."

Maury looked at his watch again. "My plan is synchronized."

"With whom?" I asked.

"Tell you later," Maury said. "Put the gown on. The way I organized it, we gotta walk through the front door of the building over there at 12:01. Exactly."

4

Maury and I crossed Lombard, me giving my gown a flourish, and arrived in the condo's lobby right on the minute. The condo building was relatively up to date in style, eight or nine years old at the most. The lobby had marble floors and several nice framed prints of ye olde Toronto on the walls. The reception desk was made of wood polished to a dark glow. Flanking the desk on either side, trying to look casual about it, were two muscular guys in tan trousers and dark grey blazers. Security, for sure. Behind the desk stood a tall reddish-haired kid with a metal clip on the lapel of his blazer, which was also dark grey. "Kevin Walker," read the name on the clip.

"Kevin, nice to meet you," Maury said in a big voice, reaching out to shake the kid's hand. As he spoke, Maury nodded in my direction. "This gentleman is a judge of the Superior Court of Ontario, Kevin," he said. "I'm his clerk. The judge is going to marry Emily Drake next week. Reason we're here today, Emily wants the judge to brief her on what'll happen at the ceremony."

Kevin looked at me, more puzzled than dazzled. He had the expression of someone who faced an inexplicable quandary. I couldn't blame him.

"I don't really know about this," he said, his glance flicking between Maury and me.

"Just give Emily a ring on your phone, Kevin," Maury said. "She'll set things straight."

"I guess I can do that," Kevin said. He reached for the house phone. "But I should tell you she's hardly ever in at this hour."

Maury was holding his own cell in his hand. The cell rang. He clicked it open and waited a beat while the person on the other end said something.

"Emily!" Maury said enthusiastically into the cell. "We're downstairs right now, talking to young Kevin."

Kevin took the house phone from his ear. I could hear it ringing at the other end.

"Hey, Emily," Maury said to his cell, "that's a heck of a cold you got. Makes your voice very husky ... Yeah, one of those summer colds, I understand ... Hang on, I'll let you make husky sounds at Kevin here."

Maury handed his cell to Kevin. "Good afternoon, Miss Drake," Kevin said. He listened for a minute or two, then said, "Yes, if you say so, Miss Drake. I'll send them up. Thank you, Miss Drake."

He gave the cell back to Maury.

"That's strange," Kevin said. "The two years I've been here, today's the first time she ever called me by my first name."

"Well," I said, getting into the spirit of the fraud, "she's probably giddy about the wedding."

"That's no joke," Kevin said. "Why's an eighty-year-old spinster getting married in the first place?"

"Kevin, my boy, I've married older in my time," I said. Nice recovery, I thought.

"And I wonder what's happening with her sister in all this," Kevin said.

"Her sister?" I said, not recovering quite so adroitly. A sister? What else had Maury missed?

"You must have heard about her," Kevin said. "Miss Drake visits her at the seniors' residence in York Mills every day."

"That sister, yeah," Maury said, sliding into the conversation. "Very nice woman."

"Hard to tell what she is, a person like her with Alzheimer's," Kevin said.

"All right, Judge," Maury said to me, talking fast. He had my right arm in a grip like a vise. "Better not keep Emily waiting. Big day coming up."

Maury turned to Kevin. "Nice making your acquaintance, Kev."

"You too," Kevin said, doubt still registering in his voice. "Go ahead, gentlemen, I suppose."

There was a bank of eight elevators beyond Kevin's desk. One elevator was open and empty on the ground floor. I thought for a moment about the kind of judge-like aura I ought to project. A lot of judges, when they entered a courtroom, they tucked the left arm under the back of the gown and kicked into a swinging stride. I gave that a try, walking past Kevin and the security guys. It seemed to impress Kevin.

"Have a good day, Judge," he called in friendly tones.

"You too, young man," I said.

Maury and I stepped into the elevator. He pressed the button for the fourteenth floor. The elevator doors closed.

"Nice planning, Maury," I said.

"Couldn't anticipate every damn thing that might happen," Maury said. "Timing with the cell was perfect, you have to admit."

"Who was the woman with the summer cold?"

"Girl works at a bar out my way," Maury said. "I told her, reward for the favour, I'm having her over to my place for a shrimp dish I cook. Specialty of mine."

We rode to the fourteenth floor with no stops, got off and walked down the stairs to the eighth. We didn't encounter anybody on the way.

In front of apartment 808, Maury took a set of small picks out of his pocket.

"Glad they don't have electronic key cards in the damn building," he said.

"Your B and E skills don't extend to more modern technology?"

"I can do it," Maury said, sounding defensive. "Just I'm slower."

In well under a minute, Maury unlocked the door and pushed it open. Maury and I, side by side, looked into the apartment. Both of us were surprised into temporary silence.

"If there's a clue in here," I said after a few seconds, "it won't take us long to find it."

5

Grace's apartment door opened into the living room. If I were describing the room's decor for a home-furnishing magazine, I'd call it minimalist.

In an isolated island in the middle of the otherwise empty room, there was a sofa and two armchairs. All three pieces were done in a dark blue satiny material. In front of the sofa there was a coffee table. Two small tables stood at either end of the sofa. The end tables held lamps with white shades. The coffee table held nothing. The rest of the room was empty, and the walls were blank, no pictures and few signs that any pictures had once hung there.

Maury opened the drawers in the end tables.

"Nothing in them," he said. "Zero."

"We're rolling right along," I said. "But not in a productive direction."

To the left of the living room, an open door led to what I could see was a large kitchen with a centre island and a table big enough for a family of four to sit down to a meal and still have plenty of elbow room. A hall ran off the living room to the right. No doubt a bedroom and bathroom were down there.

"You check out the kitchen," I said to Maury. "Look in closets and drawers. I'll do the bedroom end of the place."

The bedroom had a queen-sized bed. Its mattress was bare of blankets and sheets. The six pillows stacked on the mattress weren't enclosed in pillowcases. Definitely a pattern emerging. Furniture but none of the furnishings. I slid open the drawer in the bedside table on the left side. It was empty. I walked around to the bedside table on the right side and opened the drawer. Empty. Another emerging pattern. The closet, almost large enough to qualify as a walk-in, was bare. Nothing on the shelves. No clothes hanging on the clothes rack. Not even hangers for clothes to hang on.

The bathroom was reached by way of a door off the bedroom. I stepped in. It was as barren as the other rooms. No toiletries, nothing in the medicine cabinet, nothing in the toothbrush rack, nothing in the drawer under the sink.

Above the toilet, shelves ran up four levels. I could see that the three lower shelves held nothing on them. The top shelf was above my head. I reached up my hand and ran it around the shelf. My hand hit pay dirt, if pay dirt could be defined as a stack of magazines.

I stood on the toilet seat to make sure I didn't miss any. It looked like five magazines altogether. I carried them back to the living room and sat in one of the satiny chairs.

"What've you got?" Maury asked.

"Magazines. What about you?"

"Nothing. None of the stuff you see in movies about people who skip a joint. Sour milk in the fridge, stale crackers in the cupboard. Nothing like that."

I went through the magazines. Maybe Grace or whoever cleaned out the apartment forgot that the magazines were on the shelf. They got left behind. I shuffled through the stack. *Chatelaine*, three *Vogues*, and a *Flare*. Another magazine fell out of the bundle onto the floor. It had been stuck in the pages of one of the fat *Vogues*. The sixth magazine was something slimmer, the January issue of a full-colour monthly called *Ceramics Monthly*. The title made up in specificity what it lacked in inspiration.

"None of these magazines is dated later than February this year," I said.

"That must've been when Grace beat it out of here," Maury said. "Five, six months ago."

I flipped through *Ceramics Monthly*, taking my time.

"The other magazines seem like Grace's kind of reading," I said. "But what's with the ceramics?"

"Bowls and jugs, you're talking about?" Maury said. "Along those lines?"

I stopped flipping the pages.

"And pots," I said. "Sex pots."

I held the magazine open for Maury to take a look. The article I wanted him to see was illustrated with colour photographs of ceramic pieces in the shapes of penises and nude women with their legs spread.

"Jesus," Maury said, "you never know where you're gonna come across dirty pictures these days."

"According to the article," I said, "these ceramics were done in the sixteenth century."

"Doesn't matter how old," Maury said, "they look disgusting."

"Maury, are you going fuddy-duddy in your advancing age?"

"I like porn as much as the next guy, but it belongs in *Penthouse*. Normal places like that. On the Internet."

"You're right, Internet-porn videos seem to be the new norm."

"Google 'nude girls' and you get a couple thousand movies of females screwing guys or females screwing other females."

I leafed through the rest of *Ceramics Monthly*. The other articles seemed conventional. No more eroticism, just pretty vases, cups, saucers, flower bowls. I turned the pages, taking my time, studying every article. Something had caught my eye, but I couldn't figure out what it was. I leafed some more. Something was wrong. Or maybe something was right and I didn't recognize what it was. After three or four minutes with no reward, I tossed the magazine onto the coffee table with the other five.

"You see any reason we should hang around here much longer?" Maury said.

"What, you worried Kevin downstairs might be putting two and two together?"

Maury shrugged. "Just planning ahead."

"Another plan? What's it this time?"

"Not another plan. Just a variation on the original."

"Give me the variation."

"When we leave," Maury said, "we oughta go by way of the underground garage. I checked it out this morning. No problem."

"Way things have developed so far," I said, "there could be a squad of cops down there waiting for us with drawn weapons."

"You don't like my plan, just say so."

"Maury," I said, "your plotting is better than anything I might have thought up. Of course, I lack the subculture mindset."

"Damn right."

"Just for reassurance," I said, "I'll give the kitchen a second look, you take a turn on the bedroom and bathroom."

Five minutes later, we reassembled in the living room. Both of us had come up empty.

"Now can we leave?" Maury said. "A rule of mine in the old days, the minute I knew I was done in a hotel room, win or lose, I cleared out of there."

"Something's bugging me," I said.

I turned the pages of *Ceramics Monthly* one more quick and fruitless time. Then I put all six magazines back on the top shelf in the main bathroom.

"You convinced?" Maury said. "There's no clues in the entire apartment."

I nodded my head, agreeing but not happy about it.

Maury opened the front door and looked up and down the silent hall. "All clear out here," he said. "Let's move."

I stepped into the doorway. Then I stopped. "Wait a minute, Maury. I saw a clue, dammit. Shut the door."

I went into the large bathroom and got the magazines.

"Look at this," I said to Maury. I sorted through all six, pointing to the right-hand bottom-front corner of each. "See that?" I said.

"See what? All I see's the covers of six magazines."

"Look closer," I said. "The first five have no subscriber's sticker in the corner. The sixth is different. It's got a sticker."

"The magazine with a dick for a teapot's got the sticker?"

"Deftly phrased, Maury," I said. "Grace bought the other magazines in a store. Or somebody bought them for her. Doesn't matter. What matters is she subscribed to *Ceramics Monthly*. Mailman brought it."

I was holding the sticker in Maury's face.

"OK, I see it, man," Maury said. "It's got her name and the address of this apartment on there. So what?"

"Quite a lot," I said. "Potentially anyway. If Grace wanted to keep her subscription active, she'd have had to give the magazine her new address."

Maury got it. "You're gonna phone the magazine and ask for the new address."

"Well, not me. The person on the phone in the subscription department might notice I'm not female and probably not someone named Grace Nguyen. But you've got the general idea. I'll ask somebody to make the call for me."

"Is this a genuine clue?"

"In my opinion as an experienced seeker after clues, this is the real goods."

Maury opened the apartment door. The hall was still empty. We walked down nine flights of stairs to the parking garage in the condo's basement. There were no signs of cops with or without drawn weapons. Maury led the way through the garage to a staircase that took us up a separate flight of stairs and out a door that opened on to the street beyond sight of the condo's front door. We crossed Lombard and walked west.

In my right hand, I clutched Grace's copy of *Ceramics Monthly*.

6

When I got home, Annie was standing in our front yard talking to a short woman with a pretty, heart-shaped face. Annie B. Cooke and I were live-in companions. I couldn't account for the other woman. The front yard was the size of a postage stamp.

"Hey, sweetie," Annie said when she saw me.

We kissed lightly on the lips.

"This is Kathleen," Annie said, indicating Ms. Heart Shape. "Kathleen's our new garden designer."

"A position that was vacant until now," I said.

"The place is a mess," Kathleen said. "Front and back."

"Reassuring to know garden design is a straight-talk business," I said.

"There's a reason I'm telling you this," Kathleen said, smiling winningly as she laid on the bad news. "When you get my bill, I want you to remember what a piece of doodoo I started with."

Kathleen began to wave her arms in many directions and drop Latin phrases into the conversation. I assumed the Latin covered plant names. Since she was addressing them and the arm waves to Annie, I drifted beyond the conversation and into the house.

I changed into jeans, an ancient pair of sandals and a black Dallas Mavericks T-shirt. It had Dirk Nowitzki's number. Forty-one. Downstairs, I mixed a martini. Straight up, twist of lemon, three ounces of Polish potato vodka, a soupçon of vermouth. It had been a day of unpleasant surprises. On the other hand, I still had a chance of landing on my feet. I sat with the martini at the dining room table. It had a view through the very large rear window into the backyard. I sipped my drink and surveyed Annie's and my kingdom. Was the garden really doodoo?

Annie and I bought the house six months earlier. It was a two-and-a-half-storey semi-detached on the east side of Major Street. The address placed us in a neighbourhood that had waited decades, probably a century, to be named. Just about every other corner of Toronto got a name before us. Ours, Harbord Village, was homely but logical enough, taken from Harbord Street, a main east-west route that passed through the neighbourhood a block south from Annie and me. All of us Harbord Villagers lived below Bloor Street, the southern boundary of the ancient and envied neighbourhood called the Annex.

Annex homeowners were a proud and smug bunch. They flew into a rage if any of us on Major and environs referred to ourselves as the South Annex. It was actually real estate agents who liked to throw the term around. They thought anything with Annex in the title was worth another fifty grand on the selling price. They probably had it right.

It was our first house together, Annie's and mine. We'd been romantic partners for fifteen years but not under the same roof. Finally we took the big step and amalgamated. "Two mature people making a mutually beneficial decision," Annie said. Besides that, we loved one another. With Annie, what wasn't to love? She was petite, what my grandmother would have called no bigger than a minute. Her hair was raven, her eyes large and green, and she had a knockout figure. Currently it was knocking out the eyes of every guy who lived on Major Street.

Major was a narrow street of houses just like ours, built a century and a half ago as cottages for the working class. Now it was trendy as hell, whether or not anybody fell for the South Annex label. Most people who bought on the street spent a fortune renovating like crazy. We were lucky. The people who owned the house before us had remodelled to their taste, which happened to dovetail with our taste. A lot of professors lived on Major, people who taught at the University of Toronto a couple of blocks to the east. The rest of the population included some artsy types, some doctors and scientists at the big hospitals downtown on University Avenue, two or three actors, and as of recently, one criminal lawyer.

Annie and Kathleen had moved their discussion to the backyard. Kathleen's arms were still waving, but they seemed to radiate more enthusiasm than they had in the front. I thought I spotted bursts of joy from old Kathleen. She must have found larger possibilities in the back garden. Good for her. Good for Annie and me.

Annie came through the door from the backyard into the dining room.

"Hmm," she said, looking at the martini in front of me, "getting an early start, are we? I bought a package of almonds this afternoon if you want some sustenance with the martini."

"Prescient of you."

"I'm going to drive Kathleen home. Not far. She lives up around Bathurst and Dupont. In the Annex."

Annie gave a mock-awed emphasis to "Annex." Everybody on Major did that.

"Where's Kathleen's own car?" I asked.

"Doesn't drive. Kathleen's a bit eccentric."

"If she lives so close, she could walk."

"Honey—" Annie sounded like a teacher with a thick student "—don't you keep up to date? This is *the* Kathleen Stibbards. The goddess of the garden. Clients always drive her home. And pick her up. It's part of the hiring ritual."

"She's giving you a chance to size her up?"

Annie shook her head. "Other way around. She's sizing us up. See if we're people who'll appreciate her work."

Annie grabbed her handbag off the table and left. I went into the kitchen for the almonds. Great, the nuts hadn't been opened yet. Fresh as the day they were packed in cellophane. I sat at the table alternating sips of martini with nibbles of almond. Yummy.

Annie returned, bringing a breath of fresh air and a whiff of scent. Chloe, if I remembered correctly.

"Want one of these?" I asked, holding up my drink.

"I've got a bottle of Veuve Clicquot chilling in the fridge," Annie said. "To celebrate today's big cash inflow."

"You actually bought eighty-dollar champagne?" I asked.

Annie nodded. "Tonight we go first class."

"Ah, yeah."

"What?" Annie said, picking up the downer note in my voice.

"We can still drink the champagne," I said. "It'll just lack the sense of occasion."

Annie's smile dropped away. "You didn't get the seventy-five thousand from Grace whatchamacallher?"

"Nguyen. Doesn't matter you not remembering her last name. The judge doesn't either. Or her first name. And, no, I'm not yet in pocket with the cash."

"Oh my god, what happened?"

It took ten minutes to tell Annie about most of my morning adventure. I skipped over the part about *Ceramics Monthly* and its subscription sticker because I was saving it for later. When I described the search of Grace's condo, me in the guise of a judge, Annie's eyes went wide, then narrowed. Damn, I should have left out the unlawful details. I wound up my recital with an account of the short session in Judge Keough's courtroom after lunch when he put the sentencing over for three weeks. Then I braced for the storm sure to come from the other side of the table. Why did I mention the masquerade? Did I have a death wish? Or was it all the new domesticity, living together in our very own house? Had it made me honest and transparent even with information I knew wouldn't make Annie swoon with delight?

She leaned over and took a deep drink from my martini. In the single swallow, she finished off everything left in the glass. Then she sat back.

"Crang, my love," Annie said. Her hands were folded in her lap, and her tone of voice was deliberate. "I know you're addicted to fairly stupid stunts like this pretending to be a judge. And I'll concede the stupid stunts are always in a worthy cause. Nothing I can say will change that side of you, and I've given up on even dreaming I could rein you in. Stuff that the rest of the civilized world might consider dangerous, if not idiotic, is actually basic to your nature. Therefore, eliminating all that from discussion, I want you to promise me just one thing. And I'm dead serious about this. Please, I mean pretty please, don't ever get caught by the fucking cops."

A swear word passed Annie's lips about once every eclipse of the moon. This was a solemn moment, and she was letting me know she meant business. I started to form a response that was appropriately contrite, but I was too slow off the mark.

"Now that I've unloaded," Annie said before I opened my mouth, "would you mind uncorking the champagne. I intend to get a tiny bit swacked tonight."

I fetched the champagne from the fridge and pulled out the cork with a mighty pop. On my way back to the dining room table, I picked up a pair of champagne flutes and got *Ceramics Monthly* out of my briefcase.

"Before you begin the course of action involved in getting swacked," I said to Annie, "may I request a service?"

"If it's the service I think you're talking about, don't we usually take that up post-prandial?"

"This is something where we leave our clothes on."

I put the magazine on the table and poured the Veuve Clicquot. Annie and I clinked flutes and tasted the bubbly.

"Hmm," Annie murmured, her eyes shut. "That is so lovely." She let a moment go by before she opened her eyes and said,

"Since when did you develop an interest in pottery?"

"This is where the service I mentioned comes in," I said, picking up the *Ceramics Monthly*. "Right here."

"That probably figures, but I don't see how."

I told Annie about the rest of the events in Grace's condo, the part about the subscription to the ceramics magazine.

"I'll do it," Annie said before I finished.

"Do what?"

"You want me to phone the magazine's subscription department and bamboozle them into giving me Grace's current address."

"Your opinion is this doesn't qualify as a stupid stunt?"

"I'm about to impersonate somebody on the phone. That's the logical method of ferreting out the information, if I'm not mistaking what you've got on your devious mind?"

I nodded.

"Normally I'd think twice about deceiving a complete stranger," Annie said. "Especially when it's on behalf of a client of yours who doesn't rank among your top ten favourites."

"True," I said. "Grace isn't somebody who grows on a person."

"But since the phone call relates to the question of getting the seventy-five thousand dollars you worked very long and hard to earn, I'm willing to suck it up for the cause."

"I'll be in your debt."

"And I won't let you forget it, fella."

7

Annie wanted to know where *Ceramics Monthly* was published. In what country?

"The U. S. of A," I said.

"Down there," Annie said, "aren't magazine subscriptions handled by anonymous companies in some place like Omaha, Nebraska, and probably never respond to anything as mundane as a phone call?"

"*Ceramics Monthly*'s too small for that," I said. "On the masthead, the number for the subscription department is the same as for the editorial department."

"Cool," Annie said. "My next question, if I'm pretending to be Grace, what accent do I attempt?"

"You should sound like any girl who grew up in Toronto. That's how the genuine Grace comes across."

Annie took a swallow of champagne and got out her cell.

"Hold on a sec," she said. She tapped a bunch of numbers into the cell, muttered something I didn't catch, started over again with more tapping of numbers until she seemed to be satisfied.

"Blocked out my name and cell number," she said. "Otherwise the folks at *Ceramics Monthly* might wonder why the real me is calling instead of the Grace me. Catch my drift?"

"Puts you one step ahead," I said. "As always."

"Another thing, we're now on conference call. Meaning you can listen in as long as you're quiet as a mouse."

"You're calling Atlanta, Georgia, by the way."

I gave Annie the number, and she dialed it.

"*Ceramics Monthly*," a woman's voice said. The voice dripped with the Old South.

"Hi there," Annie said. "I've got a major subscription problem, and I wonder if I might resolve it with the right department."

"Oh heavens, sugah, you're talking to the right department. This late in the day, I'm all the departments. Everybody else's gone home."

"Wonderful!" Annie gave the impression she'd just picked the Kentucky Derby winner. "Name is Grace Nguyen, and I swear my neighbour's swiping my copies of your darling magazine. But I don't want to go around accusing anybody if the magazine isn't even being mailed to the right address. All I know for sure is I'm not receiving *Ceramics Monthly*."

"Can't have that going on, can we, sugah. Give me that last name again. Spell it, I mean."

"N-g-u-y-e-n. Nguyen."

We could hear a computer clicking at the other end.

"You callin' from Toronto, Canada, sweetheart?"

"The true north strong and free."

This seemed to be exciting news to the lady in Atlanta.

"Let me guess. Nguyen, that name?" she said, making a hash of pronouncing Nguyen. Everybody gets it wrong where the *n* meets the *g*. "You're, like, Eskimo?"

"Approximately," Annie said.

"Never talked to one of them before. Wait'll I tell my kids."

"I can give you a couple of my people's words, if you like."

"Oh, sugah, that would be so edifyin'," the woman said. "But hold on to that for a minute. I got your whole file on my screen. It shows *Ceramics Monthly* shipping out to you in Toronto every month."

"Know what I was thinking?" Annie said. "Both houses are on a corner where two streets meet. Me on the south side, the neighbour I'm suspicious of on the north. But I don't know whether his house is numbered on the cross street or on my street. See what I mean? What number do you show for me?"

"We show 32 on a street with a kind of peculiar name you don't mind my sayin', sugah. Maybe it's a Canadian thing. We got 32 Highbury Road for you. At funerals, d'you folks put the body in some, uh, elevated ground?"

I gave Annie a big smile and a double thumbs-up. I stopped myself. What was I doing with my thumbs up? I always thought it was a ridiculous gesture. I deactivated the thumbs.

"Highbury Road is the right address," Annie said. "And, yes, we have some peculiar old burial practices in parts of Eskimo Canada."

"Fascinatin', girl, it really is."

"You know," Annie said, "I think I've got an idea about my next step."

"I think your next step should be speakin' to your mailman."

"Just exactly what I was going to say. Instead of bothering you when you're all alone at the office."

"No problem, sugah. Now, how 'bout those words?"

"Huh?"

"In Eskimo."

"Oh, yes," Annie said, running her tongue over her upper lip. "I'll give you 'thank you and good night.' Ready?"

"Do it real slow."

"*Merci et bonsoir*," Annie enunciated with precision.

"Oh, sugah, Eskimo sounds so foreign. You've made my night."

"My pleasure entirely," Annie said. She clicked off the cellphone.

I said, "Excellent work, Agent Cooke."

Annie took a long drink from her flute.

"Don't suggest I do something like that again," she said.

"Annie, you were great. A natural."

"That's the problem," she said. She broke into a wide smile. "I might get to like the flim-flammery."

"Probably never have occasion to do it again."

"It could become addictive."

"You know," I said, "that address the nice lady gave you is more than familiar."

"Come on, sweetie, you're probably mixing up Highbury with Highland, something like that. There must be a dozen Toronto streets that start with High. Or Hy."

"I've seen it on a list."

"Forget it for now," Annie said, rising from her chair. "You go get our barbecue set up."

"What barbecue?"

"The one I bought today," Annie said. "Fella, you have to get with the program. We're homeowners now. All homeowners have a barbecue. Ours is in the big box in the alleyway."

"You're kidding, right? About me setting it up?"

It had long been established in our relationship that I was the one who suffered from mechanical klutziness. Actually, Annie did the suffering. I'd learned to live with the klutz factor.

"I was kidding," Annie said. She patted me on the cheek. "Remind me again about your skill set in domestic areas."

"Make a great martini. Fast at picking up the bill in restaurants."

"You left out stacking the dishwasher."

Annie needed ten minutes to assemble the new barbecue and set the thing aflame.

"Easy peasy," Annie said.

"Had've been me out there, the neighbours just missed a massive explosion."

Annie oversaw the baking of a nice piece of tilapia. I set the table, tossed the salad, poured the champagne and stared out the window at the dying of the light.

Twenty minutes and much of the champagne bottle later, we were cutting into our tilapia. Annie had coated it in a sauce of her own devising.

I chewed a chunk, thought about it and said, "Piquant."

"You're talking about the sauce?" Annie said.

"Uh-huh."

I chewed another chunk of fish.

"The aroma's not bad either," I said.

Annie reached for my hand and squeezed it.

Both of us ate mostly in silence for a few minutes.

"Know where I saw the address listed?" I said. "Hundred percent positive."

"We back on the subject of Highbury?" Annie said.

"Read it on the list of addresses of the houses where Grace and her partner ran their grow ops."

Annie thought for a minute. "If your memory's reliable," she said, "isn't that bad news? Suppose the Highbury house was one of Grace's grow ops, the cops would have seized it a long time ago. Not very likely Grace would go back there."

"Correct on all surmises, my very own Dr. Watson."

"Watson?" Annie said. "If I play your pretend sidekick, there're several females I'd rather be."

"How about Nora Charles?"

"Love the way Myrna Loy played her in the movies."

"Not to mention William Powell doing Nick."

"Nobody better."

"If we're pretending I'm Nick Charles right now," I said, "I'd point out to Nora that the champagne bottle seems to have emptied itself."

"Fix us martinis," Annie said. "That's what they do in *The Thin Man*."

"Why not."

I dumped the empty Veuve Clicquot bottle in the recycling box in the alley. In the kitchen, I took care of the drinks business.

Two vodka martinis, mine straight up with a twist, Annie's on the rocks with three small olives, a toothpick driven through their centres.

"Returning to the subject of Highbury, if you can stand it," I said, "Grace must've had a good reason for switching her subscription to the new address. Maybe she lives there, maybe not."

"And to find out, you're going to knock on Grace's door, wherever that is?"

"I've got a city street map in the car's glove compartment."

"Or you can look it up on Google Earth."

"Yes, I can."

"But you'll probably do it the good old analog way."

"Almost certainly."

"But, please," Annie said, "not tonight."

"Tomorrow is my plan."

"Good," Annie said. "Because I'm kind of thinking right about now I'd love a little snuggle. It's been a very long day."

"Can it wait till I load the dishwasher?"

"In words of one syllable, no."

So Annie and I jettisoned what was left of our martinis, went upstairs and snuggled away the rest of the evening.

8

The voices of *Metro Morning* drifted up from the radio in the kitchen when I came awake. I couldn't make out what they were saying, but I could tell it was the *Metro Morning* crowd from the rhythms of their speech. *Metro Morning* was what we listened to every morning, even after Annie got kicked off the program.

By the time I showered, dressed and made my way downstairs, it was coming up to ten minutes before eight. Annie was sitting at the dining room table, the radio beside her, a cup of coffee in her right hand, a stopwatch in her left. *Metro Morning*'s host was introducing the guy who reviewed movies. It was the job that had been Annie's until a few months earlier. When the movie guy began to talk, Annie clicked on the stopwatch.

I fixed my breakfast in the kitchen. A glass of orange juice, a banana sliced over a bowl of Bran Buds, a raisin bun from Cobs Bakery on Bloor. I spread raspberry jam over the bun. The kitchen was open to the dining room and up three steps. Slanting sunlight beamed through the big rear window and gave the table a summery, companionable look. The movie guy sounded excited about a new Martin Scorsese movie.

I did an adroit balancing job with the orange juice, cereal and raisin bun, and got them down to the dining room table in one trip without misadventure. Just as I sat in my chair, the host was thanking the movie guy with effusive praise. Annie clicked off the stopwatch.

"Exactly five minutes and thirty seconds for the whole item," she said.

"Your point being that five and a half minutes was the length you worked at when the producer dismissed you for going too long with your reviews," I said, feeling proud of myself.

"Technically it wasn't for going too long. More for not talking fast enough."

"Brief age of speed radio at the CBC."

"Damn producer had everybody talking like chipmunks," Annie said. "I couldn't step up the pace, he axed me. The idiot."

"You're not still holding a grudge?"

"By email," Annie said. "Axed me in an actual email."

I made crunching noises with my cereal.

"But now they're back to regular human speech," I said.

"The producer got switched to another job, but in all the readjusting, the bosses neglected to hire me back."

"I might ask," I said, "why are you revisiting the painful piece of employment history at this time?"

"Just to remind myself how fragile the life of a freelance broadcaster and writer can be."

"You've always been aware of fragility in the business."

"True that," Annie said, "but lying awake last night, I decided to take a little detour in my work trajectory."

"You've already got your book to write."

"You can bet your boots I'm not about to abandon it," Annie said. "The world may not think it's dying for a biography of Edward Everett Horton, but the man makes a great story."

"And you'll tell it with keen insight and a lot of laughs."

"Meanwhile," Annie said, "I'm going to work part-time as a member of Kathleen's group."

"Garden goddess Kathleen?"

"She asked me yesterday, am I interested? She's shy one person to dig and plant and weed. Pruning I'm not ready for yet. Exacting art, I'm told."

Annie went over to the counter and opened a green cloth bag. "Get a look at this cunning little device. Secateurs we call it in horticulture."

Annie held up a tool not unlike an extra-large and especially vicious pair of scissors. The thing's handles were separated by a spring, and it had two very sharp blades. The blades passed one another to make the cuts, presumably of plant stems and tree branches.

"Every pruner's go-to weapon," Annie said.

"Not to doubt the breadth of your talents, sweetie pie," I said, "but what qualifies you to garden professionally?"

"I hate hydrangeas."

"That's all it takes?"

"Gets you off on the right foot with Kathleen," Annie said. "The client begs, she still won't plant hydrangeas. Kathleen says I also need a love of gardens, a little muscle, willingness to follow directions."

"The last may be troublesome," I said *sotto voce*.

"I heard that," Annie said.

I finished off the orange juice and turned my attention to the excellent raisin bun and the raspberry jam on top of it.

"When does your career in the dirt and earth get launched?" I asked.

"You may want to clear off the property in the next five minutes," Annie said. "Kathleen and her other slaves are picking me up at eight-thirty for a job out in the Beach somewhere. First, Kathleen's hanging here long enough to figure out who'll work on our garden and what they'll do. Actual work won't happen for two, three weeks."

"Slaves?"

"What Kathleen calls her group," Annie said. "But she smiles when she says it."

I tidied away my dishes and walked up to Bloor. On the way, I fished my *Pocket Street Atlas* out of the car's glove compartment. At the Second Cup on Bloor, I bought a large coffee and carried it south on Spadina Avenue half a block to my office in a building I suspected was made on the cheap. The giveaway that a cheapskate was behind the construction came from the floors. They shimmied and quivered. My floor was the fifth, and walking down the hall from the elevator to the office, I felt the familiar shifting underfoot. Would my lease cover damage wrought by shimmies and quivers? It's the sort of thing a regular lawyer ought to know. I didn't.

Inside my office, the decor was simple but fetching. Three Matisse posters hung on the walls, each poster showing scenes of Nice with plenty of the great man's blue on display. The blue had its soothing effect on me when clients grew unruly. Even the misbehaving clients had been known to fall calm under the influence of Matisse's blue. Or so I told myself.

My desk was an old rolltop. I'd pushed it up against the wall opposite the one with whichever Matisse poster was my current favourite. I kept the three posters on an informal rotation schedule. When I had clients in the office, I turned my swivel chair around and faced into the room, my legs stretched out, crossed at the ankles. I felt like Clarence Darrow.

I drank some coffee. Compared to the Kenyan brand at Judge Keough's office, the Second Cup product came up short on potency. I turned the pages of my road map and found Highbury in the west end. It twisted through an upscale neighbourhood called the Kingsway. I got the impression from the map that number 32 and the other houses on the even-numbered side backed on a park forming around the Humber River. A close and personal on-site observation was called for. That afternoon wouldn't be too soon.

Continuing in my investigative mode, I turned on my Mac-Book and brought up the massive file in *Regina v. Wu and Nguyen*. The thousands of pages under my fingers presented the Crown's case against Wu and my client in its entirety. The handy-dandy section titles put me in instant touch with the list of addresses of the seventy-three grow houses. All addresses were in alphabetical order according to street names.

I hit the H's. Havelock Avenue was followed by Hyland Street. Alphabetically, Highbury Road should have fit in between the two. But Highbury was missing. I checked the rest of the H's in case it had been misplaced. It hadn't. It wasn't there. I'd swear I saw it on a list somewhere in the evidence.

I drank a little more coffee and thought about Highbury's absence. Looking out the window might help the ratiocinative process. My view was due north, but between my window and the northern horizon was a massive condo building. It had the effect of bullying the skyline. All I could see from my window were the condo's balconies. Totally boring, but in the moment of visual boredom, a memory from *Regina v. Wu and Nguyen* stirred. If I wasn't mistaken, the addresses of the grow op houses were recorded on a less obvious second list among the pages of evidence.

The cops busted Grace and Wu's grow houses in every part of the city and in adjacent suburbs and exurbs. A wide geographical spread, and thus many police forces had a hand in the busting operations. The Toronto Police Services, York Regional Police, Ontario Provincial Police, the Mounties, cops from Peel County to the west and Durham County on the east. All of them got into the act for takedowns, each force to its own bailiwick.

The less obvious second list divided the raided grow houses according to the police forces that handled the raids. Statistically speaking, the list was useful for the prosecution only as a way of singling out the forces for their individual pats on the back. Nothing legally strategic about the list. But it existed. I'd read the damned thing once upon a time.

Back on the computer, I scrolled through the case files until my eyes felt like they might fall out of my head. The second list was eluding me, a state of affairs that was irritating but not yet fatal.

Someone rapped sharply on the door, a one-knuckle knock I recognized.

"I'm here, Sam," I said. Sam was my neighbour across the hall. He opened the door.

"You want a coffee, Crang?" he said. "It's just perking."

In guarantees of satisfaction, Sam's coffee ranked midway between Second Cup and Kenyan. I'd settle for that.

"Perfect timing, Sam," I said.

Sam Feldman was in the massage business. He kept his office spic and span. He called his outfit An Easy Touch, and he received his clients dressed in spotless white trousers and an immaculate white sweatshirt. At the end of the massage, when the clients retired to the little dressing room to put their clothes on, Sam donned a single-breasted blue blazer to bid the clients a formal adieu. Sam had excellent manners.

"I think the taste came out just right," he said, handing me coffee in a white mug with "Let A Smile Be Your Umbrella" printed in crimson lettering around the lip. Sam was a tall, muscular guy with very strong hands.

"You look like a storm cloud's hanging over your head," he said to me.

"That's called intense concentration."

"I'll give you a massage for relaxation," Sam said. "On the house. A client just postponed his appointment."

"Maybe if I find the answer to my quest in the next couple of minutes," I said. My fingers were still typing on the computer keyboard.

I paused long enough to sip some coffee. "Not bad at all," I said of the brew.

I was shooting past some useless passages on the computer screen. But I kept on the move, and in not much more than a minute, the passage suddenly wasn't useless. It was the list. There it was, the list of the houses divided according to the police departments that raided the indicated addresses.

"I don't know how this happened, Sam," I said, "but I may have found the pot at the end of the rainbow."

"You could explain that to me maybe. I'm a sucker for stories about rainbows."

"Hold on, Sam."

According to the list, York Regional Police busted more houses than any other police force on the case. But they didn't nail the house on Highbury. The name wasn't on their list. But then I didn't expect to find it there. Highbury was a City of Toronto address. It should be on the Toronto Police Services list. But it wasn't there either. It wasn't on the list of any of the other police forces. Not the OPP, nor the RCMP. Highbury appeared nowhere on the arrest lists.

"I didn't just imagine the name, Sam," I said.

"What name?"

"Highbury Avenue."

"You're a very observant person, Crang," Sam said. "I'm betting on you, even if I don't know what you're talking about."

I gave Sam a précis of my problem.

"So what're you going to do?" Sam asked. He worried about his friends, a naive sort of guy, but it was impossible not to warm to Sam.

"Appeal to a higher authority."

"I never took you for a religious man."

"Not that higher authority," I said. "I'm talking about the federal Crown attorney."

I finished my coffee, shooed Sam out of the office and walked down the hall to the elevator.

9

Somebody left a copy of the morning's *Sun* on the streetcar.

I was riding the Spadina car south to King Street. Elderly ladies filled every space, standing room only. Spadina was the route into the heart of old Chinatown where the shops carried exotic root vegetables and seaweed. The dream of such delights was what enticed the aged shoppers. The ladies probably knew an illicit dealer in shark fin soup.

The abandoned *Sun* was tucked into the space under a window in the row of single seats. An ancient shopper with a crotchety expression occupied the seat. I knew enough about riding the Spadina car not to reach over her to get at the newspaper. She'd chop off my arm and boil it for the shark fin soup. I stood in the aisle, holding on to a pole for us standees, biding my time.

At the Dundas Street stop, which was action central for the shopping crowd, the stampede of elderly persons to the door threatened to carry me with the tide. I held on to the pole, teeth gritted, arm braced, feet trampled on. It was life out on the edge riding the Spadina line. All the old parties bailed off the car.

I took the seat the crotchety woman had vacated and leafed through the *Sun*, looking for Cheri Havlat's article about Grace Nguyen. It came up on page eight, the story taking the entire sheet. The headline read "Gone Grace." The *Sun* loved alliteration.

I speed-read down the story's columns, looking for quotes from me. I searched in vain. Cheri used all the material I'd given her about the great grow op plot. Her story was thorough, but it gave the impression the writer, young Cheri, was herself the source of all inside information. How about credit where credit was due, huh, Cheri?

At the bottom of the page, my name jumped out at me. My name always jumped when I saw it in print. It was in the article's final line, the one that wrapped up the story. "'Ms. Nguyen's present whereabouts are a mystery to me,' said Mr. Crang, Ms. Nguyen's defence lawyer."

I tried to remember, did I tell Cheri I was giving her the in-depth information to make up for the feeble quote of Monday morning? Maybe not. But whatever I'd said, I landed in print sounding like a cliché machine. I made a mental note to self-edit all quotes before I let them loose on the press.

At King Street, I transferred to the King car heading east. The piece in the *Sun* was illustrated with the only photograph I'd ever seen of Grace in print or on television. The *Sun* ran it with every mention of the case. I felt conflicted each time I saw it.

The photo caught her on the night of her and Wu's arrest four years earlier. It showed a bunch of drug cops in the act of hustling Grace into the station at 53 Division. In the picture, she had turned her head and was staring full face into the camera. Her expression was freighted with vulnerability.

I'd told Judge Keough that Grace was unreadable. That was true ninety-nine and ninety-nine hundredths percent of the time. The *Sun* photo represented the exception, the one time she let her guard slide. In that moment, she looked less like a beautiful but distant woman and more like a desperate teenager. It was a look that made me want to give her a hug. All the rest of the time, it was a struggle to work up positive feelings for Grace. She could be abrasive. That was on her good days. On her bad days, she was evasive and schemy. I wondered what was going on in her head.

More than once, I had to remind her I was the one guy on her side. I was her lawyer, for Pete's sake. Whenever I made my little speech, the best reaction I could hope for was one of Grace's no-expression expressions.

I went into an office tower of glass and steel at King and York and took an elevator to the federal Crown's offices on the forty-fourth floor. The feds ran tight security, but a young woman Crown I'd had a case with a couple of years earlier recognized me as she was passing through the waiting room. She buzzed me in. Her name was Kate, and she had a mouth on her.

"If it isn't the lawyer who lost his client," she said.

"Cruel shot, Kate."

"But don't you think it's got a ring to it?"

"Yeah, a Swedish ring. It sounds like the kind of title crime novelists over there put on their books."

I told Kate I wanted to see Dora Andreopoulos, the co-Crown on the Grace and Wu prosecution. Kate led me down a hall past small, cramped cubicles with open doors. We reached Dora's office. Cramped quarters, open door.

"Look who it is," Dora said, "the lawyer who lost his client."

"Second time I've heard that one in thirty seconds, Dora," I said. "The line's now officially stale."

Kate left, and Dora told me to have a seat.

"Easier said than done," I said, looking around the crowded little office. The two clients' chairs were stacked with files. So was most of the floor space. Dora told me to shove aside the papers on one of the clients' chairs.

"So, Crang," she said, "what's with the surprise visit?"

Dora was a short, dark woman with an angelic smile. During the Grace–Wu negotiations, she took a six-month leave to have a baby boy. The joke among the Crowns was that the case discussions were dragging out so long Dora's kid would grow to adulthood and finish law school before we wound up. Crown humour tended to be cute. Defence humour leaned to the ribald.

Crowns were Bob Newhart; defence counsel were George Carlin.

"Highbury Road," I said.

"Oh, that," Dora said. "I wondered if you'd get around to Highbury."

"What's to get around to on Highbury Road?"

"Not much really. But why ask now? The case is over. Your client's going to prison as soon as you bring her in. Highbury has no bearing on anything."

"Tell me one thing?" I said, a question mark in my voice. "I didn't just dream Highbury? It exists? It has a role in the case?"

"Half and half," Dora said. "No, you didn't imagine it. But, also no, it has no relevance to the case."

"Definitely I could use some background to what you're telling me."

"As long as you promise this isn't going to come back and bite me in the ass."

"Promise," I said. "All I'm doing is tying up loose ends."

Dora hesitated. I could imagine her thinking over the baloney I'd just fed her about loose ends. Wondering whether I was up to monkey business and whether it really mattered. From the ho-hum look on her face, she must have decided it was ancient history not worth fussing over.

"Okay," Dora said, "Highbury was our mistake, the cops' and the Crown's. The wiretap people heard Nguyen mention the address many, many times on the phone. In these conversations, she wasn't talking precisely about Highbury being a grow house. But at that point, we were close to the end of building our case. Everybody was in a big rush to finish things, and the cops figured with reasonably good motivation that Highbury was yet another grow house. They raided it."

"And found what?" I asked.

"Zip, zilch, nada," Dora said. "The place was clean of anything indicating the presence of marijuana ever. No equipment, no plants, no evidence that anybody had so much as smoked a joint in the entire history of the place."

"So you dropped Highbury?"

"Like a hot potato."

"Where did I see the address?" I asked. "What list was Highbury on?"

"This is why I thought you'd be upset," Dora said. "In the Crown's office, we jumped the gun just as fast as the drug cops did who raided Highbury in the first place. We included the address in a supplementary list of grow houses we sent you even before we really knew the result of the raid. Then we cancelled the list with Highbury on it as soon as the police told us the place was clean. It happened very fast, all in one week practically, Highbury on and off the list. We were hoping you'd never notice."

"This was what, three, four years ago, all the action with Highbury on and off, there and not there?"

Dora thought for a moment. "About that, yeah."

"Three, four years it took me to wonder about Highbury. Slow but steady, that's my game."

"Another part of it you may not like," Dora said, "the overall number of grow houses."

"Seventy-three is the official figure."

"Should be seventy-two," Dora said. "We forgot to change the total when we dropped Highbury."

"I'm still not sore."

"Crang, you're a pal," Dora said. She leaned back in her chair, looking like somebody who had a load, however slight, off her shoulders. "As you might gather from the mess in here, I've got new cases to worry about. After four years, I'm out from under Nguyen and Wu. I'm happy never to hear the name Highbury Road again."

"With Highbury, kiddo," I said, "I'm just getting started."

10

My car was a Mercedes four-door sedan, brown in colour and referred to by guys in foreign-car repair shops as a 304X. I had no idea what the designation meant. A mechanic named Angelo sold me the car for eight thousand bucks a few years earlier. Angelo said it was a 1983 model and had been in the hands of a little old gent who used the vehicle only to drive to *shul*. When I got behind the wheel of my big, bulky, powerful Mercedes, I felt as safe as houses.

I drove west on Dupont through the south end of the Italian district and past the north end of the Portuguese neighbourhood. At Jane Street, I turned south to Bloor West, which put me in the grasp of the west end's Anglo stronghold. I got off Bloor on the road next to the Old Mill subway station. On the other side of the station, I passed the Old Mill itself, a low-slung and aging but stout building in an English countryside style. It was split into bars, dining rooms and reception halls, much favoured for wedding receptions and for serious small-group jazz in the main lounge. I took Annie there a month earlier. A stalwart on the Toronto jazz scene named Bernie Senensky played lyrical piano that night. Annie and I had two glasses of wine each, a couple of helpings of sliders and salad, and two sets of melodic Senensky piano. All for seventy reasonable bucks.

Beyond the Old Mill, the Kingsway turned hilly, the streets got winding, and the Mercedes got lost. I stopped for a reorienting study of my road guide, and a few blocks later, I was gliding through Highbury Road's twists and turns. The neighbourhood was clean, prosperous and faithfully tended. Many architects and contractors had left their influences behind, but most of the houses ran to brick and stone, a centre-hall plan and a lot of tidy landscaping. It didn't look as if anybody like Annie's garden goddess had been let loose on the lawns and flower beds. They were too tight-assed in conception and design to be the GG's work, unless I'd misunderstood Annie's description of her creative gardening mind.

I couldn't miss number 32. The lot took up the space of three conventional Highbury lots. Around the borders, the property's lines were defined by a low wall of large whitewashed stonework. Between the wall and the house, the space was dense with ancient maples and oaks and a few tall evergreens. All trees appeared healthy. Their thickness with leaves and needles blocked any view of the house from the street. A driveway led off Highbury toward the residence, then looped back out. I parked the Mercedes on the street and walked down the driveway.

The house was brick, two-storey and larger sized than any of the other houses on the block. I rang the doorbell three times. Nobody stirred. I walked around the house. The curtains were pulled across the first-floor windows. At the rear, a flagstone patio spread out from the back door. Just off the patio, there was a large garden shed filled with an electric lawn mower and an array of shovels, rakes and other tools of the gardening trade.

I put my hand on the shed's doorknob. It turned smoothly without emitting creaks or groans. Somebody was taking good care of the shed, the implements inside and the grounds surrounding the house. Standing on the edge of the large and freshly mowed back lawn, which wasn't nearly as thick with trees as the front yard,

I had a clear view down into the valley with a faint glimpse of the Humber River in the farthest distance. All was quiet, all was peaceful. Grace Nguyen was nowhere in sight. Neither was anybody else.

I walked back to the street and into the driveway of the house directly opposite number 32. A kid wearing a University of Western Ontario sweatshirt was washing a car with a garden hose. I introduced myself and asked what he knew about the people in the place across the street.

"Practically nothing," he said. "I'm away at school year-round. Taking my master's in business. What I understand, somebody might live there, but they lie low. My parents say there're lights at night. That's the only sign of life."

The kid was talkative, genial even. I could press him a little.

"You think you could ask around for me?" I said. "It's rather important."

"I can do better than that," the kid said.

He leaned closer to me. "Don't look behind me at what I say next, okay?"

"Deal," I said.

"The man in number 29 is who you want to talk to, the house next door to us."

"Fount of information is he?"

"Mr. Griffith is his name, Lawrence Griffith. He's always peeking out his windows. I'm sure he is right now, wondering who you are."

"Sounds like just my man," I said.

"Got this nickname among the neighbours. Everybody calls him 'I Spy' behind his back. He doesn't have a clue about the name. So don't, like, give it away. He might be offended."

"My lips are sealed," I said.

I went up the walk to number 29 and gave the heavy knocker on the door a bang. A tall, lean man with thinning grey hair and excellent posture opened the door. He was wearing a dark blue V-necked sweater and a pair of beige corduroys. The sweater-and-corduroy combo looked smart and neatly laundered.

"Lawrence Griffith?" I asked.

"That is I," he said. "And you are parked across the street. The old brown Mercedes."

"Crang's my name," I said. "Or have you worked that out already?"

"You've been talking to the Edmonds boy, so you already know keeping an eye on events around here is kind of a hobby with me."

"That was the intimation."

"Closer to an obsession, some would say," Griffith said. He had exceptionally clear blue eyes for a guy his age.

Griffith gestured me to come in. I followed him through a bright and cheery hallway. Most of the cheeriness radiated from the paintings hanging along both sides of the hall. They filled practically every inch of wall space, most of them done in colours of an optimistic nature. Griffith and I sat down in the living room where the walls were just as bright with paintings as the hall.

"Now let me guess what you're interested in, Mr. Crang," Griffith said. "The house at number 32?"

"No trick to getting that one right. You saw me doing my investigative thing around the property over there."

"Even without that, I'd have guessed correctly. The sole reason for anyone from outside the neighbourhood to visit this part of Highbury is number 32. It's our mystery house. Big old place, people come and go, but nobody stays."

Griffith stood up.

"Let's wet our whistles before we get going on our little gossip. Coors do for you?"

I said by all means, and Griffith went out to the kitchen. While he was gone, I gave the paintings a once-over. Many were in styles that seemed familiar, but I couldn't quite tease the artists' names out of my memory. A few I could definitely identify.

Griffith came back and handed me a cold sweaty can of Coors and a tall glass to pour it into. The glass was cold but not sweaty.

"The painting on the wall by the door," I said, "the one with the red-checkered tablecloth, that's an early Louis de Niverville. He doesn't paint them that big these days."

Griffith grinned like a fiend. "I haven't had a stranger come here in years who recognized a painting of mine."

"We passed a Graham Coughtry in the hall."

"Outstanding, Mr. Crang," Griffith said, still with the grin. "Never thought I'd meet a cultured private investigator."

"You still haven't," I said. "I'm a lawyer."

"Even more rare, a cultured lawyer," Griffith said. The grin wouldn't quit. I'd made the guy's day. Now I had to unmake it.

"I can't take the credit," I said. "My partner is the visual literate in the house. She chooses the galleries. I store away memories of what I like."

"That gives us something else in common," Griffith said. "It was my late wife who educated me about Canadian painting."

He turned his head toward the de Niverville, getting a little misty eyed. He needed a minute to pull himself together.

"I retired too damn early," he said in a tone that told me he was getting down to brass tacks. "Had no idea retirement would be so dull. I've got my interests, Canadian art for one, but nothing has its point unless there's an objective to it."

"So you turned to snooping?"

"One way of putting it, I suppose. I've always read spy fiction. Upmarket authors. Le Carré, Charles McCarry. I love the information-gathering in those books. The techniques of it. That's what I put to work on my own neighbourhood."

The cold Coors was going down smoothly. "Score any successes?" I asked.

"I knew Roy Cameron at number 44 was having an affair with Lois Ford at 52 long before anybody else sniffed it out. Including their spouses."

"You blew the whistle on Roy and Lois?"

Griffith shook his head. "Not the point. I like the technical side of the work. Once I get the information, I'm satisfied. I sit on what I learn."

"What happened to the adulterers?"

"Both families broke up. A shame really. But Roy and Lois are living together these days in one of the condos over by the Old Mill subway station. Perhaps love prevailed after all."

It was hard to tell whether I Spy had a touch of the kook in him. He seemed rational enough. Most likely he was just a lonely guy with a weird hobby.

"But number 32, that's a horse of a different colour," Griffiths said. He hadn't touched his Coors.

"Who owns the place?" I asked.

"The Spencers had it for ages going way back. Rather a shy couple, the two of them rattling around on that huge property all alone. They died close to the same time four years ago this summer, Emma first and then Ted. No kids, so their trust company sold the house. But nobody around here knows who they sold it to."

"You never scoped out the people who moved in?"

"That's what I'm trying to tell you. Nobody's been in the house long enough to tell whether they're living there."

"How about recently?"

"Ah," Griffiths said, holding up a finger, "that's where it gets interesting."

"Glad to hear it."

Griffith's Coors was still untasted.

"You're wondering about the beer?" he said. "I don't care for it. It's just a sociable thing to get one for myself while my guests are having a drink."

"Sociable would be if you opened the can."

Griffith smiled a rueful smile but made no move on the Coors.

"To continue," he said, "this past winter, when the leaves were off the trees, and I could make out the traffic into 32, people in a black Ford Navigator became regular visitors. They still are."

"How regular?"

"Every weekday and many Sundays," Griffiths said. The guy was relishing the telling of his story. Probably not often he got an eager audience for his peepery tales. Most likely never. "One problem in viewing from my window, it's a bad angle on the Navigator. Plus the car's driver has a habit of pulling up close to the front door."

"Not much opportunity for identification?"

"It's always two people, sometimes a third. This latter one comes only on Mondays. A very large man and a Vietnamese woman are the regulars. The third person, he's a man, very tall, quite slim, has a distinctive profile, rather a protuberant nose. He accompanies the others once every two or three weeks, always on Mondays as I say. Just one more word about this other man. He doesn't come in the Navigator. Note that, Mr. Crang."

"How's he arrive?"

"Through the woods at the back," Griffith said. "That's my own guess. Only times I see him are when he talks briefly to the woman at the end. Then he disappears, probably by the back way."

"Vietnamese?" I said. "You told me a minute ago the woman is Vietnamese. How can you tell?"

"The name for one thing," Griffith said. "Grace Nguyen. Nguyen, you know, is the most common surname in Vietnam. Centuries ago, a warlord of that name had four hundred wives and about a thousand children. The name just kept spreading down the years."

I held up my hand in a stop signal. "Go back a bit, Mr. Griffith," I said. I was making an effort to keep an unlawyerly look of gloating off my face, now that I seemed to be close to pinning down one of Grace's current locations. "How did you get the name?" I asked Griffith. "How do you know she's Grace Nguyen?"

"From the postman. Ernie his name is, and he's a member of my team."

"Your what?"

"Well, he doesn't know he's a member of my team. He likes the generous Christmas tip, the occasional Glenlivet or cup of coffee when he's on his rounds, that kind of thing. He's only too glad to answer my questions."

"Anybody else besides Ernie on your team?"

"The gardener, a fellow named Andreas. German, I think. He got hired by phone and is paid by mail. So, as you might imagine, he's not a ready source of information. Nice chap, though."

"Summing up," I said, "Grace Nguyen receives mail over there, but doesn't stay the night. Have I got that straight?"

"Approximately."

"That implies I'm missing something."

"The hours," Griffith said. "Whatever's going on in there, they keep strange hours."

"But I bet you've taken their measure in that department."

Griffith's face filled with satisfaction. "They arrive at six o'clock. Always about six in the afternoon, maybe ten or fifteen minutes before or after the hour. They don't leave until two or three in the morning. Sometimes a little earlier. Their departure time isn't as precise as the arrival time."

"You're up and around at three in the morning?"

"My nightly visit to the bathroom happens around then. Some nights I loiter awhile and watch until the Navigator leaves. It's a random sampling perhaps, but I can pretty much vouch for the times."

I polished off the Coors. "Just a couple more questions, Mr. Griffith."

"The licence plate number on the Navigator would be one," Griffith said. "Got something for writing it down?"

I made a habit of carrying a small notepad and a black Uniball pen. Griffith recited the plate number from memory. I bet he was the insufferable kid in grade school who beat everybody to the answer. Hot shots who carried notepads and Uniball pens were slackers compared to our Lawrence Griffith. I wrote the plate number into my pad.

"According to Ernie the postman," Griffith went on, "no other mail comes to the house except pieces addressed to Homeowner. And we don't know who that is, do we."

Griffith smiled at his small joke.

"A couple of questions you said, Mr. Crang?"

"You just covered them," I said. "But one more. What about the police raid three or four years ago?"

Griffith made a sound best described as a chuckle. "By gad, you're well briefed, Mr. Crang," he said. "The raid was pretty much a non-starter. Police went in with a massive force, all guns blazing, as it were. They had the misguided notion someone was growing marijuana over there. Nobody was, the police left, and that was the last we heard of that."

"They should've checked with you first. Think of the saved manpower."

"Indeed," Griffith said. He got up from his chair. "Leave me your cell number, Mr. Crang. I'll ring whenever something else develops at 32. All that's happened so far could be only a prelude to more interesting events over there. I have that feeling."

"Bigger than Roy and Lois having it off?"

"In a different league, Mr. Crang."

We walked to the front door. "You've been a big help, Mr. Griffith," I said.

"Call me Lawrence."

"Thanks, Lawrence."

"Or," he said, "you can call me I Spy."

I stopped and turned to him. He was wearing a look somewhere short of smug but way beyond satisfied.

I said, "I might have known you'd have sussed that out."

"It's just a matter of paying attention, Mr. Crang. And besides, I'm rather fond of the nickname."

"How so?"

"It's what I do. The same as the characters in le Carré novels. I spy."

11

Annie played tour guide on a shortcut to a restaurant new to us named John's. It was on Bathurst Street twenty minutes north and west of our house. Annie's route sliced through the southwest corner of the Annex.

"Built in the 1880s or thereabouts," she said, pointing at the steeple and other features of a church on Howland Avenue called St. Alban's. "It was supposed to be the cathedral for Toronto's entire Anglican diocese."

"Looks on the truncated side for something that grand."

"Exactly," Annie said. "The diocese ran out of money. Never finished the church. What we're looking at right now is one-quarter of the planned cathedral. Kind of sad."

"Never made it to diocese status?"

"Not for as long as they counted on. Now a boys' school owns the place."

"'Royal St. George's College,'" I read from a sign on a small building next to the church. "Imagine that, an institution in the Annex that's royal. No wonder they're so snooty around here."

We crossed Bathurst and went into John's, a small narrow room, done in dark wood and restrained decor. It seemed to be trying for a New York feel.

I studied the menu. Venezuelan platter, Colombian empanadas, Milanesa de pollo, a lot of dishes with a choice of shredded chicken or shredded beef.

"The place ought to be called Juan's," I said.

"Latin American cuisine is why we've come," Annie said.

"How'd we get lured way up here? Off the beaten track, isn't it, not a chic section of town. Maybe there's no such thing as a chic section of Bathurst."

"Word of mouth got us here," Annie said. "Specifically the mouths of our neighbours."

"Which ones?"

Annie smiled and leaned a little over the table. "Ones who're like me. Freelancers. Tons of my kind live on the block. Every day, I'm taking a break, out there in the front yard. Somebody walks by. We chat, and in no time, five or six of us freelancers are mingling." Annie glanced around John's as if she was checking the place for Major Street residents.

"These freelancers," I said, "what do they freelance at?"

"Mostly at being retired. But they seem to be occupied with many things. Busier than they've ever been in their lives is what they say. Dining out is a preoccupation. So the other day I ask what restaurants around here they recommend. Charles said John's, and everybody else went nuts with their opinions."

"Nuts in a positive sense?"

"Unanimously."

"Which one is Charles?"

"In the house with the ironwork bench out front. Sixtyish guy, I'd say, nice looking with the beard. Everything else's average. Average weight, average build. Not average brain."

"The guy who always seems to be wearing the baseball cap, that's him? Drives the red Jeep?"

"You've met Charles?" Annie asked, pleased with me if I had.

"He nods, I nod. We have a nodding acquaintanceship."

Annie squeezed my hand. "Isn't it fun being a homeowner in a neighbourhood all our own."

The friendly waiter who looked more Italian than Latin American took our order. A bottle of the house red. The Venezuelan arepas for Annie. Milanesa de pollo for cautious me. It was billed as lightly breaded chicken with rice, beans and plantain. Sounded tasty.

"Wait," I said, puzzled momentarily. "What's plantain?"

"Relax, fella," Annie said, "it's of the banana family."

"Got you," I said.

Anne and I toasted ourselves with glasses of the red wine, and Annie said, "Want to feel my biceps, big guy?"

"You've only been gardening one day."

Annie flexed her right arm.

"Should've seen me," she said. "Turning over great shovel loads of earth. Carrying a tree. Actually it was helping carry a tree. Called a paperback maple, this one was. Looked like an innocent little thing, but those mothers are heavy. Takes four people to lift. Practically tears your arms out of the sockets."

"What about the creative side? That's what you're in it for, right?"

"Still to come," Annie said. "Kathleen's drawing a plan for what she wants to do with our backyard. We'll look it over in the next couple of weeks. And then—" Annie spread her arms wide "—we go wild."

The friendly waiter brought our food. Annie's Venezuelan arepas featured corn cakes. She said they were delicious. I felt the same way about my pollo. Everything on the plate tasted light, as if the chicken, rice and beans were floating over my taste buds. The plantain wasn't bad, though the banana connection seemed a stretch.

"Made a crucial purchase this afternoon," Annie said. "Something rare and vital. A VHS machine."

"Is this retro week? I should get my rotary phone out of the closet?"

"Put a sock in it, sweetie. The VHS is going to be an essential working tool for the Edward Everett Horton book. Most of his movies, my problem with them, they haven't reached DVD. Is that crazy or what? Especially when you consider the star of a bunch of his films is nobody less than Fred Astaire. You'd think the whole world would want to see Fred Astaire on DVD or Blu-ray or whatever technology."

"No argument from me."

We chewed happily, and Annie burbled further on the subject of Edward Everett Horton until Horton led back to Astaire who reminded her of another topic.

"Speaking of tap dancing," she said, "what's your next move in the hunt for Grace Nguyen and your seventy-five Gs?"

"Got Gloria on the case."

"Oh goodie, the first thing you've done in the Grace thing I fully agree with."

Gloria Allard was my part-time secretary. Nobody who worked for me was full-time. I shared Gloria with three other criminal lawyers. I had her services for a day and a half every week. Billings, filing, badgering clients delinquent on paying their bills. In a pinch, Gloria expedited tracing jobs that were beyond Maury's range of effectiveness. The Highbury search was one of those. Annie loved Gloria. Everybody loved Gloria. She was a very even-keeled person.

"The stage of the game I'm at," I said, "I've got the address where Grace is working at god knows what, and I've got the licence number on the car that takes her to the address and back. What Gloria's going to do is find out who owns what. Check out the title to 32 Highbury. Trace the ownership of the Navigator SUV. Get all my ducks lined up."

Annie chewed on her corn cakes, simultaneously looking at me as if I might have once again lost my moorings.

"What's it matter who owns what?" she said. "All you have to do is follow the black SUV to Grace's current residence and brace her for the seventy-five thousand."

"I don't think the situation's that simple," I said.

"I know you don't. You can't stand it when things aren't complicated."

"My lawyer's training."

I swallowed a bit of wine and said, "Shall I make the case for taking my investigation into Grace a step or two further?"

"If you insist," Annie said.

"Suppose Grace is in there at the house on Highbury running some kind of scheme. Probably one with a crooked angle. A consequence of that, among many potential pieces of trouble, the agreement I worked out with the Crown in the grow op case could blow up."

"You don't think she's still in the marijuana business? Really?"

I shook my head. "According to my sources, namely the Crown, the Highbury house showed no signs of grow op activity."

"Whatever dumb thing it is these people do with condensation on the windows? None of those kind of signs?"

"Nothing in evidence," I said. "And anyway, just one grow op house isn't enough to earn bucks that would seriously lead Grace to take a chance on getting back in the dope business."

"So what's she doing in there five nights a week, sometimes six?"

"That's the whole problem," I said. "I've no idea about her activities, her intentions, her financial status. Especially the latter. Can she pay me the seventy-five grand? Where's her money?"

"I don't quite trust your reasoning," Annie said. "But I can't think of an argument against doing whatever it is you're thinking of doing. Common sense tells me you shouldn't. But since when does common sense come into the picture if you've made up your mind otherwise?"

"I think it's helpful to nose around before I ask Grace for my money."

"It's not ask her for the payment, honey. It's demand the payment. You've done the work. Remember?"

"That's the step after the next step. I nose around, then I get the money. That's my order of attack."

Annie had nothing more to add.

Both of us ordered an espresso. I paid, we agreed retired Major Street people knew what they were talking about when they recommended restaurants, and we walked home to watch a VHS of a 1937 Fred Astaire movie called *Shall We Dance*.

"This is out of the chronological order of the Horton movies we've watched so far," Annie said. "But who cares?"

Not me. The movie had a couple of great songs. "They All Laughed" and "They Can't Take That Away From Me." It had Astaire, Ginger Rogers, a bunch of terrific character actors including the one-and-only Edward Everett Horton. He was a tall, slightly hunched-over guy. In the movie, he looked like a fussbudget and said "oh dear" a lot.

"He does befuddled better than anyone," Annie said.

Befuddled?

At the moment, on the Grace Nguyen case, I could relate to that.

12

When I arrived at my office next morning, Gloria Allard was already there. She'd gone across the hall for two cups of Sam Feldman's coffee.

"Sam just poured it," Gloria said. "It's the way you like it. Hot. Practically scalding."

Gloria looked like the woman with the long shiny white hair in the Eileen Fisher dress ad. She had the same hair as the ad woman, and wore clothes the same way, loose and billowy. Gloria was close to sixty, but her face was without wrinkles. I was pretty sure she had a great figure, even if I couldn't see much of it under the white top and the blue skirt she had on this morning, both loose, both billowy. It was her standard everyday uniform.

I drank some coffee. It was almost as hot as Gloria described. "You know," I said to her, "I should rig my own coffee setup in here."

"You probably owe Sam a couple hundred free cups, the rate you drink his coffee."

"That's not counting the cups I mooch for my clients."

"When you get your own setup, what brand of coffee are you going to be offering? I got an idea, if you need one."

"I have an idea too," I said.

"Kenyan," Gloria said.

"You took the word out of my mouth," I said.

"What about Maury?" Gloria said.

"If he knows it's Kenyan, he'll say, 'Goddamn foreign shit.'"

"What he'll say," Gloria said, "he'll say, 'What's wrong with Maxwell House?'"

"We won't tell Maury it's Kenyan."

"I'm on board with that."

"Done," I said. "Now, let's get down to the other business."

"Plenty of it," Gloria said, opening her slim, black leather briefcase. "And all of it revelatory. Of what exactly, I'm not sure. But I have a feeling you'll be intrigued."

"Go ahead," I said, "intrigue me."

"First, the Highbury house," Gloria said, leafing through a pad of paper from her briefcase. The paper was yellow and legal sized. The sheets were covered in Gloria's small, neat handwriting in black ink. In combination, the paper and ink made an old-fashioned and reassuring sight.

"A little under four years ago," Gloria said, "the property was transferred from the estate of Edward Ronald Spencer to Elizabeth Anne Janetta. All cash deal, no mortgages. Million and a half dollars on the button. And there's nothing on title since the sale. No more transactions. The property remains in the hands of the aforementioned Ms. Janetta."

"It happens I'm aware of a Mr. Janetta."

"Sit on that for a minute, my man," Gloria said. "Next, we turn to the vehicle, to wit a 2010 Ford Navigator SUV. Black in colour, and it's registered in the name of, ta da, Elizabeth Anne Janetta."

"I love consistency."

"Nothing owing on the car either as far as I can tell."

"Ms. Janetta must be rolling in dough."

"She married a bundle," Gloria said. "That much I know."

"The Janetta who occurs to me is Luigi Janetta, crime figure."

"That's Elizabeth's guy," Gloria said. "They got hitched nine years ago. No kids so far."

"Maybe the Highbury house and the Navigator are Luigi's. He puts them in wifey's name for tax reasons."

"That's one possibility," Gloria said. "He much prefers Lou, by the way. Sounds more Metro Toronto and less Calabrian Hills than Luigi."

"Where did you get the Lou Janetta material?"

"I Googled him."

"Of course," I said. "Doesn't everybody Google everybody else?"

"For a guy who avoids publicity like the plague, the way Janetta does," Gloria said, "he's got a hundred thousand Google items."

"I seem to remember a libel action a few years back. He sued a newspaper for something like putting his name and 'racketeer' in the same paragraph."

"You're close. It was a magazine trying to take some of the market away from *Toronto Life*. Did a lot of sensational coverage of the Toronto scene. This one article they carried, it named the names of people they identified as Toronto mob figures. Janetta was in the group. Money laundering. Drug trafficking. Loan-sharking. All the standbys. The story said Janetta was a kingpin. He sued, and it was all settled out of court pretty fast. The magazine apologized, and took back everything it said about Lou. A little money changed hands. And the magazine folded."

"Wow, victory couldn't have been more complete."

"As for the missus, Elizabeth Janetta, I've got material here," Gloria said. When she turned the pages in her yellow pad, she gave each sheet a snap. All business, that was Gloria.

"Elizabeth'd be a woman with a large crooked nose?" I said. "Wart on the nose, a hair in the wart?"

"Geez, Crang, you think in stereotypes," Gloria said. "Inaccurate stereotypes I might say. The real Ms. Janetta happens to be a looker. Grade-A-certified gorgeous."

Gloria handed me a colour printout of an Internet photo. It showed a blond woman in a black evening gown barely held up by two thin straps. She wasn't posing for the picture. She didn't seem aware it was being taken.

"This was last year at some annual Italian-Canadian ball," Gloria said. "Two things in reference to the photo. You'll note there's no Mr. Janetta in it even though he was at the ball. And, two, I'm sure Ms. Janetta was alarmed when she found out the camera caught her."

"She's classy," I said, studying the photo longer than I needed to. "Bet that's her real blond hair, and she's got the high cheekbones and the fresh look. Healthy and tanned. Probably plays tennis."

"A third thing about the photo, the Janettas didn't attend this year's Italian-Canadian ball."

"Once photographed, twice shy."

"I don't know if the picture actually appeared anywhere except on the Internet," Gloria said. "It didn't turn up in any magazine or newspaper as far as I could tell."

I drank the rest of my coffee, and debated whether to hit up Sam for a refill. I decided against it. The next cup of coffee poured in the office would come from my very own machine.

"What about the Janetta family home?" I said to Gloria. "We know they don't live at 32 Highbury. Nobody does. So where's the homestead?"

"Up Bridle Path way," Gloria said. She turned a couple of sheets of the yellow paper, doing it with the usual snap. "Very chic place, architecturally speaking. I drove by first thing this morning. They have about an acre just off Bayview Avenue, the part south of York Mills. Got a high metal fence around the property, but you can still get an appreciation of the architecture through the bars."

"Is it in Ms. Janetta's name the way the other stuff is?"

Gloria shook her head. "A numbered company owns it. I haven't gone behind the numbers. You want, I'll look deeper."

I thought about it. "Probably no need," I said. "Let's stick with Ms. Janetta for now. What was she before she married the mob?"

"Alleged mob," Gloria said.

"Point taken."

"Her surname was Kieran, the family being a wing of the Baldwins," Gloria said, a touch of glee in her voice. "Can you believe it? I'm talking the ultimate FOOF Baldwins, the ones who go way back in our proud province."

"Fine Old Ontario Family Baldwins? We're talking Robert Baldwin himself?"

Gloria nodded. "What was he called when we studied him in Canadian-history class?"

"The Father of Responsible Government. Do schoolchildren get taught that stuff anymore?"

"Mine didn't," Gloria said.

"Kids today," I said, "they'd probably laugh at the idea of 'responsible' and 'government' appearing in the same sentence."

"Cynical bunch, kids today," Gloria said. "Anyway, getting back to Ms. Janetta, a tiny share of the Baldwin-Kieran money trickled far enough down the generations to reach her."

"What's your idea of tiny?"

"No more than a couple million."

"I wouldn't mind a sum that minuscule in my bank account."

"Elizabeth sounds like she might have been the family wild child in her youth," Gloria said. "Got kicked out of Havergal College. Never quite finished her English course at Trinity where all good FOOF children still go."

"What's she do with her time now, besides lend her married name to properties her husband probably owns?"

"Not a whole lot I've discovered so far. Not involved in the usual ladies' committees. Not the ROM, the AGO. But then I really didn't expect our lady to be among that crowd."

"Probably not what mob wives do."

"Want me to expand on Lou himself?" Gloria said, flipping her pages. She looked up at me, smiling a teasing smile. "Give me your stereotypical version of Mr. Janetta," she said. "The physical Lou. What's he look like?"

"Short and rotund. Swarthy. Uses a lot of Brylcreem. Needs to shave three times a day or else his face goes all blue."

"So in your version Elizabeth wouldn't have married him for his looks?"

"You asked for the stereotype. Not reality."

"Needless to say," Gloria said, "there's no photo I could find of Lou. But the magazine article I told you about described him as 'dashing' in one place and 'movie-star handsome' in another."

"There goes that stereotype."

Gloria bent her silver head over the yellow pad, flipping pages.

"Lou ever been busted?" I asked.

"Charged with a crime twice in his life, convicted of neither. One was for dealing cocaine, the other a bunch of gobbledygook that boiled down to money laundering. In both, the Crown withdrew the charges before anything reached the courtroom. Lou was in his twenties back then. Hasn't been a whisper of a charge since."

I made a snorting noise. "No wonder Lou's libel lawyer made mincemeat out of the magazine."

Gloria snapped her yellow note pages a couple of times until the pad was closed. "That's pretty much all I've got on the Janettas," she said. "So what's next with you? You're going to call on the dashing Mr. Janetta?"

I shook my head. "On the lovely Ms. Janetta."

"Want to see those looks in the flesh? So to speak."

"I'll just pretend I didn't hear your trivialization of my investigative purposes."

"Be my guest, Crang."

"Ms. Janetta's the one attached to Highbury," I said. "On paper, she is. If I press her, I can make some yards whether she denies her attachment or admits it. She says she never heard of Highbury, then I thank her and take my questions to Lou. On the other hand, if she tells me, yeah, so what if she owns the place, then I commence my interrogation."

"The straight-on approach, huh?" Gloria said. "I can see maybe that'll work. When do you plan on carrying out this astounding display of forensics?"

"My motto, strike while the iron is hot."

13

Legal representation for the two or three of the ritzier clients in my stable of accused persons had sometimes taken me through the prosperous neighbourhood in the northeast suburbs known as the Bridle Path. So I already knew that a high percentage of the houses up there were teardowns.

Going way back to the years right after the Second World War, E.P. Taylor owned most of the Bridle Path acreage. E.P. was everybody's favourite Canadian tycoon. He looked the part, portly and genial, a pair of qualities Toronto expected to find in its fabulously rich guys. And E.P. had his grasping hand in the kind of investments ordinary folks could understand. Beer companies, grocery store chains, racehorses. Northern Dancer was his, Kentucky Derby winner, greatest racehorse in Canadian history.

I drove north up Bayview Avenue, past Lawrence Avenue, the very Waspy Granite Club on the left. Then turned right off Bayview where the real estate I was cruising through was once Windfields Farm, the headquarters for Taylor's horse operation. When the market for Toronto suburban residences leaped in the 1960s, E.P. moved Windfields east into the country way out near Oshawa. He broke up the former horse property on Bayview to build developments of houses bordering on mansion size on very large lots. Now, E.P. having long since kicked the bucket, the houses were well into the process of redevelopment. The nouveau riche bought up the lots, tore down the mini-mansions and erected imposing castles of bleak grey stone.

The one architectural exception on the block I soon found myself negotiating was the Janetta home. Its lot was as large as the others. The house probably was too, but its élan disguised the vastness. The prime building materials were glass and weathered British Columbia redwood. Combining the two produced an overall architectural effect that, my opinion, rated adjectives like organic and integrated, maybe even wholesome. My list of adjectives was beginning to sound like a list of the sterling qualities of multi-grain bread. But the house looked stunning, and I liked the symbolism of all the glass. The owner may have been a mobster, but he had nothing to hide. The cheek of the guy.

I saw what Gloria meant about the fence. It was high and metal, and perched on every available surface were so many security cameras that nobody entering or leaving the place could avoid appearing on tape. The driveway had an impressive gate, but it was open. I drove in and parked behind a black Navigator SUV. It had the licence number that I Spy Griffith had given me. Ubiquitous was what this Navigator was. It turned up in all the wrong places. Parked next to it was a red Jaguar convertible with a canvas top. The shade of red belonged to the tomato family, and the canvas was light brown. One glance at the licence plate revealed the car's owner. LIZ'S JAG, it read. If I were comparing my ponderous car to Elizabeth Janetta's nifty little number, I'd say hers was Fred Astaire to my Peter Boyle doing "Puttin' on the Ritz" in *Young Frankenstein*.

Getting out of the Mercedes, I was aware of movement behind the glass where the living room was probably placed. But I didn't stop to wonder who was doing the moving or why. More security, I supposed. I pushed a button beside the front door, heard chimes go off inside and waited.

A short, compact woman opened the door. She wore trim black slacks and a tailored green blouse. She deserved congratulations for carrying off the simple outfit so successfully at her age, which I figured to be about the same as Gloria Allard's.

"May I help you?" she said. Her voice had a slight Scottish accent. Or was it Irish? I wasn't good on accents.

"I'm hoping Ms. Janetta might be free to talk with me," I said. "I haven't an appointment, you'll excuse me. But I'm a fan of her home's architecture. May I come in?"

"Aren't you just the pushy one," the woman said.

"But good natured."

The woman smiled, revealing pretty dimples and laugh lines around the eyes. Her hair was dark brown going gracefully to grey, and her eyes were as green as her blouse.

"You look presentable enough," the woman said. "I'll say that for you."

I had on freshly washed jeans, a blue button-down shirt and a lightweight black jacket. I thanked her for the compliment and said, "My hope one day soon is to build something along the same lines as Ms. Janetta's home."

The woman with the dimples looked at her watch.

"Elizabeth swims her laps starting about now," she said. "I'll just see if she has a minute for you first."

"Ms. Janetta might care for my card," I said, taking one out of my wallet.

The woman reached for the card. "Wait here, if you would, good sir," she said, not quite closing the door all the way.

I bounced a little on my toes and tried whistling the opening bars to "Take the 'A' Train." It was harder than I thought.

The woman with the Scottish or Irish accent returned. She no longer had my card in her hand.

"Follow me, you lucky man," she said. The woman definitely had a jolly streak. Would that be more likely Irish or Scottish? Maybe I'd find out one day.

We went across the foyer into a large, bright room furnished in chairs and couches just few enough in number to make the room feel uncluttered and airy. The furniture featured black coverings and cushions. Was the woman leading me the housekeeper? Or one of the family? On the whole, I thought she probably fit the housekeeper role. She kept on moving past the black furniture, me behind her, finally concluding the journey in a reasonably spacious office. It too featured black chairs, cushions and a shiny black desk. I sat in what looked like a director's chair. It was amazingly comfy.

As if all the black called for a little balance, the walls were hung in watercolours in shades of yellow, orange and light blue. All had a kind of playful charm. Behind the desk hung something completely different. In form, it looked like a certificate of graduation from an institution of higher learning, but it announced itself as a notice that Elizabeth Anne Janetta was a member of the board of directors of the Levin Museum. The Levin? The name rang a bell. Faintly.

I was busy digesting this information from the vantage point of my comfy chair when Ms. Janetta herself arrived in the office. I recognized the blond hair and the athletic but delicate superstructure from the photograph Gloria had shown me. Ms. Janetta had on a white bathrobe, uncinched at the waist, hanging open, and under it, a one-piece black bathing suit. Her figure in the bathing suit was lush, almost all of it revealed by the fit of the suit, not leaving much that a guy's imagination needed to work on. I stood up to greet her. She reached out a hand, and I shook it firmly. The hand was slim and warm.

"Please sit down, Mr. Crang," Ms. Janetta said. She took a seat in another black director's chair. "You happened to be driving by?"

"Not quite, Ms. Janetta," I said. "I've made a point of passing the house three or four times in the last month. Scouting it, you might say. This visit is spur of the moment. I felt something like a compulsion to introduce myself to the owner of such a striking home."

"Our housekeeper said you're building a place yourself."

I patted myself on the back for getting it right about the dimpled woman's place in the household.

"Still in the planning stages," I said to Ms. Janetta. "But I know of a property I'm thinking of putting something on, and when I do, I'll use your house as my architect's model."

As I talked, I noticed for the first time that we weren't alone. A man was standing in the doorway from the living room to the office. He cut a formidable figure, tall, big body, probably lifted a lot of weights judging by the bulging muscles under the T-shirt he had on. He kept his hands crossed at his waistline. The guy was definitely one of the help, not a Janetta. In his left hand, he held what I felt certain was my card.

"The property you're talking about, Mr. Crang," Elizabeth Janetta was saying, "is it in the Bridle Path near here?"

"I wish," I said. "No, it's out in the west end."

"There're nice places in that part of the city."

"In the district they call the Kingsway. Do you know it?"

Ms. Janetta crossed her legs. With her, that was maximum provocation of a sexual sort. "Everybody knows the Kingsway," she said.

"On a street called Highbury," I said.

Ms. Janetta didn't flinch or do anything else overt. No looking over at the help in the doorway, no flushing or blushing. But there was a definite shift in the air around us. Her eyes did something funny, as if they had lost focus for an instant. It wasn't much, the changing atmosphere and the eye thing, but I felt pretty certain my mention of Highbury had caught Ms. Janetta way off balance.

"I don't think I know the street," she said.

"What I like about it," I said, "the lot out there is extra large. Just needs several trees taken out, and of course, I'll have the present house levelled."

"That's very ambitious of you."

"All I need to do is buy the property."

Elizabeth Janetta uncrossed her legs. It was very hard to keep my eyes meeting her eyes. She said, "How does the present owner feel about that?"

"Something of a mystery there, Ms. Janetta," I said. "The house appears to be unoccupied."

"Really?"

"No one answers when I knock on the door."

"Perhaps the owner is on holiday."

"Maybe," I said. "But I intend to persevere."

Ms. Janetta seemed to give that some thought, then she stood up abruptly but gracefully.

"You'll excuse me, Mr. Crang," she said. "Fitness calls. I like to keep in shape."

"And all of us are the better for your fitness, Ms. Janetta."

"Good luck with your house plans," she said.

Ms. Janetta walked back through the living room, turning toward a door that led to the backyard. I could see a swimming pool out there, about fifty metres long. There were no slides in it, no beach balls, no toys. It was a working pool for serious swimmers.

I felt someone's light touch on my arm. "This way, Mr. Crang," the housekeeper said. Just as she spoke, I was watching Elizabeth Janetta as she dropped the white robe and raised her arms to dive into the pool. It was a sight to make a man groan.

I followed Ms. Dimples to the front door. The muscular help trailed along, studying my card.

"Hang in there, sport," I said to him. "You'll have it memorized in no time."

14

On the way from the Janetta place to my office, I pulled onto a side street off Bayview long enough to text Gloria. I asked her to dig up whatever she could find about the Levin Museum. The bell that the Levin's name rang for me still tolled faintly. But persistently. The texting done, I detoured to the Loblaws at Dupont and Christie to buy one package of Kenyan coffee and another of number two coffee filters.

Back in my own neighbourhood, I circled around our block twice, looking for a parking space. I found none, and headed back up to Bloor, went east a few long blocks all the way to Huron, south to Washington, back to Major and around one more time until, fifteen minutes after I'd reached the neighbourhood, I finally found room to park on Brunswick a block west of Major. Nobody thought about parking cars when the houses in the neighbourhood were built. For one thing, none of the working people who bought the houses could afford a car. For another, cars weren't such a big deal a century or more ago when the houses went up. The result was that only a couple of homes on our block had garages today, and the rest of us battled over street parking spaces. We paid the city one hundred and ninety bucks a year for a permit and the privilege of entering into the parking fray. I figured it was the inability to park one's car that would sound the death knell of Toronto, maybe of all cities everywhere. Drivers would be stuck in their cars for days without end, hunting desperately for a place to ditch the car, going mad from the frustration of never being able to get out from behind the steering wheel.

I locked the car and walked back along Bloor to a crowded little store that sold discounted appliances. Toasters, blenders, items like that. I picked out a Cuisinart coffee maker. The literature on the box said it made four cups at a time, but the clerk said it was actually no good for more than three cups. I bought it despite the false advertising. Before I lugged all my packages to the office, I got a tiny table on the patio at By the Way, a Bohemian sort of restaurant on Bloor at Brunswick. Or maybe it was just casual. I ate a vegetarian sandwich and ambled back to the fifth floor on Spadina.

Gloria Allard was still there.

"Not still here," she said. "I went out and did the research on the Levin Museum. Now I'm back to write a memo."

"Forget the memo," I said. "Just talk me through it while I set up the office's brand new coffee machine."

"Did you see the dame married to the mob?"

"Did I ever."

"And?" Gloria said. She was getting her notes lined up.

"She certainly does things to a bathing suit."

"I can imagine. Are we talking bikini?"

"A form-fitting one-piece."

"Must have been thrilling for you," Gloria said.

I put the new coffee maker on a little table that sometimes held a vase into which I sometimes put flowers.

"Looks nice, doesn't it?" I said.

Gloria was studying her notes some more. She raised her head. "Are we still on the subject of Ms. Janetta's figure?"

"I could wax lyrical. But, no, the coffee maker."

"It's well designed and appears functional," Gloria said, giving the Cuisinart a study. "But where's a spoon for measuring the coffee into the maker? How about milk and sugar? Not to mention cups? We always depend on Sam for cups. It's a slippery slope you put yourself on, Crang."

"A miniature fridge to keep the milk from going bad, yeah, I'll need one of those too. Not that I use milk. Or that you do. Or Maury. But the fridge'll be nice for clients who aren't so fastidious about coffee purity."

"You're beginning to sound like a TV food show host."

"Grace Nguyen's a milk-with-her-coffee person, now that I think about it."

"Which brings us back to the case," Gloria said. "You asked me to dig around for the bathing beauty's pursuits in her spare time, one of them being her position on the Levin Museum's board."

"I know the name, but I've forgotten where it is."

"How can you forget?" Gloria said. "Pay attention, Crang. It's the one on College, shows only one kind of art. Guess what the kind is."

"Hey!" I said. The faint tinkling of the memory bell was suddenly loud enough to break an eardrum. "Is that the ceramics place?"

"Four floors of nothing except pots and vases and cups and mugs."

"So," I said, feeling something close to euphoric, "what we have is Grace Nguyen subscribing to a ceramics magazine and Elizabeth Janetta sitting on the board of a ceramics museum."

"Not enough to support a case for any proposition you might be contemplating."

"No," I said, "but more than enough to build hopes on."

Gloria rolled her eyes in a give-me-a-break look.

"Who's Levin of the Levin Museum when he's at home?" I asked.

"Crang, old pal, you've based your question on two false assumptions," Gloria said. "Levin's dead, and when Levin was alive, she was a woman named Victoria."

I thought about the implications of the Levin Museum. Whatever they were, did any of them reach into Grace's life? My first-hand knowledge of the museum and its workings was just about zero. The place was only a fifteen-minute walk from Annie's and my house, but neither of us had ever passed through its portals. Ceramics weren't our cup of tea, so to speak.

"You got more about the museum's background?" I asked Gloria.

"Quite interesting," she said. "Victoria Levin's husband was Mr. Steel in these parts. He made large sums of money in the building boom of thirty years ago. Then he kicked the bucket, and not long after that, in the 1990s, the widow Levin spent fifty million of her inheritance on the museum."

"How public-spirited of her," I said.

"There's more," Gloria said. "While she was at it, Ms. Levin made a kind of feminist statement. She saw to it that the board of directors was then and forever entirely female. All employees at the museum have to be women too, except for volunteers. Men are allowed to do the nonpaying grunt jobs."

"That's cute," I said.

"But," Gloria said, "the place's feminism isn't as pure as they'd like you to think."

"Are you showing your catty side?"

"Just about all of the women on the board got there because their husbands kicked in with big donations in the wives' names."

"Not necessarily the case with Elizabeth Janetta," I said. "You pointed out this morning she brought some inherited money into the marriage."

"Yeah, she may get a pass," Gloria said. "Her donation, wherever the money came from, added up to half a million."

"Generous enough to be serious," I said. "I'm putting a trip to the Levin on my agenda."

"What else've you got in mind?"

"An immediate return visit to Highbury," I said. I studied the coffee maker on its stand. "And I'm going to complete the conversion of the office into a coffee bar."

"Mini-fridges you can get for a song at Walmart."

"Not me," I said. "I've gone through life so far without setting foot in a Walmart. Not a McDonald's either or a Tim Hortons. No chance I'll break my streak now."

"A life without a coffee and a Timbits from Timmie's? Crang, for heaven's sake, where's your Canadian pride?"

"Never been in a Red Lobster either."

"What's all this denial of pleasure and convenience get you?" Gloria asked.

"Not far in practical terms. Means I have to scratch around to find a little fridge. But my god, girl, imagine how virtuous I feel."

"You're actually talking about virtue?" Gloria said. "You, the guy who recently gained entry to a private residence by way of subterfuge and impersonation?"

"That was business," I said. "Not crossing the threshold of a Tim Hortons belongs in the category of moral crusade."

Gloria did another of her oh-how-bogus-can-you-get gestures. "Back to the Janetta family and whatever nonsense it's involved in," she said, "what's your next move?"

"A piece of midnight creeping out on Highbury," I said. "It'll be a whole lot more about business than moral crusade."

15

It was a few minutes before three in the morning. Maury and I were sitting in the front seat of my car drinking Kenyan coffee out of plastic cups. We poured the coffee from a large Thermos. The car was parked in I Spy Griffith's driveway, facing at an angle across the street from the grounds of 32 Highbury. I'd called I Spy for parking privileges that afternoon. On the phone, I Spy sounded thrilled at the prospect of being within observing distance of whatever action might occur.

"This's pretty tasty," Maury said of the coffee. "What is it, something new from Folgers, some shit like that?"

"Just bought it the other day," I said, hoping evasion would carry the day.

"Not some foreign shit?"

"Maury, you've got to enlighten me about the way you toss around the word 'shit.' Just now, the first time you said 'shit' it meant something positive. Folgers was 'shit,' but that was a good thing. The next sentence, 'shit' and foreign went together, and nothing was good about either. You'll pardon me, but a person can get confused."

"It's all in the context," Maury said. "What's confusing about that?"

"I reasoned that out, but the reasoning out came in retrospect, if you follow me. When you said 'shit,' both times my immediate reaction was negative."

"Follow you, my ass. It was only negative the second time. Anything foreign is negative shit. Practically anything. You remember Bobby Jaspar? Tenor saxophone player?"

"Very nice musician," I said. "Was once married to Blossom Dearie."

"Bobby was Belgian, but he wasn't shit. He was one of the exceptions. Everything else not from North America is shit." Maury turned to me, making sure I was taking in his lecture. "That's not so hard to remember," he said.

"True," I said, hoping he wouldn't ask me again about the origins of the coffee he was drinking.

"I'm used to working late hours from the old days," Maury said. He'd moved along to another topic. "But not under these crappy conditions."

"What's so crappy about in here?"

"Hotel jobs like I did, I kept on the move every night. Going room to room. Good exercise when you think about it. Tonight, crissake, it's all this sitting in a car getting a numb bum."

Maury and I had been in the Mercedes in I Spy's driveway for almost two hours. When we arrived sometime after one, I'd sneaked across Highbury to number 32, all the way up to the house, to check for the black Ford Navigator. The car was where I Spy said it would be, close to the front door. The house's curtains were still pulled across the windows. Light showed around the edges of the curtains, but I wasn't going to risk a search to see if any of the edges allowed enough room for me to peek in. I was playing it safe.

In the Mercedes, waiting for the Navigator to leave, Maury and I drank from the Thermos. Annie made the coffee after I told her my plans for the evening. A break and enter with Maury, I said. Annie shrugged. She didn't say anything much, but her general demeanour told me she thought this was a stupid stunt on a par with the one at Grace's condo. Still, she fixed up the Thermos of coffee and gave me a big hug. That must have counted for something.

Annie had put in another day of heavy lifting for the goddess of the gardens. One of the other slaves came home with Annie for dinner. She was a tall, fit blonde named Rita who looked like she spent time in a gym toning her muscles. When I left, Annie and Rita were pulling the cork on what they said was their final bottle of wine.

"I never used to drink anything on a night I was working hotels," Maury said. "Not coffee, not booze, not anything."

"Why was that?" I asked.

"Avoid having to take a leak when I'm in the middle of somebody's room."

"That would've been an adventure."

"Adventures, oh shit, I had different kinds of those," Maury said. "I ever tell you about the time I went into this famous Canadian actor's suite? Was at the Windsor Arms Hotel behind Bloor and Bay, around that neighbourhood?"

"New one to me."

"In the guy's suite," Maury said, "he had thousands of dollars' worth of stuff. A watch, jewellery, a little cash. Jesus, he had a huge collection of sex toys. The guy's libido must've never quit. Anyway, I took everything worthwhile in sight. Then a couple of weeks go by, and this guy, the famous actor, he turns up on Johnny Carson's show talking about the burglary at the Windsor Arms up there in Toronto. I'm at home watching the show, and the actor said he lost one thing he really missed. I thought he was gonna say one of the fucking sex toys. But, no, he said he was broken-hearted about the burglar taking his Order of Canada medal. The guy was practically weeping in Johnny Carson's arms. So what else could I do? I got the guy's address, and mailed the medal back to him. I been waitin' ever since for this famous actor to go on somebody else's talk show, and thank the burglar with the heart of gold."

Across the street, headlights beamed out of the long driveway.

"Here they come," I said.

"About fucking time," Maury said.

Both of us slid down in our seats. I Spy's driveway was to the left of the spot where number 32's driveway met the street. I Spy said the black Navigator would turn farther to our left and drive away. I Spy had that straight. The Navigator stopped at the street, paused, turned to his right, which was our left, and sped out of our sight down Highbury.

Maury and I got out of the Mercedes. We shut the car's doors softly, not to cause undue racket in the still of the night. I led the way across Highbury and up the driveway. Both of us carried flashlights. I was wearing an all-black outfit. Black jeans, loose black shirt, black Nikes. Maury had asked why I hadn't rubbed black shoe polish on my face. "Like a fucking commando," he'd said. As far as I could make out, Maury wore his usual clothes, even a tie with a Windsor knot.

Neither of us turned on our flashlights until we reached the front door to the house.

"Shine your light on the lock, you don't mind," Maury said. I did as I was asked, and Maury leaned close to examine the lock.

"They got an Abloy on here," he said.

"Is that bad news?" I asked.

"Very reliable lock," Maury said. "Except when a guy like me comes along."

He turned on his own flashlight and beamed it around the door and over to the window closest to where we were standing.

"Looks like there's no security system," Maury said. "The kind that calls the cops and a private outfit at the same time."

"Maybe they got something inside they wouldn't want the cops to see," I said.

"Probably," Maury said. "Private security companies aren't worth shit anyway."

"Really?"

"I mean 'shit' in the negative sense," Maury said.

"I deduced that."

"Keep your light on the lock," Maury said. Maury spoke in a commanding voice when he put himself in charge of events.

He performed some sleight of hand with his picks, and in a couple of minutes, he swung open the door.

We stepped over the threshold, shining our flashlights ahead of us.

"What's with this Grace dame?" Maury said. "Everyplace she goes, it's got no furniture."

He was right. The very large room on the other side of the foyer was mostly bare. But grouped over by the far wall, there were three large and significant pieces of working equipment. Maury and I walked over to check out the pieces. The first was a table with a chipped surface that held several small tools arranged in orderly rows. There were small artist's brushes on the table and many containers of enamel. To the right of the table, a silver tank dominated everything within range. It was enormous and sleek. Closer to the wall, there was a supersize pail that appeared to be filled with scraps left over from whatever enterprise was being carried out on the table and in the silver tank. Underfoot, as we moved around the arrangement of table, tank and pail, there was some faint crunching.

"Smells like cement in here," Maury said.

"To be exact," I said, "I think it's clay we're sniffing. It's what we're probably walking on too."

"Like for pottery, that's what you're talking about?"

"The silver tank right there is a kiln," I said. "The little I know about pottery, the last step for a potter, or close to the last step, he sticks the pot he's shaped out of the clay into a kiln at a very high temperature."

"How do you know that Jesus big thing's a kiln?"

"It says so," I said. I shined my flashlight beam on the side of the tank where it carried the manufacturer's name plus a word in big letters, "KILN."

"What about all the crap on the table?" Maury asked. "Those brushes and all the little tubes?"

"To paint the decorations on the pots or whatever it is they're making in here," I said. "Just as a guess though, it's probably not pots or anything else big they're making. It looks like the place is scaled for smaller work."

"This is what you came to see?" Maury said.

"Let's just say we might be getting closer to answers."

"I'll leave you to it," Maury said. "I gotta check the back door."

"What for?" I asked.

"Here's another rule of the business," Maury said. "You should have two places of ingress and whatever the hell the other thing is."

"Egress," I said.

"For getting out in an emergency."

Maury disappeared down a hall to the back of the house.

Shining the flashlight over the tools on the table, I picked up some of them one by one. They must have been used for shaping clay. They were impressive little things, delicate in appearance but strong and firm and probably unbreakable. Shaping the clay? Yes, almost certainly, but where was the clay? I pointed the beam along the wall behind me. There it was, the grey clay, in rows and rows of thick plastic bags. Some of the bags were open and spilling out at the top; the rest were still waiting for the summons to usefulness.

I turned my light and my attention to the big refuse can. There was some scrunched-up newspaper in there. There were a few small pieces of solid clay of no particular shape. The pieces had the look of leftover chunks. Rejects, I'd say. Somebody was working with clay, and when the work didn't come out right, the person threw it in the major-sized garbage pail. It was a theory, but was I certain what I was talking about? Not nearly.

I held the flashlight in my right hand, and with my left I messed around in the pail's debris. The left hand found something solid. It was a larger piece of clay that might have a shape of some possibly identifiable sort. The bottom of the thing kind of resembled a pair of fat legs, the top half was lumpy and indeterminate. It was an unfinished piece, and looked to me quite a bit bigger than the size of the metal soldiers I used to play with when I was a little kid. As far as I could make out in the beam from my flashlight, the figure I was turning over in my hand was much heavier than a toy soldier and not nearly as specific. On the other hand, the object was too incomplete for me to make any judgment about. What it most looked like at the moment was a lump that a figure was waiting to emerge from.

Then the cell vibrated in my pocket.

Whoever was phoning me at three-thirty in the morning must have something very important to report. Or it was a wrong number.

I chose to answer.

"Crang," I said in a low voice.

"The Navigator is coming back!" a man said, speaking in a rush close to panic. "It's two seconds from reaching the driveway!"

"Mr. Griffith, that you?" I said. "I Spy?"

"Yes," he said. "The car's making its turn to the house now!"

At the same moment, I saw the headlights shining through the trees at the front of the house.

I switched off my flashlight. Closed the cell. And turned toward the darkness Maury had disappeared into.

"Maury," I said in a low voice I hoped had carrying power. "Put your flashlight out. The people in the Navigator are back."

"Then get the fuck down here," Maury's voice answered. He sounded calm. He must have been caught in this sort of jam before. Surprised in the act of burglarizing a room.

I bumped into a wall, lost my bearings in the dark, stumbled once, then found the hall and hustled down a short flight of stairs.

Maury was standing at the back door, holding it open.

"Another Abloy," he said, nodding at the lock on the door.

"That's a very professional observation, Maury," I said. "But now we got a different problem. You know, escape?"

Both of us stepped on to the flagstones of the back patio. I looked around while Maury did some tricky thing about relocking the door behind us. We could hear the door at the front of the house swinging open and banging hard against the foyer wall. A man's angry voice said something, but the only word that reached my ears was a loud and insistent "Fuck!"

"We can't run across the lawn," I whispered to Maury. "They'd spot us."

"Got no choice, Crang."

"Let's try the garden shed," I said, pointing at it behind me. "Oughta be a couple of hiding places in there."

I was closest to the shed door. When I pushed it open, it swung as smoothly and silently as it had when I visited the place earlier. I moved to the right and ducked down below the window on that side. Maury did the same on the left side.

"Oh, no, shit," I whispered.

"Crang, shut the fuck up," Maury whispered back.

"Shit," I said. "That's what I'm in. Manure over my ankles."

"Relax, pal," Maury said in a comradely whisper. "This probably won't last long."

For a guy crouched almost shin deep in animal excrement, the time in the shed had already stretched too long.

16

Hunkered down in the Highbury shed the way I was, my nose hovered about a foot and a half above the manure. In such a tight space, the stench just about knocked me out. I tried shifting position by an inch or two. My shoes generated faint sucking noises in the muck. The change in posture made no difference in the strength of the stink. It was growing more powerful by the second.

I heard the back door to the house open. Then footsteps on the patio.

"Nobody's out here," an angry male voice said. It was the same voice we'd heard at the front door a minute or two earlier. Whoever the guy was, he was in a foul mood.

"You're the only one seen a light," Mr. Angry said, apparently to someone with him. "I never."

"You were too busy bitching about everything else," said a voice I knew only too well. The voice belonged to my client. Elusive Grace Nguyen. "I saw a light moving in the house when we were coming back up the driveway," she said.

"If a light was turned on in the house," the guy said, "I woulda caught it."

How many people were out there? Just Mr. Angry and Grace? This wasn't a Monday night. I Spy said another man often showed up at Highbury, usually on Mondays. So he probably wasn't out there, though one never knew.

"Look in the shed," Grace said. It sounded like she was directing operations, though the angry guy seemed to think he was in charge.

Footsteps crossed the patio. The steps belonged to the angry guy. I squatted down, even closer to the manure. I was holding my breath.

The door to the garden shed swung open.

"Oh, Jesus," the angry guy's voice said. "It stinks in there."

He shut the door without spending time on anything like a real check of the shed's interior.

"This is fucking ridiculous, Grace," he said. "Get your stuff out of the can, wherever the hell you left whatever the hell it is."

"My makeup kit," Grace said. "It's upstairs in the powder room."

"Why don't you carry a purse like a normal broad?"

"Because I'm taking precautions." Grace's voice was fainter than when she first spoke. She'd probably turned to go into the house.

The guy with the angry voice was still on the patio. I could hear his footsteps. They sounded as if he was walking in a direction away from the shed toward the long stretch of lawn in the yard. I risked a quick look out the window.

At first, my body didn't like the idea. My legs and back felt as if they were glued in place. They resisted movement. But I levered myself a foot or so upward. I thought I heard my bones cracking. I intuited two inches of space would be enough for my peek from the window. I peeked. The angry guy had his back to me at an angle to my left. He was about six or seven yards away. But his back and his all-round contours told me who he was. He was the muscular gent from the Janetta house when I called on the lovely Elizabeth. I ducked back down. My legs and back were screaming in agony.

A few minutes of silence went by. They felt like a few hours. The angry guy stayed on the patio until the back door opened.

"All right, Rocky, we can go now," Grace's voice said.

Rocky?! I could hardly believe the guy's name was so appropriate. Rocky suited him, all muscles and wrath. What else was someone like that going to be named except Rocky?

Maury and I didn't budge. We heard Rocky go back in the house, slam the back door and head out the front door. The Navigator's motor revved a couple of times. That was the way a guy named Rocky would drive. Lot of revving of engines, though with the Navigator, the revving had a muted quality. The sound of the engine soon faded down the driveway. Things at 32 Highbury became once again still and quiet.

Maury stood up from his crouching position.

"Give me a hand, if you would, Maury," I said.

"Depends," Maury said. "Forget it if your hand's covered in fucking manure."

"My pedal extremities are the problem," I said. "They're what soaked up the stinky stuff."

Maury yanked me to a standing position. Both of us stretched and groaned on the patio's flagstones. My back and legs loosened up, but the odour coming off my shoes, socks and the bottoms of my jeans wasn't going anywhere except with me.

The two of us walked back to the Mercedes in I Spy Griffith's driveway, Maury striding, me squishing. I Spy stood in the second-floor window at the far right end. He had a big smile on his face, and he was giving me the damned double thumbs-up. I answered him with an ordinary wave of my hand. That ought to be enough to convey gratitude for the heads-up cell call.

After I scraped the muck off the bottom of my Nikes, Maury and I got in the Mercedes and drove away.

"Put down the windows, if you wouldn't mind," Maury said. "All of them."

I did as Maury asked.

"The house back there has a safe," Maury said. "In a cupboard on the landing before you get to the back stairs."

"Could you have opened it?" I asked.

"Not without a couple sticks of dynamite," Maury said. "But I know a guy."

"I'll keep that in mind," I said. "Might be helpful if I learned what's in there."

I put a Lester Young CD into the car's player. The idea was to take Maury's mind off the smell I'd brought into the car.

The first tune out of the speakers was "Lullaby of Birdland."

"Ah, Prez," Maury said. "I love the guy."

We drove in silence except for the exquisite sound of Young's tenor saxophone all the way back to Spadina. Maury had parked his car in a small lot next to the Spadina subway station just above Bloor.

After I dropped Maury off, I spent twenty minutes circling the blocks south of Bloor. If it was tough finding a parking space during the day, it was completely hopeless at night. The cars were parked bumper to bumper. I couldn't spot a hint of room on any of the streets. I gnashed my teeth, cursed my luck and ended up back at the parking lot on Spadina, pulling into the space Maury had pulled out of almost half an hour earlier. Parking Armageddon had descended on the neighbourhood. In my frustrated car parker's opinion, it was certifiably impossible to park a car on all streets south of the Annex. I would have explored the Annex's own proud streets for a spot, but my permit only applied on our side of Bloor.

I reached into the back seat for my black jacket and headed home. As I walked, my Nikes made more squishing noises, and I trailed behind me the odour of horse excrement. Or was the manure from cows? Our house was dark except for the two lights on the porch. I unlocked the front door, reached in and switched off the porch lights. I planned on taking off my shoes, socks and jeans, but didn't feel like performing the mini-striptease under lights.

Standing in the gloom of the porch, I unloaded all objects from the jeans pockets and transferred them to the jacket. Wallet, roll of bills, key chain, the beginnings of what looked like a clay figurine from 32 Highbury. I barely remembered confiscating the hunk of clay in the rush to flee the joint. The next thing I did on the porch, still standing there, was take off my smelly shoes, socks and jeans, roll them up in a bundle and crush the bundle into the outdoor mailbox.

My bare feet made no sound when I stepped into the hall on my way past the living room to the first-floor bathroom. I was going to wash off the stink before I joined Annie in bed. Halfway to the bathroom, me wearing nothing except underwear, shirt and jacket, a voice came from out of the dark of the living room.

The voice said something resembling "Eeek!"

My head snapped around, and my heart felt like it was doing a somersault. Now what? I'd had enough stress and strain for one night.

The voice was female, and it wasn't Annie's.

I turned the hall light on.

"No, no," the voice said. "I don't need the light."

I didn't need it either. Why the hell had I turned it on? Automatic reflex. I did what the voice said and turned the light off.

"It's Rita," the voice said. "Annie's gardening friend."

I switched the light back on. It seemed the courteous thing to do for a guest. Rita was sitting up on the couch, wrapped in a blanket, bare shoulders showing.

"Love your outfit," she said.

"You appear to have no outfit at all," I said.

From upstairs, I heard Annie's feet patter across the master bedroom to the hall and start down the stairs.

"Where are your pants?" she asked me.

"In the mailbox," I said.

"Of course," Annie said. "I should've thought of that."

"It's a long story," I said.

Annie gave me a light kiss on the lips.

"I seem to have sobered up," Rita said from the couch.

Annie turned to her. "Crang sometimes has that impact on a girl."

"With me," Rita said, "it's usually the reverse. The better men look, the drunker I get."

Annie said to me, "After you left, Rita and I finished the bottle of wine, and we both thought she shouldn't drive home."

Rita said, "Either Crang's wearing a strange new aftershave or my nostrils are stuffed up with the manure we were heaving around on today's job."

"You are kind of ripe, sweetie," Annie said to me.

"I think I'll have a shower," I said. "Excuse me, ladies."

I walked over to the stairs. Halfway up, I heard a whistle. I looked back. Both women were staring at me.

"His buns are pretty nice," Rita said to Annie.

"I'm a fortunate girl," Annie said. "But I don't think I'm going to like whatever the story is about his pants and the manure."

After a long, hot shower, fatigue hit me. When I came out of the bathroom, Rita had left for home, and Annie was waiting in bed. I gave her a rundown of events on Highbury.

"I was right," Annie said. "I don't much like what happened." She let out a long sigh. "But at least you're sort of narrowing things down. Aren't you?"

I said, yes, I was, though I would have been hard-pressed at that moment to put my finger on what exactly was narrowed. I kissed Annie, she rolled over and fell back to sleep within seconds.

I wasn't so lucky. I still felt the fatigue, but my mind wouldn't quit thinking about Grace and the Highbury house. She was the only logical person to be doing things with the clay. I couldn't imagine Rocky as a man of artistic leanings. No one could imagine Rocky that way. Not even his loving mother, if he had a mother, and if she could manage to love him. And the third guy, he only showed up at the house now and again. If he was just a part-timer, it was unlikely he'd be working with the clay and the table and the kiln. Maybe he was a consultant of some kind. He came around to check on whatever Grace had fashioned. He might be a guy who gave her technical advice. Grace had to be the one with the creative touch. Nobody else I'd met in the general mess of recent events qualified.

But in all the years of acting as Grace's lawyer, I hadn't heard a word out of her about sculpting or clay or ceramics or firing up a kiln. If she was any good at that kind of art, it must have taken a big piece of her time. But she didn't talk about it. Not to me. Grace and I rarely got beyond the subject of the grow op case. No personal stuff. But she must have discussed her ceramics work with somebody, some friend or some person in her family. The trouble was I couldn't remember her ever mentioning anybody from either category, family or friends.

Maybe George Wu, her partner in crime, fit the role of friend. I got the idea they'd had an affair at the beginning of the grow op plan. I'd always kind of speculated the affair was part of Wu's strategy to get Grace on side with the scheme. Wu was the one guy I knew of who got close to Grace. Maybe I ought to speak to him about her interest in ceramics. That sounded like something an intrepid investigator would do. I'd think about it some more after the sun came up, which was probably any minute now.

I reached over for the MP3 on the little table by my side of the bed. I fitted the earbuds into my ears. The MP3 was set to the live recording of Bill Evans and his trio at the Village Vanguard on June 25, 1961. Most gorgeous album ever. The first tune up was a waltz, "Alice in Wonderland." Calm and peace began to settle over me, and somewhere near the end of another waltz, "Waltz for Debbie," I began to drift off.

17

When I woke up next morning, I was surprised to find it wasn't morning. It was two in the afternoon, and rain was falling outside. While I slept, Annie must have untangled me from the MP3 and put it back on the little table. She'd done a neat job of it. I had a shower, got dressed and went downstairs to two more surprises, both courtesy of Annie.

She had pancakes on the go and a suggestion for the afternoon.

"Let's play hooky," she said. "The Bloor's doing a bunch of Kristin Scott Thomas movies. One's on at four."

I gave Annie a hug.

"That's an affirmative?" she said.

"As long as it isn't *The English Patient*."

"I'm with you on that one."

"Remember the *Seinfeld* episode when Elaine went off on *The English Patient*? Great and classic."

"According to you, all *Seinfeld* episodes are great and classic."

"But Elaine was right about the movie."

"Pretentious, long-winded, boring, whatever," Annie said. "I agree."

I poured maple syrup on my pancakes.

"Today's movie," Annie said, "is *I've Loved You So Long*. First time we saw it a couple of years ago, you got tears in your eyes the size of golf balls."

"That's what makes it worth a revisit?" I said. "Not that I'm against weeping in movies."

"Know what I like about Kristin Scott Thomas?" Annie said. "Her *je ne sais quoi*, her . . ."

Annie, shaking her head, said, "The way she speaks French, I can understand every word she's saying."

We strolled to the Bloor, using one umbrella for the two of us. It felt cozy underneath. The Bloor was our local rep theatre, running a lot of documentaries but making room for retrospectives like the Scott Thomas series. Even though the place had been fixed up a little, it still felt like the movie theatres of my childhood. Annie and I bought one large popcorn with imitation-butter topping. The movie started right after we sat down, without previews, commercials or thundering soundtrack.

The story was about Scott Thomas's character coming out of a French prison after serving thirteen years. There was an explanation for why she did the time. It involved a child and death, and was all too overwhelmingly triste for words. I got weepy on cue.

When we left the theatre, the rain had stopped. The sky was clear, and the sun shone obliquely from halfway down in the west. We crossed Bloor and went into Green Beanery. It was a place I'd never figured out. Half of it was given over to elaborate displays of high-end coffee makers and related devices for the perfect kitchen. Too high end for me. The other half sold ice cream.

Annie made a beeline for an empty table while I went to the counter and ordered two dishes of vanilla. The vague young woman in charge said they were out of vanilla. How could an ice cream emporium be short of the world's most basic flavour? It was against the laws of nature. We settled for chocolate, feeling a touch grumpy about it.

A few tastes of chocolate cured the grumpiness affliction, and in the good mood that followed, Annie asked, "Do you know what this is?"

She was holding the clay figure I'd removed from 32 Highbury.

"Stands to reason it's a ceramic piece," I said. "But I can't do identification past that. It's the beginnings of a toy figure?"

"A figure, I agree, but not a toy," Annie said. "It's intended to be a fairly serious kind of adult work."

"You've been giving the thing some thought?"

"I saw it on your bedside table and got curious."

"Your curiosity tell you anything?"

"From the figure's waist up," Annie said, "there's nothing going on. All we got is a lumpy mass. But down below, the legs are almost fully developed."

"Fat-looking legs, you ask me."

"It isn't the legs that are fat," Annie said, running her index finger up and down the figure's sides. "It's the pants. These are a really early style in pants. Historically speaking."

"Pantaloons?"

"Not them, they were nineteenth century," Annie said. "Besides, pantaloons fit tight, not loose like these. The pants on this figure predate the nineteenth century. Renaissance pants these are, if I'm not mistaken."

"Where'd you learn all this stuff?"

"Fashion history was one of the courses I took for my master of fine arts."

Annie turned the figure over in her hands a few more times, giving it a concentrated inspection from different angles.

"These things below the pants could be the beginnings of feet," she said.

"Actual appendages you think? Or shoes?"

"Too crude to tell."

Annie put the figure on the table.

"Where in the Highbury house did you pilfer it from?" she asked.

"Technically it may not qualify as a pilfer," I said. "I got it out of the garbage pail."

"A reject, huh? Whoever made it wasn't satisfied with what they were making," Annie said. "Maybe the pants are all wrong."

"Why did you ask me what location in the house I found it in?"

"I was wondering if it was among other figures of a similar type."

"Not that I saw," I said. "The work table was more or less tidied up. Equipment right out there for anyone to see, but no ceramic pieces in sight. Just the spoiled one in the trash."

"It's usual that figures come in multiple groupings. That's how collectors gather them. Not just one, but a whole bunch of related figures."

"One with the pants is no doubt a reject, like you said. But Maury told me the place had a safe. Maybe the completed figures, the unrejected ones, are kept under security."

"Surprising your friend Maury didn't blow the safe."

"At the time," I said, "we had more pressing concerns."

Annie scooped up the rest of her ice cream, then leaned over and took a spoonful of what was left of mine.

"One guy I gather knows his way around ceramics is our neighbour Charles," she said. "He's got a studio in his backyard. Or maybe he had a studio at one time. Very aware of the field anyway, so I hear."

"If I need help, I'll knock on his door."

"You ever heard of the *Monkey Orchestra*?" Annie asked me. "My question's relevant to your little piece."

"Is this a derogative term?" I said. "As in, 'an orchestra of monkeys would sound better than Guy Lombardo's band'?"

"I'm talking ceramics," Annie said. "A famous group of figures is what the *Monkey Orchestra* is. It features all the instrumentalists in an orchestra except they're monkeys, not people. Collectively the figures are worth a lot of money. Millions maybe. I don't really know. Everything I'm telling you now is getting to the far edge of my limited knowledge."

"Big bucks in ceramics, that's your message?"

"Huge, oh yeah," Annie said. "There was a time in Europe, seventeenth century, in around then, ceramics replaced gold as the monetary standard. I've probably got the terminology wrong. But you get the idea."

"If the people on Highbury are messing around in the ceramics business, then they could be looking to score a major profit?"

"An illegal profit, given the people involved," Annie said. "I mean, come on, the Janetta family? The mob and all that? I just bet they play rough."

"You'll note it's Ms. Janetta who might be the person connected to the ceramics business. Not Mr. Janetta, mob kingpin. But you're right, people of the Janetta calibre usually come with violence attached."

"So do ceramics," Annie said.

"What's violent about ceramics?"

"Seventeenth century I'm talking about," Annie said, leaning forward and lowering her voice as if she were revealing a great confidence. "Nations fought wars over ceramics."

"Wars?"

"That's the kind of passions ceramics can raise," Annie said. She pointed her spoon at me. "Watch yourself, big boy."

18

I arranged on the phone to meet my friend Fox for lunch at Harold's, a restaurant on a side street a couple of blocks north of Osgoode Hall. Fox's real name was Phil Goldenberg, but everybody called him Fox. When he was fresh out of law school, and took nothing except drug cases, which was what beginner criminal lawyers started with in those days, he won a slew of acquittals. His trick was to put original twists on his cross-examinations of Crown witnesses. Somebody said he was smart as a fox, and we all got into the habit of pinning the name on him. When his hair turned prematurely grey, the name stretched to Grey Fox. He dyed it black, and the name switched back to Fox. It stayed that way even after he quit the dye jobs.

He and I acted in some drug cases together where we were co-counsel, each of us acting for a jointly charged client. We weren't partners exactly but we shared information and ideas when it saved one or both of us time and inconvenience. *R v. Wu and Nguyen* was one of those cases. He represented George Wu, and when I asked him on the phone to bring Wu to lunch, he said, sure, no problem, George was just sitting around waiting to go to prison anyway.

"Locate your own client yet?" Fox asked, still on the phone.

"I'm hoping Wu can help me," I said.

"So the answer's no, you haven't found her."

"She's floating out there somewhere," I said. "Maybe she's getting herself in some different kind of legal jam. That's part of what I'm going to ask Wu if he knows about."

"And how will it play out if my guy happens to incriminate his own self?" Fox said.

"If anything of that danger appears on the conversational horizon, you can excuse yourself from the table."

"Naturally you don't expect that to happen."

"Naturally."

"Then I can just sit there, keep my mouth shut and eat the lunch you're going to pay for."

"That sounds like a scenario," I said.

"In that case, why don't we lunch at Splendido, Canoe, one of those restaurants neither of us can afford? Put on the dog?"

"Tell you what," I said. "If something Wu says leads me to Nguyen, then later on after the dust settles, I'll book us at Splendido, just you and me, old pals together."

"You being the old pal who picks up the bill?"

"Champagne even."

When I got to Harold's at a few minutes before twelve, Fox had already ordered beers for himself and Wu. George Wu was a short guy with a lot of slicked-back black hair and a whimsical manner, though the wrinkles around his eyes were showing the wear and tear of recent years. His English was more relaxed than Grace's. She talked in precise sentences, trying for an upper-class accent and coming reasonably close. Wu had made himself so at home with English that he'd worked up a variation of the slang from the stoner culture.

"Cool to see you again, dude," he said to me.

"I can dig it, man," I said.

"Crang, if I've got to sit here in silence," Fox said, "at least you can make it less grating on the ears."

"I hear you, gate," I said.

"Hey, dog," Wu said to me, pleased.

Fox grimaced. He knew perfectly well what I was up to. Currying favour with George, talking the same brand of speech dysfunction, getting on his sunny side, softening him up for the questions. The idea might work if I didn't suffer a giggling fit first.

When the waiter came, Fox ordered another beer, I asked for coffee, and all of us settled for a different kind of omelet, plain for me, cheese and tomato for Fox, western for Wu, toast all round. Harold's was the kind of restaurant where you could count on the omelets, a plain, busy, affable place.

"You don't mind, my man," I said to Wu, "I want to get in your head about Grace."

"In Grace's head through my head?" Wu said, a big grin on his face that made him look dopier than he really was.

"Let me ask you about Grace's life apart from real estate," I said.

"And apart from grow ops," Wu said cheerily.

"What about ceramics?" I asked. "Was Grace into making clay bowls, kitchenware type of implements, coffee cups?"

"Hey, she gave you one of those damn mugs, bro?" Wu said. "Grace isn't a generous person, you may have noticed. But, like, every birthday, I could count on a friggin' coffee cup from her. I must have seven, eight of the mothers at home, one for every year since I met her. My wife has the same."

"She make anything else besides coffee mugs?"

"Got a soup bowl once."

"How about smaller pieces? Human-type figures?"

"Like, little soldiers you're talking about?"

"Sure. Or a character with balloony trousers."

"Nothing looked like that, dude."

"Only larger pieces? Mugs and bowls?"

"Yeah, but, man, the handles on the cups were shaped like what you might call figures. My wife got a kick out of that. She had a handle on a mug, it looked like Brad Pitt. Pretty clever. It was, like, early Brad in *Thelma & Louise*."

"This is good, George," I said. "Did anybody ever tell you Grace was particularly talented at that kind of thing? An opinion from an expert perhaps?"

"Nobody said that, bro. But Grace was, like, obsessed about making ceramic cups, bowls, handles, that kind of shit."

"As far as you know," I said, "it didn't get past the hobby stage?"

Wu shook his head. "Leastways I don't think she made money out of selling them."

The waiter brought our orders, and for a few minutes, the omelets took everybody's attention.

"Let me try another approach," I said to Wu. "Is there anybody besides you who's been particularly close to Grace in the last three, four years? Somebody knows her better than other people do?"

"You wanna count her husband, yo?" Wu said.

"Grace's married?" I said. I looked at Fox. He shrugged. It was the first he'd heard of a husband too. Not that he'd be more knowledgeable than me about Grace's personal life, though I thought it was possible Wu might have dropped a confidential tidbit on Fox sometime in the past. Wu apparently hadn't.

"The dude she married," Wu said, "he's got a zed in his name. Bulgarian, something like that. Romanian."

"A husband, huh? I was told about a boyfriend, but not a husband." I would have routinely asked Grace about her marital status when she retained me. I felt pretty sure I'd marked her down on my client's file as single.

"Grace kept secrets," Wu said. "But I know about the marriage because, dog, I was at the wedding. Me and the wife, that's all who attended. Back a few years when we were still flying high."

"Any kids?" I asked.

"Whoa, man, it'd be a crime against children if Grace gave birth," Wu said. "She's not a person who softens up. You must've noticed it yourself. But like I said about secretive, that was Grace. What I know is she and her husband live in a condo downtown. Lombard, dude, you know where I'm talking about?"

"Not anymore they don't live there," I said.

Fox ordered his third beer. Wu asked for a coffee, and I got my cup refilled.

Wu didn't show any interest in Grace's change of address. He had shifted along to other attributes of Grace's.

"For a chick, Grace's a heavy intellectual type of person," Wu said to me. "Like, she's artistic and cereal."

"Cereal?" I asked, looking at Fox.

"I think you'll find George means cerebral."

I turned back to Wu. "How about the opposite of close friends of Grace's? Is there anybody in particular you know of she hasn't been getting along with? Somebody who might mean her harm, if you dig me?"

"Her enemy, dude, is my enemy," Wu said. "She and I are as one in the mind of the evil man."

I could sense Fox rolling his eyes.

"Are you speaking metaphorically, George?" I asked. "Or is this a real flesh-and-blood bad guy out there you're talking about?"

"I never personally met the dude," Wu said. "But he walks this earth, let me tell you, man. He sent his henchmen to do the dirty on me and Grace."

"Narrow this down, George," I said. "You're talking about the grow op business?"

"The evil empire was supposed to market our product."

"Now we're getting somewhere."

Vietnamese grow farmers of any substantial size didn't deal their own marijuana to the users. They weren't set up for the retail trade. Strictly wholesale as far as big marijuana growers like Grace and Wu were concerned. They sold their crops to an outfit that had the marketing machinery already in place. These were the dealers, and they made the biggest profit of all, bigger bucks than the farmers ever realized. The dealers paid low and sold high. And the farmers were the saps who exposed themselves to most of the risks. When the cops took down grow operations and busted the farmers, they rarely nabbed the people with the drug apparatus. The drug guys were too smart at keeping low profiles and staying anonymous. Nobody ever caught them on wiretaps.

"What went wrong between you and the drug people?" I asked Wu. "I imagine it involved money."

"You talking about the money Grace and me never saw, yo?" Wu said. "Like, man, that kind of grief? What happened was . . . It was a case of . . ."

Wu couldn't find the English word. Or words.

Then he burst out. "They erectioned us!"

Fox and I looked at one another.

Five seconds of silence went by before a smile broke across Fox's face.

"Think penis, Crang," he said.

I thought penis.

"Got it," I said. I turned to Wu. "The drug people stiffed you."

"Stiffed! You're on it, dude," Wu said. "The cops busted Grace and me, and the evil drug king wouldn't pay us anymore after that. They had all our dope, but they still owed us millions of dollars, man. They didn't pay us, and they never will. They left us high and dry, dude."

"Grace never mentioned that," I said. "Even if she had, it wouldn't help us get lighter sentences for you guys from Judge Keough."

Fox laughed and said, "I can see it now, us whining to Keough about our clients deserving a break. He asks, on what grounds? We say, the poor people got cheated out of their illegal profits by other bad guys. It'd be like the boy who murdered his parents then begged for mercy because he was now an orphan."

"George here never revealed to you this duplicity among thieves?" I asked Fox.

"First I've heard of it."

I went back to Wu with questions. "You and Grace would have received an original down payment from the dealers? Something that got the arrangement on track long before they crossed you up?"

He nodded a grim and weary yes.

"How else," I went on, "could Grace have afforded the condo?"

"Right on, bro," Wu said. "The wife and I bought a big place in Markham. A frigging mansion, man. But we hadda let it go on account of we didn't have enough to pay the upkeep. The evil mastermind left us broke when he wouldn't pay up."

"Now for the million-dollar question," I said.

"More like ten million," Wu said.

"Who was the drug guy that stiffed you?" I asked. "His name?"

I expected at this stage in our conversation Wu would clam up. He might not want to be known as the guy who ratted out a big-name drug boss. Not that I intended to use the name as anything other than an aid in my analysis of Grace's situation. But big-time crime guys had ears in unexpected places, and Wu might be scared silly of the consequences of his own loose lips. That was what I thought.

I thought wrong.

"Lou Janetta, dude," Wu said.

"That's who you dealt with?" I said. Why wasn't I surprised?

"Like I said, not him personally," Wu said. "But his people came around, they said, don't worry about getting a fair dollar because the Janetta organization goes, like, first cabin all the way. Dude, I heard that so many times. Now I could puke, the way things ended."

Fox spoke up. "Crang, you're taking the revelation about this guy Janetta with remarkable calm."

"Probably because I'm running into his name a lot this past week. His name, his house, his reputation, his wife. Can't be a coincidence, coming up against Janetta at every turn. He must fit into the story in some major way."

"His wife? You're running into the mob guy's wife?"

"Once seen, never to be banished from the mind."

"A real babe?"

"You bet."

Fox laughed. "Well now, how's the lovely Annie these days?" he asked.

"Unfair insinuation, Fox," I said. "On the subject of Elizabeth Janetta, I'm speaking purely as a dispassionate connoisseur of female beauty."

"Glad to hear it," Fox said. He swallowed the last of his beer. "What else can George help you with?"

I turned my attention back to Wu. "Who did the negotiating with Janetta's people? Just you? Or you and Grace both?"

"Mostly Grace," Wu said. "Dude, everybody seems to think I was, like, the mastermind of the grow op thing, beginning to end. You and Fox probably still think that. But it really was Grace who came to me in the first place, man. And it was her got me into bed. Like, physically in bed, dude. That's when she brought up the idea of the grow houses, right there in bed. Told me how we could set up our pot business. Man, that woman ended up costing me a ton. I almost lost my marriage, and now I'm headed to the big house."

Wu was beginning to look like a guy who'd just run a marathon. Depleted, his dopey grin no long in sight. But he wasn't finished talking.

"Thing you reminded me of, dude," he said to me. "Talking about Janetta's wife, there was one time Grace mentioned the wife to me. It was some kind of big deal to her. To Grace."

"In what connection?" I asked.

"Same thing you and I were talking about earlier. Ceramics," Wu answered. "Grace said she went to some gallery, museum, whatever, where they showed bowls and all that, and she saw Janetta's wife there."

"How did she know the woman was Elizabeth Janetta?"

"Because there was a little photograph of her on the wall with her name underneath it," Wu said. "Dude, the Janetta babe is on the board of this museum."

"Did Grace just happen to notice Ms. Janetta? Or did you get the impression from Grace that this was a little more? In other words, was it an accidental encounter? Or a planned meeting maybe? Did Grace have a real conversation with Elizabeth Janetta?"

"Lot of questions all at once, dude."

"Just give me your impressions, George," I said. "The connection between the two happened at a ceramics museum, right?"

"The Lubin Museum," Wu said. "I remember that."

"Levin Museum?"

"Right on, dude," Wu said. "Grace used to go there all the time."

"You're doing great, George," I said.

"All I asked Grace when she told me about meeting the wife was, did Grace bring up the subject of the money the Janetta woman's weasel husband owed us?"

"So the meeting took place after your deal with Janetta had gone south?"

"Right again, bro," Wu answered. "But Grace said she didn't talk money with the wife. She said they just discussed ceramics. When I heard that, I lost interest in the whole subject of Janetta's wife. I could care less about ceramics and all that shit. I had other things on my mind. You dig it, dude?"

"I dig, George," I said. "You've been a big help. Anything more occur to you? About Grace's connection to the Janetta couple?"

"Haven't really seen much of Grace since the big score of our lives fell in the dumper. A painful story, dude."

"Perfectly understandable, George," I said, feeling pretty certain I'd worked Wu for everything he knew.

After a few moments when nobody said anything, I turned to Fox.

"Fox, old pal," I said, "I think we're getting closer to lunch at Splendido."

"On you," Fox said.

"How could I possibly forget that part?"

19

Back in my office, I was in an expectant mood. The man at the bargain appliance store on Bloor promised his guys would deliver a mini-refrigerator that afternoon, sometime between two and four-thirty. On the stroll from Harold's to the office, I bought a pint of milk and a small box of sugar cubes. I'd already stocked up with four mugs from the gift shop at the AGO. The mugs were in cobalt blue. By the end of the afternoon, I'd be in the full-service coffee business. I planned to present my neighbour Sam Feldman with the ceremonial first cup.

Someone knocked on the office door. It wasn't Sam's familiar knock.

"C'mon in," I said, a breezy tone in my voice. I thought the fridge guys must have arrived early. I rose to greet my new appliance.

The door opened to reveal the most dapper gent I'd come across since I last watched George Clooney in one of the Oceans movies. I had the immediate and overwhelming sense this visual paragon was Lou Janetta.

"You're Crang?" the man said. "The lawyer?"

"The guy with his name on the door, that's me," I said, getting out of my chair. "And might you be Luigi Janetta, better known as Lou?"

"How do you know my name?" he said. The question was asked in a pleasant enough tone.

"The fame of your home's architecture precedes you," I answered.

Janetta was a shade under six feet, a little shorter than me. He had a slim build, handsome features, a light suntan and black hair. The hair fell in natural waves, the kind a barber had no need to encourage. He wore a white linen double-breasted suit and a dark blue silk shirt with a matching handkerchief in the appropriate jacket pocket. He did without a tie, and kept the shirt's top two buttons undone. A modest glimpse of black chest hair showed at the top of the shirt.

Dashing Lou stepped into the room followed by the all-too-familiar figure of my adversary, Rocky. Good thing for me Rocky wasn't aware of my adversarial feelings. The closer he got, the bigger and meaner he loomed. He had on jeans and an unadorned white T-shirt, the better to show off the rippling muscles. The guy probably went about 220 pounds, not an ounce of it fat. Rocky's nose, flattened at the tip, announced that he might have done a little fighting in a ring. Or maybe in a cage like those guys on television who fight in their bare feet.

"This's my associate, Rocky Galenti," Janetta said, making the introductions with a gesture that was both suave and abrupt.

"Gentlemen," I said, "have a seat."

Janetta sat in one of my three clients' chairs. Rocky stayed on his feet, standing just behind Janetta, his arms crossed in front of him in the same way he'd stood in the Janetta living room when I visited the madam of the house.

"Rocky and I have met," I said to Janetta. "After a fashion."

"You went to see my wife," Janetta said, "when I wasn't there."

"In point of fact, it was your physical house I called on," I said. "It would have been my pleasure to meet you if you'd been on the premises."

"Nobody told me about you dropping into my place until I overheard the housekeeper mention your name."

"That so?" I said. Strange things were happening to my vocal system, all the rigid lines I was spewing, "physical house" and "on the premises." Janetta had me in a wary state of mind. His line of palaver wasn't quite an interrogation, but it was much more than just shooting the breeze.

"My wife never said anything about it," Janetta said. The sound in his voice was neutral but scary. That seemed to be his habitual conversational position.

"Would you gentlemen care for a cup of coffee?" I said. "I can offer a delicious brand from Kenya?"

"Never mind the coffee," Janetta said.

I looked up at Rocky. "How about you, Mr. Galenti?"

"Rocky's answer's the same as mine," Janetta said.

There was nothing in Janetta's voice I could describe as pure menace. That only made everything he said seem to have even more potential for danger.

"I'm not fond of guys calling on my wife who got no reason," Janetta said.

"I agree with your point of view, but I had a reason," I said. "I'm interested in your house's design."

"That's what Elizabeth said you said."

"I'm glad she confirms my purpose," I said.

"She said you want to build a house like mine."

"So I did," I said. "I did, uh, say that."

"Crang," Janetta said, "you and I both know you've got as much chance of financing a house like mine as you have of getting appointed to the Supreme Court of Canada."

"A man can dream."

"If you were still married to your first wife, you could afford any house you wanted," Janetta said.

The guy had done some research. My first wife, who was my only wife so far, was Pamela, the heiress to a fortune that reached back through generations of her family's trust business and expanded from there. Heiress was Pamela's financial situation when she and I were husband and wife. Now we'd been divorced many years, and she was no longer a mere heiress. The inheritance had kicked in. Today Pamela could buy and sell anybody in the Bridle Path.

"On the other hand," Janetta said, "now you live with a free-lance writer. Crang, with all respect to Ms. Cooke's skills and maybe yours, you can barely afford the house on Major."

What was my best strategy with Janetta? Should I bring up his fleecing of Grace and Wu out of their marijuana profits? Would that give me any leverage in finding out what Janetta's current business relations were with Grace, if any relations existed? And what was up at 32 Highbury? The posing of the question might offer a pretty good wedge into a deeper investigation of what was going on with Grace. Or was I spinning my wheels, whatever choice I made?

"Mr. Janetta," I said, "if I may be so bold, I have some concerns about your property in the west end."

"West end's not where I do business," Janetta said.

"Specifically Highbury Road."

Janetta, an impatient expression on his face, started to speak, but Rocky's rumblings interrupted whatever his boss was about to say. Rocky muttered something I couldn't make out, but there was no mistaking his physical intention. He was coming around Janetta's chair, moving in my direction. The guy had all the looks of somebody about to bop me with a punch.

"Rocky, what are you doing . . . ?" Janetta said. He radiated annoyance. I had the feeling that my own face, if anybody besides me cared, showed a high degree of unease.

Needing to act, counting on surprise tactics, I jumped out of the swivel chair and let fly with a left hook aimed at Rocky's oncoming head. My punch landed flush, high on Rocky's right cheek. It left a bright red mark, the beginnings of a bruise. But it didn't come anywhere close to slowing Rocky's progress or giving him second thoughts about his plans for me.

He swung a short right-hand punch at my solar plexus. It was perfectly executed. Rocky's fist buried in my stomach at a spot just below the rib cage. It knocked every wisp of wind out of me. I couldn't breathe. My eyes were wide open, registering everything that was happening in front of me, but it was as if the events were taking place in a silent movie. I watched Rocky relishing his great punch, Janetta trying to drag him away from me, the closed office door behind them swinging open, Sam Feldman materializing from the hall. I saw all of this, but I couldn't offer any response, verbal or otherwise. I couldn't talk or hear. The way I felt at that moment, I wasn't sure I would ever breathe again.

In front of me, Sam steamed across the room in impressively quick strides. He grabbed Rocky from behind, his big hands squeezing Rocky's head just back of the ears. Sam lifted the big guy in the air, his feet off the ground. Rocky's choices were limited. He flailed his arms and legs, but within a second or two, he went still. Sam seemed to be applying some kind of sophisticated chokehold. He kept Rocky hoisted aloft, swinging him around and aiming him for an exit out the door.

Janetta looked at this rapid turn of events with an expression of bemusement. He seemed much less a participant in what was going on and much more a member of a surprised but entertained audience.

My hearing was beginning to kick back in. The first sound I heard was the rasping, coughing racket of somebody struggling for air. It was my own throat giving off the funny noises.

"Crang," Janetta said, leaning over me, "you hear me okay?"

I realized I'd slumped back in the swivel chair.

"I don't know why the hell Rocky whacked you," Janetta said. "But you probably did something to deserve it. All I gotta say, keep in mind what I told you about my wife."

I gave a shaky nod of my head and struggled to get upright in the chair.

"No more turning up at my house when I'm not there," Janetta said. He started for the door, then stopped and turned back. "I'm gonna rephrase that. No more turning up at my house any time. Doesn't matter whether I'm home or not."

Sam came back through the door. He seemed to have dumped Rocky, and was now looking as if he might have more mayhem on his mind. Janetta put up his hands in a gesture that said Sam would get no trouble from him. Janetta still wore his bemused expression. Sam left him alone, and Janetta disappeared, softly closing the door behind him.

Sam kneeled beside the swivel chair and put an arm around my shoulder.

"The big thug must've got you in the breadbasket," Sam said. "Actually, that's the best place he could've landed a punch. Hitting you there isn't going to break any of your bones." Sam eased me against the back of the chair. "Just take it slow," he said. "Your breath'll start up as good as normal."

My hearing had already returned to its regular acuteness. And my breathing grew smoother. There was no more gasping or wheezing. I decided to test my speaking capabilities.

"You came on like the cavalry, Sam," I said. My voice felt comfortable again. "Glad you and I are on the same side."

"I wondered about those guys when I saw them going into your office," Sam said. "Especially the big bozo. He looked like bad news."

"Where did you deposit Rocky?" I asked. "That's the big bozo's name."

"On the elevator," Sam said. "He probably got his consciousness back by the time he reached the ground floor. All I gave him was a squeeze of the windpipe. Cut off enough air to knock him out."

I stayed in the chair, waiting for a complete zone of natural functioning to arrive. Sam leaned over me again, and undid my belt. "Let you have more breathing space," he said.

Someone knocked on the closed door.

"Not those guys again, do you think?" Sam said.

"If they came back," I said, "I doubt they'd knock."

Sam called out, "Enter." He faced the door, his hands raised in a posture that indicated he was on danger alert. I stayed slumped in the chair, my belt hanging loose.

The door opened slowly. Two men wearing overalls stood in the open doorway, taking in the scene.

"Is this not a good time?" the guy on the right said. His eyes kept moving from Sam's hands to my undone belt.

"It depends on why you're here," I said.

"Got a delivery," the same guy said, gesturing toward the hallway behind him. "A small refrigerator."

I came out of the chair like a man who'd found new life.

"Right this way," I said.

The two guys unpacked the fridge and plugged it in. I did up my belt and asked the two guys if they'd like to stay for a cup of coffee. They said they had more deliveries. They seemed to be in a hurry to leave. I tipped them twenty bucks, and they shut the door behind them.

"Okay, Sam," I said. "It's you and me for the inaugural coffees."

"I got a client waiting," Sam said.

He left too.

My renewed energy was beginning to leak away. I made enough coffee for two cups. Four or five minutes went by while the little coffee maker did its duty. I poured the first cup and added a lump of sugar. That was unusual for me, a sweetener of any kind in my coffee, but I thought it'd have therapeutic effects on the shock my system had taken.

My diagnosis and prescription were pretty much on the money. By the time I finished the second cup, I was feeling close enough to normal to face Annie with the story of my two-punch showdown with Rocky. Annie wasn't going to be pleased.

20

When I got home, Annie had so much of her own news hot off the presses that I didn't bother steering the conversation straight to the tale of the rumble in my office.

"Look at all the zeros on this baby," Annie said, holding up a printout of her account at our Bloor branch of the Bank of Nova Scotia. The account showed an online deposit the day before of a sum I recognized as significantly large, especially for a first-time author.

"From Columbia University," Annie said. "My advance against royalties for the Edward Everett Horton biography, and no fooling."

Annie gave me an enthusiastic hug. "Things are on pace," she said. "Maybe ahead of pace if I move fast."

The hug shot a jolt of pain through my sore stomach muscles. For a moment, I could just barely keep myself upright. Annie didn't notice any of the struggles because she was occupied with the happy business of rushing for the refrigerator to get out a celebratory bottle of white wine.

I knew from Annie that Edward Everett Horton had been a native New Yorker and a Columbia alumnus. About four weeks earlier, the university had reacted to her proposal of a Horton biography with what anybody would call alacrity. The sum that had just arrived as an advance against royalties was marginally higher than the figure she suggested in her pitch. Annie said that was unheard of in the publishing world.

While she dashed around the kitchen, I sat in the dining room looking into the garden, surreptitiously stroking my tender stomach.

"You got indigestion, sweetie?" Annie asked when she came back to the table. My rubbing hadn't been as surreptitious as I thought.

"Probably too much coffee today," I said.

Annie was carrying the wine bottle, a corkscrew and two wine-glasses. She performed the opening duties and filled each glass to the halfway mark.

"Here's to a bestseller," I said, raising my glass in the air.

Annie shook her head at the extravagance of the toast. "Let's not go completely overboard," she said. "Just getting a contract is fabulous enough. Never mind sales." She sat back in her chair and hiked her bare feet up on the edge of the chair I was occupying. "You know how I feel right now?" she said.

"Overjoyed?" I said. "Oh, wait, inspired? Determined?"

Annie made a waving-off motion with the hand that wasn't holding her wineglass. "What I feel is terrified."

"Well, a new venture and all, I guess terror is a natural reaction."

"It's the size of the thing. I mean, a whole book? The longest piece I've written until now is a ten-thousand-word maga-zine article. For *Premiere* a few years ago, the profile of Heath Ledger."

"How long is your long book supposed to be?"

"Eighty thousand words."

"That works out to what in book pages?"

"More than three hundred."

"Now I'm impressed," I said. "How long's it take to write three hundred pages?"

"It better take one year," Annie said. "What the contract calls for is a year till I hand in the manuscript. Time started running on June first."

"Makes your deadline closer to eleven months than twelve."

"Which is the reason, my love," Annie said, "I'm leaving for New York on Sunday."

"Sunday? The Sunday only two days away?"

Annie said yes, and explained that Columbia had an Edward Everett Horton archive. She was invited to put the archive to whatever research use she wanted. Columbia would even make a small suite on campus available for her to live and work in. No charge, but the offer expired at the end of June when summer students would be moving in. Annie needed to work fast. She'd already booked her flight to New York, leaving on Sunday and returning at noon a week from the following Monday.

"All the wheels in motion," I said.

"They are," Annie said. "Now let's talk about what you'll be up to while I'm away."

"Meaning you want to hear about Grace and my seventy-five grand."

"Let's have it," Annie said.

I told her about Lou Janetta calling on me that afternoon. I included a description of Rocky's assault, but downplayed its ferocity, and wound up with Sam Feldman's deed of heroism. Sam was another of Annie's favourites. Practically everybody in my circles were her favourites except Maury Samuels. She thought Maury was a bad influence. I thought not.

"Whole thing sounds weird," Annie said. "What I'd like to know, sweetie pie, did you learn anything helpful from these rude people?"

"I get the impression Lou Janetta knows absolutely nothing about the Highbury house or the fooling around with ceramics."

"But the big bully sure knows what's up," Annie said.

"Rocky you mean?"

"What other big bully you met lately?" Annie said. "A crime baron like Janetta might be a bully by definition. But from what you say, he's kind of Mr. Neutral. What's that all about?"

"Matter of his style," I said. "He's powerful and successful and untouchable. Cops haven't laid a glove on him. He can afford to act like he's the coolest bad guy in town."

"And so?"

"And so Janetta is an incidental figure for my purposes. That's my current view anyway. He's a big-time mob guy, but he's a side-show to the real plot I'm looking into."

"I just wish you wouldn't call it a plot," Annie said. "Makes it sound dangerous. I mean, all you really need to do is collect your fee from Grace."

I poured each of us enough wine to bring the level in the glasses back to halfway up. The wine, I noticed, was Sancerre. Annie had got out the really good stuff for the occasion.

"Janetta didn't appear to react at all when I mentioned High-bury," I said. "Like you say, Rocky is deep into whatever's going on with the ceramics. I think he threw the punch at me to deflect the conversation from getting any deeper into the general sub-ject of the Highbury house."

"Janetta's got nothing to do with Highbury, but you think Janetta's beautiful missus is in it up to her neck? Words to that effect?"

"My hunch."

"She and Rocky?" Annie said.

"From all signs to date."

"Makes for an odd team. The chatelaine of the Bridle Path house and the thuggy bodyguard," Annie said. "A little D. H. Law-renceish."

"I completely doubt there's any sex going on. Rocky's no more than the obedient servant carrying out Elizabeth Janetta's orders."

"Even though Rocky's first responsibility is probably to the mister of the house?"

"Complicated, isn't it?"

Annie appeared to think about what I'd just told her. "I may not have everybody in focus," she said. "But it's obvious where Grace fits into all of this. She's the one who works with porcelain."

"I get the shivers when somebody says a thing is obvious."

"Your lawyer's training."

"What appears to be obvious," I said, "is Grace working for Ms. Janetta."

"Yeah, because whatever she's doing with porcelain is happening in a house owned by the allegedly stunning Janetta woman."

"Yeah, hypothetically," I said. "The part about Elizabeth Janetta's looks is for sure. The rest is conjecture."

"Geez, Crang." Annie sounded impatient. "I'll tell you one part that isn't hypothetical or conjecture or anything else that comes with a trace of doubt attached to it. Actually I can tell you seventy-five thousand parts."

I sipped some of my Sancerre and couldn't help noticing how mellow I was beginning to feel. Even my stomach muscles seemed not so bothersome.

"I think it's time to have a face-to-face talk with Grace," I said to Annie. "See about the cash and ceramics and whatever else she cares to let me in on. I'm still her lawyer. It's my obligation to advise her."

Annie leaned over and patted me on the knee.

"Good thinking, my man," she said. "At last."

"First step is to follow her from Highbury to wherever her home is when Rocky drops her off."

"Great," Annie said. Her voice had a ring of decisiveness that made me nervous. "Let's the two of us do the tail job tonight. Maybe actually converse with her."

"Tonight? I had next Monday night in mind. And what's this 'us' stuff?"

"I'm the perfect cover in the tail car," Annie said. "None of the black Navigator people would expect to be followed by a car with both a man and a woman in it. We could act lovey-dovey in the front seat. Grace and Rocky and whoever else is in the car will think it's just a couple who can't wait to make out."

"Well, yeah, that's nice thinking. But the idea is for them not to notice us at all."

"See!" Annie said, sounding as if she'd scored a major point. "Now you're referring to 'us.'"

"Noticed that," I said.

I got out of my chair, and stared some more at the backyard, the plot of land soon to be rescued from the doo-doo category. I was staring, but I wasn't thinking about gardening. I was thinking about the logistics of following Grace, Rocky and company.

"Something else about the stakeout," I said.

"Love this," Annie interrupted. "First a tail job, now a stake-out. Technically, unless I'm mistaken, the stakeout precedes the tail job."

"I better rent another car," I said. "The Mercedes is becoming a familiar presence on Highbury. Might stir questions among the people we're tailing."

Annie sat up very straight in her chair.

"Borrow Charles's car," she said. Her tone had escalated from triumphant to jubilant.

"Charles who drives the red Jeep?"

"He told me if we need to cart things around for the new garden, the Jeep would be far more practical than the Mercedes. He said we could borrow it any time."

"But," I said, "tonight we won't be doing garden errands."

"It all hinges on where you put the italics," Annie said. "Myself, I put them on the 'any time' in Charles's invitation. Charles said we could borrow the Jeep any time."

"Sure you're not a Jesuit?" I said. "That's as fine a piece of sophistry as I've heard in a while."

Annie let the remark float past.

"I'll nip up to Charles's place and get the Jeep's keys," she said, sliding from the chair. "And while I'm at it, I'll pick up some Japanese takeout for dinner."

"From which restaurant? There's only about a dozen sushi places every block."

"One on the north side that took over from the Thai joint last month?" Annie said. "That one. Good reports on it from the street's retired persons squad."

Annie shot out the front door.

I sipped some Sancerre and wondered whether I'd lost control of events. Not really, I thought. Or was I just rationalizing a sticky situation? In my version, rationalized or not, Annie had merely speeded the timetable. Since I intended to confront Grace anyway, what was the difference between sooner and later? The answer was, not much, though having headstrong Annie along on the mission might unduly stir things.

I went upstairs and changed into an outfit appropriate for a stakeout. How about a loose pair of summer pants and the same in a shirt? I had both. I got out the old Nikes, which no longer smelled of my visit to the garden shed. Before I left the room, I opened the little table on my side of the bed, and took out the clay figure. As I hefted it in the palm of my hand, it felt and looked just as enigmatic as it had when I'd first held it. What would the figure have turned into if Grace had finished her shaping and given it the kiln treatment?

21

The Jeep was a bouncy little thing. Maybe too bouncy. I was used to driving the big old Mercedes, which was wider, longer, heavier and more earthbound. By comparison, the Jeep felt awfully damn frisky. That might lead to trouble. The last thing I wanted was to return damaged goods to good neighbour Charles. I hardly knew the guy.

I whipped along Highbury Road past I Spy Griffith's driveway, past the property at number 32 and farther along Highbury until I came to the first cross street. It was called Bramble Crescent. I cut a brisk left onto Bramble, continued a half block, then whipped through a U-turn and coasted back to the corner of Bramble and Highbury. I parked the car, nose out, and snapped off the lights.

"Well," Annie said, "that was an exhilarating experience."

"The driving, you mean?"

"For a few minutes there, I thought Danica Patrick was at the controls."

"How do you happen to know a woman named Danica Patrick is a race car driver?"

"Sometimes when you leave the *Globe* open at the sports pages, I find myself paying attention to what's written in there."

"Maybe we could discuss the sports results regularly? Preferably basketball?"

"Sorry, sweetie pie, I won't be paying that much attention."

I settled a little in my seat.

"Our position right here on the corner ought to do for the stakeout," I said. "Navigator comes out of the driveway back there, it'll turn to its right, and drive past where we're parked."

"How can you be sure it won't turn in the other direction?"

"According to I Spy," I said, "it always comes this way. My limited experience leads to the same conclusion."

"Think it'll be long before that happens?"

I looked at my watch. Ten minutes past two. "Probably an hour," I said.

"Want to snoggle while we're waiting?" Annie said. She rubbed her hand up and down my thigh with a luxurious touch.

"Annie, we're on a business mission here."

"Aw, come on," she said. She put her face close to mine, her lips puckered.

Beyond her head, car lights shone from 32 Highbury's driveway.

"Duck," I said. "They're coming already."

Both of us crouched in the front seats below the level of the car windows, waiting for the Navigator's lights to swing past.

Thirty seconds ticked by, but no lights lit up the road or the Jeep.

What was taking them so long? I lifted my head for a view out the window. Nothing in sight. No Navigator and no other vehicle.

"Rats," I said. "They've gone the other way."

I started the Jeep, switched on the lights and started off down Highbury at a cautious rate.

"Shouldn't you speed it up?" Annie asked. "Drive more like Danica?"

Annie had a driver's licence, but didn't drive often. Her style behind the wheel tended to be damn the torpedoes, full speed ahead.

"Streets around here are twisty," I said. "I might surprise myself and run too close to the Navigator."

Just one car besides us seemed to be out and about in the whole visible neighbourhood. It was somewhere in the blocks up ahead of us. All I could see of it were the car's headlights flashing against the upper reaches of the trees when the wheels bounced over the speed bumps that dotted the roads. The bouncing, flashing car had to be the Navigator. I figured it was heading on the route that led past the Old Mill and out to Bloor Street. If it wasn't the Navigator, our tail job was kaput.

We pulled around the curved road outside the subway station. No car was stopped for the Bloor red light.

"We lost them?" Annie asked. "So soon?"

I looked east and west. About a dozen cars were in sight on Bloor. Most seemed to be eastbound, coming from the suburbs into the city. A few stragglers were driving the other way. One of the vehicles going east, a couple of long blocks away from us and headed for a curve in the road that would put it out of our sight range any minute now, was dark coloured and SUV shaped.

"Don't know whether it's a Navigator way up there," I said.

"Could be a Model T for all I know about cars," Annie said.

"Listen, kiddo, if you've got a particular talent in tail job situations, what might it be?"

"Intuition is what I bring to the table," Annie said.

"Has intuition got a message right now about the black car?"

"Intuition is mute on the subject," Annie said. "But reason says the car up there has the best chance of anything on the road of being our Navigator. Simple matter of percentages. More cars going east. Ergo, more eastbound cars could be the one we care about."

I turned left onto Bloor with the green light, and zipped in pursuit of the flock of cars that included the suspect vehicle. The little red Jeep performed like a speedy marvel. At the stoplight on Bloor at Jane, just before Bloor turned into the neighbourhood known as Bloor West Village, we caught up to the car that looked like a Navigator. It was stopped at the red light in the middle lane of three. I positioned us in the curb lane and one car length behind.

"That's not just a Navigator," I said. "It's our Navigator."

"How can you tell?" Annie said. "The city's full of cars that look exactly like the one right there. Black, SUV, sitting up like that, so damned haughty the way they're built."

I looked at Annie. "You finished?"

"What?"

"The licence plate tells me it's ours."

"Oh."

The Navigator took the Jane green light and stayed on Bloor for a couple dozen blocks. It wasn't hard to follow its trail. The traffic was not too heavy and not too light, just right for us in our cute wee Jeep to lay a car or two behind the target vehicle without attracting the attention of Rocky or Grace. At least, as far as I could tell, the Jeep wasn't rousing suspicions.

Then, a block or two east of Lansdowne Avenue, everything about the situation changed, beginning with the Bloor traffic.

"What's this?" Annie said. "Where did the traffic jam come from all of a sudden? And what's with all the people out there?"

Our Jeep's pace fell from slow to dead halt, lined behind cars stopped up ahead for as far as we could see. The sidewalk on the south side of Bloor seemed as busy as on a noon-hour shopping day. Almost all of the people out there were guys in their twenties and thirties. They seemed in high spirits and maybe a little drunk. Some might be a whole lot drunk.

I looked up at the sign on a building on the south side.

"Here's the answer to all questions," I said to Annie, pointing at the sign.

"The Duke of Lancashire?" she said, reading the name in lights. "That's a strip club, have I got the right place?"

"Explains why everybody on the street looks so jolly."

"Your friend Fox took that famous case in the Supreme Court, the one made it okay for girls in strip clubs to take off every stitch of their clothes."

"They don't have to leave on the little pieces of fabric between their legs."

"Gross," Annie said.

The Jeep was moving forward in the traffic at not even a snail's pace. Cars seemed to be looking for parking places. Even at this hour, patrons were flocking into the Lancashire. Here and there, women appeared among the guys on the sidewalk. The women looked like strippers on a break between pole dances. The clothes they had on were highly informal, and the girls tended to be busty and wear their hair long, all the better, I imagined, for whirling in the air when they danced with the pole.

"They offer sexual favours in there?" Annie asked. "I mean apart from the opportunities to ogle boobs and private parts, no doubt shaved. What about actual sexual contact?"

"Lap dances," I said. "Which adds up to the same result as sexual favours. Naked girl sits in a guy's lap squirming around until the guy experiences, you know, a moment of sensation. Or so I understand."

"Never mind what you understand," Annie said. "Did you notice where the Navigator went?"

"It was two cars in front of us until we ran into this mess," I said. "All these drivers trying to ditch their cars, I lost track of our people."

"I did too," Annie said, reaching for the door handle on her side. "But my intuition suggests a possibility. I'm going to take a look around. Don't jerk the car forward when I open the door. I'm getting out."

"Hold on a minute," I said. "Those people on the street don't look like safe company for a nice girl like you."

"We've lost the Navigator anyway. What's the harm in me taking a look for it and its passengers somewhere around here?

You and the Jeep are going to be stuck in this traffic for God knows how long."

"You don't know what the Navigator people look like. You've never even met Grace."

"Yeah, but now I know the car's licence number. And besides, I got a hunch about what's going on."

"A hunch? That the same as an intuition?"

"I'm betting our friend Rocky is stopping to get his ashes hauled," Annie said.

"Language like that, maybe you're not such a nice girl after all."

Annie got out of the Jeep, turned back to the side window and said, "Park on the next street up, and wait for me. This shouldn't take long."

I needed about ten minutes to turn on to the side street Annie pointed out and slide into a parking space another car was in the act of pulling away from.

I got out of the Jeep, and when I looked back down the side street, the first thing I saw was Annie coming toward me lickety-split.

"In the parking lot," she said, out of breath. "Somebody who's got to be Grace is sitting in the passenger seat."

"Alone?"

"Attractive woman? Dark, slim, kind of tragic looking?"

"First time anybody's called her tragic," I said. "But it must be Grace if it's the right Navigator, and the woman's Vietnamese."

"She is, and, yes, she's alone," Annie said. She climbed into the Jeep. "I've no doubts Rocky's in the club for the purpose previously stated."

"Ashes hauling?" I said.

Annie nodded. "I'll wait here," she said, "resting on my laurels."

I walked up the sidewalk to the lot behind the club. The Navigator was easy to spot at the far end of the second row of cars. I got myself at an angle to see the woman in the car's front passenger window without attracting her attention to me. No doubt at all, the woman was my client. Grace hadn't changed in any way in the couple of weeks since I last saw her. If she was under some new stress, she didn't show the cracks.

I studied her and the car for another minute, making sure she was alone. It was awkward in the packed lot to get a straight line on the whole car and its human contents. But I couldn't waste more time reconnoitering. Who knew how long Rocky would take for an act of sexual congress, if that's what he was bent on? I had to quit stalling. Suppose Rocky happened to be a premature ejaculator.

22

Grace spotted me before I reached the Navigator's door. She paused for just a flash, long enough to give me a baleful look, as if she was saying to herself, oh, damn, does this guy have to show up now, of all lousy times?

She rolled the window on the passenger side halfway down.

"Have patience, Mr. Crang," she said. "I'll go to court with you when it's time."

"Time expired a couple of weeks ago, Grace."

"I needed space for myself. That was why I couldn't meet you."

"Might be tough to sell that one to Judge Keough."

Grace looked to her left in the direction of the Lancashire's back door. "The man with me will be back very soon. You don't want him to see you."

"Rocky engaging in, ah, sex inside?"

"He is totally a pig," Grace said. "He does this because he thinks he's humiliating me."

"Is he?"

"Just makes me impatient." Grace looked my way more intently. "Tell me, Mr. Crang, how do you know Rocky's name?"

"He and I traded punches the other day," I said. "You'll notice I'm still standing."

Grace gave me another expression conveying her profound wish that I get lost.

"I'm your lawyer, Grace," I said. "It's my job to see you through the sentencing process without anything else going wrong. That's my concern."

"Why might I think collecting the rest of your fee is your real concern, Mr. Crang?"

"Now that you mention it . . ."

"I have your seventy-five thousand dollars," Grace said. "It's put aside. Ready for delivery to you. Just wait a week. Mr. Crang, I'm in the process of looking after all my responsibilities, to you and to others."

"George Wu says you're married, Grace," I said. "To a Bulgarian or a Romanian."

Grace gave one of her rare smiles.

"George gets things wrong," she said.

"You're not married?"

"My husband is Hungarian," Grace said. "A lovely man."

Grace's mood turned into something that was, for her, practically goo-goo.

"Glad to hear it," I said. "Your Hungarian husband got a role in what you're doing on Highbury?"

The goo-goo mood fled as swiftly as it had arrived.

"How do you know about Highbury?" Grace said. "And how did you find me in the parking lot of this awful place?"

"All part of the service, Grace. Now, please, a few answers to my questions."

"Following me around is part of the service I don't appreciate."

Grace flicked another look toward the Lancashire door, then turned back to the half-open window. "Trust me, Mr. Crang, I know what I'm doing."

"I'm sure you do, but you've got to trust me too. As long as I'm your lawyer, you and I have to honour the agreement I made with the Crown and the court. If I allow you to get into some kind of trouble that messes up the agreement, I won't be carrying out my duty to the court."

Grace wasn't looking at me. She kept staring straight ahead, as if she could outwait the bothersome presence I represented.

"Or my duty to you," I said.

No response.

"Help me here," I said. "What's going on with you and Rocky and Highbury?"

Grace gave no sign she would answer any time soon.

"Sorry, Grace," I said, "but you're forcing me to wheel up the heavy artillery."

I reached into my pants pocket and pulled out the clay half-figure from the Highbury waste pail.

"Tell me about this," I said.

Grace looked at what was in my hand. Her eyes went a little narrow, and her mouth shaped an "Oh." For once in the years I'd known her, Grace was showing distress in my presence.

She took a moment to get her thoughts together.

"You were the man in the house the night I saw the lights," she said.

"That was me," I said. "Now, what's this little clay piece?"

"Mr. Crang," Grace said, "you've no idea the trouble you could cause me."

"Trouble is what you're paying me to keep you out of."

Grace ran her tongue over her upper lip, taking more time to think about her next lines. When she spoke, it was to ask a question. "I'm your client, Mr. Crang," she said, "and as your client, you must take orders from me, do I understand our roles correctly?"

"It's more a case of you telling me the facts as you see them, and I provide you with advice."

"In this particular case," Grace said, "I'm not asking for advice. I'm telling you to stay away from me until we appear in court together. I'll be there, fully co-operative. I'll pay your bill, and serve my time in prison. You can't ask for more."

"Grace, my friend, I can ask for one thing more . . ."

A bang from the Lancashire's back door interrupted my final plea. It was Rocky making a noisy exit from the club. The guy was incapable of opening a door without producing a racket.

"If he sees you, Mr. Crang," Grace said, "all my plans could be ruined."

"I'm not keen to duke it out with him either," I said.

"Then go away. Please."

"I'll never be far," I said. Geez, would I never stop talking in clichés? I thought of rephrasing it, but Rocky was bearing down on the Navigator. He hadn't seen me, and I planned to make sure he didn't. He looked supercharged and extra threatening. Probably the act of ashes-hauling had invigorated him.

I slipped away in the aisle between another SUV and a pickup truck. The Lancashire seemed to do a lot of business with customers who drove the larger-sized vehicles. I came out on the side street where I'd parked, and hustled down to Charles's Jeep.

"What'd Grace say?" Annie asked.

"She's in denial," I said.

I made a U-turn, pulled the Jeep ahead a couple of car lengths and stopped just short of the Lancashire parking lot.

"Can't we go home now?" Annie said. She sounded tired and plaintive.

"Need to finish the tail job," I said. "Find out Grace's home address."

"We're waiting for the Navigator to get going?"

"Yes," I said, "but listen, Grace said she's put aside the seventy-five thousand for me."

"You believe her?"

"What I believe is she'll give me the money the Monday after next when we get back to court."

"Oh yeah, I've heard that one before."

Up ahead, the Navigator began to pull out of the parking lot.

"We're on the move again," I said.

Annie sighed. "Let's just hope Grace hasn't shifted addresses to Scarborough, someplace like that, the remotest suburbs."

"Oh, lord, not way out there."

Both of us got our hope. The Navigator drove straight along Bloor no more than a half mile, and turned right on a street a couple of blocks east of Dufferin. Rocky stopped in mid-block not far south of Bloor. He waited barely long enough for Grace to get her feet out the car door, then tore away with his trademark screeching of tires.

I parked at a hydrant and killed the lights. Annie and I watched Grace cross the street to the east side and up a walk to a triplex. The building had a small lighted foyer with a row of three mailboxes on one wall. Grace opened the unlocked front door, then used a key on the door from the entranceway into the building.

"Wonder if we can tell from out here which apartment is hers," Annie said.

"I put my money on the top floor," I said.

Annie poked her head forward and looked up.

"Top floor's the only one with the lights still on," she said.

"That'll be hubby staying up to greet her after a long night at the kiln."

"The Bulgarian guy? Or possibly Rumanian?"

"Hungarian," I said. "Grace says so."

"Bravo for us, the stakeout has solved one mystery. The husband's nationality."

Annie and I waited. No lights went on in the lower two apartments. The lights on the third floor remained as they were, the shining beacons in the darkened building. We watched a bit longer, then I got out of the Jeep.

"Back in a flash," I said to Annie.

I stepped into the triplex's foyer and checked the mailbox for the top apartment. The name on the box read "S. Lazslo." Mission accomplished.

"S. Lazslo's a Hungarian name, right?" I said to Annie back in the Jeep.

"The S is probably for Steve," Annie said. "Hungary teems with guys named Steve."

I started the Jeep and looped back to Bloor.

"Wonder if Steve's related to Victor?" Annie said.

"Who're you talking about?"

"Victor Lazslo."

"The guy married to the Ingrid Bergman character in *Casablanca*?"

"Go to the top of the class, sweetie."

"Annie," I said, "maybe you're not cut out for late-night stakeouts. Why are you bringing up Victor Lazslo?"

"Paul Henreid played him."

"Fatigue is making you loopy," I said.

Annie went silent and soon fell asleep. I steered the rest of the way home in the restful hush of the early morning.

23

On Sunday morning, I took Annie to the airport. It was a quick trip, down to the foot of Bathurst Street. Annie was travelling to New York by way of a Porter Airlines flight to Newark out of the Billy Bishop Airport on Toronto Island.

I hung around Billy Bishop long enough to watch her plane take off. We'd been having a discussion in the car about whether I could see Annie's face at a window on the plane. The Porter planes were much smaller than at Pearson International. Shorter and slimmer. On the inside, they had one aisle and seats on either side for two passengers each. No wide-bodied aircraft, no teeming hordes of passengers.

When Annie's plane taxied out to the runway, I stared hard at the little windows. I was able to make out the pilot and the co-pilot. But passengers? Annie? I could see her only in my imagination. I waved anyway. If I couldn't see her, I made sure she could spot me, the maniac flapping his arm like he was witnessing the first plane takeoff of his life.

I drove home, made a salmon salad sandwich, ate it at my leisure with a glass of white wine, then set out by foot down Major with the Levin Museum as my destination. The day was overcast but plenty warm. Walking west on College Street, busy and hopping even on a Sunday, took me to the eastern edges of the long strip of Italian restaurants that fight one another for supremacy in fresh pasta.

The Levin was on College's south side, the entrance set well back from the street, a small plaza rising in long steps to the front door. The building was four storeys high, done in a nice combination of traditional and contemporary architecture, almost the entire exterior made of glass. I stepped into the airy lobby. Nothing was especially large about the building, but all the glass gave it the feeling of generous space.

To my right, there was a reception desk, also in glass. A guy standing behind it leaned his bum against a tall stool, stacks of programs and pamphlets spread on the counter in front of him. Since the Levin's founder mandated only female employees, the guy had to be a volunteer.

The volunteer guy was beaming at me. He made me feel warmed and welcomed and singled out. This, I thought, was a hell of a friendly museum. I smiled back and prepared to buy a ticket from him. A discreet little sign advised me admission was eight dollars. I peeled a ten off my roll of bills.

"Welcome to the Levin, Mr. Crang," the volunteer said.

He had an English accent. He was medium height and wore a small greying beard. He looked familiar, but I was damned if I could attach a name to him as easily as he could to me. The guy could sense my dilemma.

"It's the hat," he said. "I'm not wearing it in here, old sport."

He made a motion like he was pulling a baseball cap onto his head.

"Charles, sorry," I said. "Just I've never seen you anywhere except on the street. You're Charles the good neighbour."

"The Jeep did its job the other night?"

"Like a dream," I said.

"If I have my dates correct, your dear Annie must be off to the Big Apple."

"Landing in Newark practically as we speak."

"And you're devoting your first hours as a temporary bachelor to porcelain," Charles said. "How admirable, old lad."

"Not as devoted as you, working here among the real articles."

Charles smiled a beatific smile. He leaned forward on the counter, appearing to set himself for a confidential chat. I could tell he had time on his hands. Nobody else had entered the museum since I arrived.

"Ceramics and I have what you might well call a love-hate relationship," Charles said. "When I retired from business, I took a course in ceramic art out at Sheridan College, three years of it. Thought I'd do my own work. Be creative, you know. I put together a studio in our backyard. Kiln and all. My stuff turned out to be good enough. Workmanlike, you could describe it. But I lacked the gift of the great ceramicists. Bit of a disappointment, old bean."

Charles hardly looked crushed. He seemed one of nature's cheerful souls.

"You volunteering in this place," I said, "you must still have the hots for the art form."

"I love being close to the real artists' work," Charles said, waving his arm in a gesture that covered every ceramic pot and bowl in sight. "It's just the art doesn't love me back. Not enough to let me be one of the sodding artists myself. You see what I mean, old sport?"

A flurry of new arrivals diverted Charles's smiles and attentions. I wandered away to look at the large pots on the first floor. They were mostly products of eighteenth-century China. Not old as Chinese history went, but ancient in terms of the western world.

In the little I'd learned from Annie and my own Googling, I gathered vaguely that porcelain art emerged as a form in China and Japan many centuries ago. In the 1700s, European explorers and other nosy persons began hijacking the products to the western nations. Fairly quickly, the inventive minds of European artists were applied to finding the formula for creating porcelain out of their very own local clay.

The first guy to hit on the porcelain's precious arcanum—the fancy word they used in the field for formula—was actually looking for something else. The guy in question's name was Johann Frederick Bottger, an employee and more or less prisoner of the heinous King Augustus the Second of Poland and Elector of Saxony. Bottger was supposed to nail down the arcanum for gold. But he failed at the assignment several times. Eventually he lucked out and stumbled on the right combination of Meissen clay and heat and other elements that created not gold but porcelain. The discovery elated just about everybody, but it didn't persuade Augustus to spring Bottger from the royal clutches. The unlucky sap died impoverished, confined and a drunk. Meanwhile, the rage for porcelain swept across Europe.

I went at all four floors of the Levin in rising order starting at the first and looking at almost every pot and cup and mug and vase and all other household items that a person with a talent for porcelain could think of making. They were attractive enough, but my brain started going fuzzy with the repetition. My basic problem was that I couldn't find any objects in the size and shape I was looking for.

What I wanted was an exhibit that featured smaller pieces along the lines of the thing in my pocket. I'd brought along to the Levin the unrealized figure I liberated from 32 Highbury. My thinking was that if this hunk of clay got everybody so heated up—everybody being Grace and Rocky and probably Ms. Janetta—then it must relate to something of value in the legitimate world of ceramics.

Did that make sense? Not much added up to anything coherent in this confusion of a case, not so far, but it was at least a possibility that Grace was using her talent with porcelain to make copies of some legitimate ceramic pieces. The pieces would necessarily have to be of a high monetary value. The only reason for making the copies would be to sell them at exorbitant value as the real thing to some sucker of a collector. Given that scenario, where might such legitimate pieces be on display? All signs pointed to the Levin Museum where Ms. Janetta was a director, where Grace often visited, where I was now prowling.

I reached the fourth and top floor, parading up and down the first two aisles cursorily checking out yet more damn bowls. But, aha, down at the end of the second aisle, set aside in a large space close to the floor's big front window, stood a tall glass cabinet displaying an arrangement on three glass shelves of what appeared from a distance to be several smaller figures. Before I investigated the figures, I took a moment to appreciate the glass cabinet. It made a show all by itself, about seven or eight feet high, standing on four powerful-looking legs, pure and thick glass on all sides, a barely noticeable small door in the back equipped with a small lock. The door was no doubt the means by which the little figures were placed inside the formidable cabinet.

As I got closer, the figures revealed themselves as just about the very articles I had in mind. A sign on the middle shelf inside the cabinet read "*A Company of Fools* by L.L. Schwartzmann, 1774." The "fools," I recognized right away, were of the clownish sort. Jesters and entertainers in the Europe of four centuries ago. I counted the figures. Twenty-seven of them I got, each one in a slightly different costume, nothing too elaborate but all colourful and amusing.

And each figure came with a gimmick. None of the fools' faces was human. All were of a different animal type. The whole arrangement seemed to be a variation on the *Monkey Orchestra* Annie told me about. Except here, the figures were jesters, not musicians, and their faces weren't confined to monkeys but came from the entire range of the animal kingdom. I ticked off the beasts in the case. Three or four different kinds of dog. At least two cats. A lion and a tiger. A monkey and a gorilla. There was even a snake head if I was reading the silly-looking reptile-type figure correctly.

I took the unfinished hunk of clay out of my pocket. All I had to go on by way of a comparison test were the hunk's pants. Did any of the animal-faced jesters in the case have pants similar to those of the half-man I held in my hand? Dumb question, as it happened. Just about all jesters, almost every single one, wore pants that billowed. It must have been the jester style. I gave each jester a good long stare, but couldn't narrow them down to one or two with a pants shape that exactly matched my guy's. The investigation stalled.

But surely not permanently. I counted on the search becoming ongoing.

I checked the clock on the fourth-floor wall. It was a quarter to four. At that moment, a woman's voice on the public address system announced that the museum would close in fifteen minutes. We should all prepare ourselves for departure.

Excellent, I thought, the closing would free up Charles for a consultation.

I took the elevator to the first floor. Charles was at his post behind the counter in the lobby, alone and available as the small crowd streamed out of the place. I showed Charles my hunk of clay with pants.

"This piece remind you of anything in the museum?" I asked.

"The left shoe is all wrong, the right shoe is not bad, and the trousers are close to very good." Charles looked up at me. "Good enough, old chum?"

"You recognize all that?" I said.

"It's the jester with the fox face from the *Company of Fools* on the fourth floor. Or the beginnings of something like our fox-faced friend. Rather like it, to be even more accurate. Don't want to overrate something that's a primitive start to a piece in the clay you're holding there in your hand, Crang old boy."

"The part I don't get, how're you able to spot it so fast?"

"*Company of Fools* is the great prize of the Levin. I was up on the fourth earlier this morning, just getting my regular fix of *Fools*. I love it for its own glorious self, Crang old laddie. So do thousands of others. Experts come from all over the world to study it."

"Puts a glow on the museum's reputation?"

"Indubitably, my dear Crang," Charles said. His phrasing wasn't comic or ironic. That was Charles's normal talking mode. "Replicas of *Company* sell briskly among even non-expert fans of ceramics, old chap."

"But this thing I've got, it's not a replica in the sense you're talking about?"

Charles took the piece from me and turned it in his hands. "No, some overly ambitious maker of ceramic pieces seems to have set about making a copy, then flamed out badly before he finished."

As Charles and I talked, I sensed that somebody behind me was hanging on the edges of the conversation.

Charles looked up and smiled. "Hello there, Hugette," he said to the person behind me. "What do you make of this, dear girl?" Charles said, holding up my piece for Hugette to examine.

I turned around and took in Hugette. There was a lot to take in. Hugette was very tall, more than six feet. Slenderly built, though it was the kind of slender that conveyed an impressive aura. She had large features, particularly her prow of a schnozz, but the whole package was attractive. She wore her hair cut short, and she had youth on her side. She was no more than twenty-five.

"Somebody fooling around with Mr. Fox," Hugette said, taking the piece out of Charles's hand.

Charles introduced Hugette and me. Her last name was Jennings. "Hugette," Charles said to me, "is the Levin's deputy chief of security."

"You worked on this, Mr. Crang?" Hugette asked me, indicating the piece of clay. She seemed intense about getting the answer.

I shook my head. "Can't tell a kiln from a kit and caboodle."

Hugette wasn't amused. "Who did it then?" she asked.

"A friend with aspirations," I said.

Hugette continued to examine the piece, still giving off the waves of intensity.

Charles said, "Isn't Sunday one of your two days of rest, Hugette?"

"Anita's going to be late," she said. "I'm filling in the couple hours till she gets here."

Hugette thrust the figure in the general area of me. She turned on her heel and left without a goodbye.

"Can be a bit brusque, our Hugette," Charles said in a whisper.

"Probably the security mentality," I said.

"Boring job actually," Charles said. "Hugette sits up all night in the security room on the fourth floor looking at the cameras."

"Boring you say? I call it inhumane. Chair-bound for an entire work shift?"

"She gets small breaks, old bean. Every hour, she leaves the cameras and makes a quick in-person inspection of all four floors."

"But the idea of cameras in the museum," I said. "That's to make sure no thieves're prowling the place in the middle of the night?"

"Lot of paranoia in the gallery world these days, my lad," Charles said. "Even affects us in ceramics."

"There's good value in the pieces on these floors, huh?" I said. "What do you figure *Company of Fools* would go at? How much we talking about?"

"The price if somebody swiped it? That the bee you've got in your bonnet, Crang old chappie?"

"Idle curiosity, Charles."

"It's academic, you know. *Fools* isn't leaving its home in the Levin."

"Humour a neophyte. Hundreds of thousands?"

Charles made a sputtering sound. "Good lord, old bean, millions. They're priceless, those twenty-seven pieces taken altogether. But if you're talking about some fishy business with the entire *Company of Fools*, then you're into eight figures."

Charles and I stepped away from the reception counter and got ready to leave the museum. I was still thinking about the size of the numbers Charles had just hazarded a guess at.

Charles said, "Why do I get the feeling there's more to your curiosity about *Fools* than idleness?"

"For now," I said, "that's for me to know and you to guess, me old lad."

24

On Tuesday morning, I got to the office before nine. I made enough coffee to fill three cups, one for Sam across the hall, two for me. The measure of water to coffee wasn't quite right. Little too strong in the resulting taste. The day before, it'd been a touch on the weak side. My coffee-making was a work in progress. But fun.

I put in the first of my two daily phone calls to Annie. She said the curator at the Columbia archives was treating her generously. "A swell dame," Annie called her. Annie's slang was showing the influence of a 1930s Edward Everett Horton vocabulary. I told her about my surprise that Charles spoke with an English accent. "You should hear his wife," Annie said. "Must've been born within the sound of Bow Bells, she's practically impenetrable in the vocal department." We signed off with expressions of love and yearning. Annie said it seemed a decade since she'd left our little home. She'd try to get back earlier than Monday, but that was probably doubtful. She had a treasure trove of Hortoniana to go through.

I worked on the files of cases I'd been neglecting for the past couple of weeks. These concerned miscreants still to come to court, probably sometime in the next months. I drank my two cups of coffee, and answered the first phone call of the day at eleven-fifteen.

"I Spy here, Crang." I Spy Griffith sounded pumped. "Much police action across the street this morning."

"Tell me why," I said. "Also who and what."

"A death, I'm positive. Police cars arrived an hour ago, sirens blaring. The policemen must have called an ambulance. It pulled up about ten minutes later. That brought more sirens. Everybody's still there. I'm looking through my window as I speak to you. Yellow police tape blocking off number 32. Three cars of plainclothes people got here thirty minutes ago. Homicide detectives, I would wager."

"What about the who? Anything to identify a victim, assuming there is one?"

"Not yet," I Spy said. "But I'll tell you who a key person in the who category is. My friend Ernie."

I needed a moment to process the personnel in I Spy's world. "The postman?" I said.

"He's the one who called the police, that's what I surmise. After the police and everybody got here, a half hour or a little further in, a Canada Post truck dropped off another postman outside 32. He waited till a plainclothes person, a woman, brought out Ernie's bag of mail. This second postman is finishing the route."

"I'll wager you buttonholed the new guy."

"Very close-mouthed, this second fellow," I Spy said. "I doubt he was told much anyway. Just that Ernie needed to help the police, and wouldn't be doing any more mail delivery today. That's what this fellow told me. Name's Gus."

"Thank you for the tip, I Spy. Appreciate it. Soon as I hang up, I'm on my way out there."

"That's how I expected you to respond, Crang." I Spy sounded bubbly with enthusiasm. "Don't try driving your car all the way into Highbury. Media's taken over the street."

"One thing to keep in mind till I get to your place," I said. "The police will be canvassing the Highbury houses. They'll want to know what you saw across the street last night."

"Absolutely nothing."

"Wait a minute, I Spy," I said. "You can't lie. Not to the cops."

"It's no lie, Crang," Griffith said. "My two children and their spouses came for dinner last night. We got to reminiscing about the kids' lives around the house when they were young and their mother was alive. My son-in-law got bored stiff. The rest of us kept talking till midnight."

"You didn't glance out the window? Maybe spot the black Navigator?"

"Didn't take so much as a tiny peek."

"What about your 3 a.m. urination? You look out the window then?"

"Slept right through till seven this morning."

"An atypical night for you."

"I have to tell you I woke up this morning with a strange emptiness. As if part of my life had gone missing."

"Turns out somebody else's life may have gone missing permanently."

"Exactly my reaction."

I couldn't think of anything else to ask I Spy or warn him about.

"Heading your way," I said, and hung up.

25

I made good time to the Kingsway, parked my car on one of the back streets and hiked a couple of long blocks to Highbury. Three TV trucks clogged the block, one each from CFTO, Citytv and the local CBC channel. People wearing makeup and holding microphones stood around talking to one another; they were the on-camera reporters gossiping, keeping loose, ready for the moment their field producers figured there was something worth updating. Camera guys, sound people, makeup artists, all of them waited for the action. A truck selling coffee and sandwiches had opened for service, doing rush business. A whole village had sprung up on Highbury, all in the interests of a dead person. I was getting antsy, wondering who the victim was.

There was no need for me to knock on I Spy's door. It was open, and he was standing on the porch. We shook hands, then he led me into the living room.

A man in a Canada Post shirt was slumped in the chair I'd sat in when I first visited the Griffith house. He was about forty with a small paunch, a goatee and a look of exhaustion. He was gulping coffee.

"You must be Ernie," I said to him. "I'm Crang."

"Mr. Griffith's been talking about you," Ernie said.

I went over and shook Ernie's hand. He didn't get up. His hand felt clammy.

"You've had a bad jolt," I said. Nice line, Crang, I thought. Deep stuff.

I Spy stepped into the conversation. "The police let Ernie take a break, but not go home yet, not talk to the press."

I said to Ernie, "Mr. Griffith told you I have a client involved in some of the events been going on in number 32?"

"Grace Nguyen?" Ernie asked. His eyes went to me with something sudden in them, something very much like shock.

"Grace's the victim?" I said.

"I didn't think she was dead when I first saw her," Ernie said. He talked with a lot of hesitations. "Then I got closer. She was lying in the trees a few yards in from the driveway. Soon as I saw the way her face was broke up, her eyes staring wide open like that, I knew nobody looked that way could be alive."

My legs felt as if they could turn wobbly. I sat down. I'd never had a client killed before. It wasn't a pleasant sensation.

"Coffee, Crang?" I Spy asked in a soft voice.

"Please," I said.

I Spy poured a cup from a carafe on the living room table.

I took a swallow and looked over at Ernie.

"You mind going through this with me?" I said to him. "All in confidence. I won't use your information for reasons other than my professional connection to Grace."

I seemed to be rallying from the first effects of the news.

"The reason I was there in the driveway in the first place," Ernie said, "I was just making my usual delivery."

"About what time?" I asked.

"Not long after ten, maybe earlier," Ernie said. "Funny thing this morning, not ha-ha funny, but coincidental funny, I delivered the magazine she gets about glass or whatever it is, bowls, cups and so on."

"*Ceramics Monthly.*"

"That's the one," Ernie said. "Never met the lady on deliveries, never laid eyes on Grace Nguyen, but I felt I knew her. You get that way about all your customers, just from seeing their names on the envelopes. But most of these people I usually run into in person from time to time. Grace Nguyen, I only knew her strictly from her name. Which was distinctive, specially in this neighbourhood."

"You ever meet anyone else at number 32?"

"Not a soul," Ernie said. He drank more coffee, still gulping. "Not anybody as far back as I can remember being on the route."

"When you walked up the driveway this morning," I said, "on your way to put the magazine through the mail slot, you didn't see anything out of the ordinary?"

"Not the body, that's for sure," Ernie said. "Might not have noticed anything on the way out of the driveway either except a couple squirrels made a heck of a racket. Just chasing one another in the trees and bushes. Couldn't help looking over, that's when I saw this flash of bright blue colour on the ground. Turned out to be Grace Nguyen's blouse."

Ernie stopped to take a deep quavery breath. "So, like I said earlier, I went a few steps into the trees, far enough to see the woman's face smashed up. I backed away from there fast as I could. Got out my cell and hit 911."

"No doubt in your mind the woman on the ground was dead?"

"Wasn't going back in to see for myself. But later in the driveway, when everybody started arriving, I heard a medical guy from an ambulance tell a plainclothes detective, 'This one's been chilling a few hours.' Something like that. 'Chilling' his word for sure."

"A few hours?" I said.

"Way he put it."

"One big question, Ernie. We're supposing the dead person is Grace. But have the cops confirmed the identity, far as you know?"

"Kind of wondering about that myself," Ernie said. "I'm the one told the officers I delivered the ceramics magazine to the house in the name of Grace Nguyen. Poor woman on the ground was Asian, so I sort of connected the two things in my own head and said so."

"The police had no other verification?"

"They went back and forth on their cellphones about who she was, the 'vic,' they kept referring to her. But nobody told me in so many words, yeah, you're right, the dead person's Grace Nguyen."

"You didn't overhear anything specific about identity?"

"Why would they want me to know what they're thinking?"

I Spy had a question for Ernie. "What about a handbag? Did you notice if Grace had one?"

"Oh boy, Mr. Griffith, the state I was in, I doubt I would have seen a steamer trunk if she was lugging around one of those."

I had my own ideas about Grace and handbags. From over-hearing her conversation with Rocky during my confinement in the garden shed, I felt pretty certain Grace didn't make a habit of carrying anything like a handbag or purse. A makeup kit seemed the limit of her carry-alongs on her trips inside number 32. I sus-pected it was a case of Grace wanting nothing on her person that gave away her identity. I'd heard her say so myself.

I sat back in my chair, thinking Ernie had been wrung dry of information. What came next? I turned to Griffith.

"Cops talk to you, I Spy?" I asked.

"A uniformed woman did. Asked me about last night, and I told her what I told you. I was entertaining my kids the whole evening."

"Anything else come up? More general questions?"

"Did I know who lived at 32? I answered no."

"No deeper than that?"

I Spy shook his head. "I expect a real detective will come call-ing later. Somebody from Homicide. When that happens, should I mention your involvement, Crang?"

"Answer whatever questions you're asked, but don't volun-teer anything they don't bring up. No harm mentioning me. I'll eventually be speaking to them on my own anyway. Me being Grace's lawyer."

"That what you're going to do next, talk with the police?"

"First thing for me to do," I said, "I need to break the news to Grace's husband."

"The murdered woman was married?" I Spy said, looking and sounding astounded. "Can't say why, but I didn't imagine she had a husband."

"Unless I tell him, he won't be finding out about Grace anytime soon. Not if she left no easy clues lying around about who she was."

"That's your thinking?"

"For the time being."

"A husband." I Spy shook his head. "I know what it's like to lose a wife. Poor fellow."

"You're right, I Spy," I said. "The guy's world is about to get rocked."

26

Looking for the triplex Annie and I had seen Grace go into, I turned south off Bloor on the wrong street. There was no triplex the whole length of the block. The next north-south street to the east was a one-way coming north. On the street after that, I spotted the triplex. A cop car was parked out front.

I sat in the Mercedes and waited. It would have been too much of a coincidence if the cops were calling on anybody in the building except Lazslo. Lazslo must be their guy, which meant I was wrong about Grace and her secrecy. Somehow the police figured out her address fast off the mark. But I was still ahead of them on Grace's connections inside the ceramics business, the scam or whatever it was I imagined she was involved in. If I hung around, and talked to Lazslo, maybe I could add to my store of information. Maybe I could sort out her killing and pin down the murderer. Maybe I could find a way to collect the seventy-five grand.

The money kept coming up in my thinking. Was I letting my mercenary side control the rest of me? A woman had been murdered, and almost my first thoughts were of how much she owed me? Maybe I should recalibrate the whole mess in a light that was marginally more flattering to my good self. Something like, I solve the murder, then let the chips fall where they may? That seemed a fair and moral approach, the chips in this case being the seventy-five Gs.

I waited a half hour before the cops came out of the triplex. One was young and female, a brunette, in uniform. The other was an older guy, more portly than detectives were supposed to be, wearing a dark suit and tie, white shirt. He was doing all the talking as the two got into the patrol car, the woman taking the wheel. They drove off.

I went into the triplex's foyer and pressed the button for apartment number three. The door buzzed open. Nobody asked who I was on the intercom. I looked around, but didn't see an intercom. Maybe the building worked on the honour system. I opened the entrance door and walked up two flights to the third floor.

A tall man in shirtsleeves waited in front of an open door, the numeral 3 on it. The tall man looked at me for a moment, his expression showing a hint of surprise.

"Thought police come back," he said. "You a police also?"

"I bat for the other side."

"You criminal lawyer."

"Very nice. You got it right away from the baseball analogy?"

The man shook his head. "Don't know what means baseball analogy," he said. "I'm recognizing from when I drive Grace to appointment at Spadina office. You walking into building, Grace say man out there Mr. Crang."

"May I come in?" I said. "I'm on a serious mission, but if the police have been here, you must already know."

"Grace dead," he said. "Police tell."

Steve Lazslo was lean as well as tall, and he had a lachrymose expression. I didn't get the impression it was a look brought on by the occasion of his wife's death. It looked natural and permanent. Could be a Budapest thing. People from Buda were said to be happy-go-lucky, people from Pest were lachrymose. Or the other way around. Lazslo must have come from whichever was the grim side of town.

His apartment was crowded with furniture. Probably every-thing that was missing from the condo on Lombard had been squeezed into this place. Lazslo sat on the sofa. I took a plush armchair. When I sat, I sunk down about two feet. It would take a hell of an effort when the time came to extricate myself from the depths of the plush.

"Okay if I call you Steve, Steve?" I said.

"Please." The way he said it, the word came out "pliz."

"I'm sorry for your loss, Steve. The reason I'm here is to fin-ish my duties as Grace's lawyer."

"Grace say you good lawyer."

"She never offered an opinion one way or another in my pres-ence."

"Grace never person for saying compliment."

"That's not just kidding."

"She never do that, what you say, kidding."

"Probably made you and Grace an ideal couple," I said.

"Two peas in pod. Grace say all the time."

"Speaking as one of the peas, Steve, you know what Grace was doing all those nights at 32 Highbury?"

"Never heard this Highbury until police say today. Grace tell me better I not know nothing. Have no information about where she go, what she do. She go out at night, do job, come home, say nothing. Just she glad to be home. Go on like that for five months. But she say yesterday, soon be over. Very soon, any day now."

For Steve, the tall, dark, silent Hungarian type, that qualified as an oration.

"Tell me this, Steve. How did the cops find you so quickly?"

A very small smile flickered across Steve's face. "Good ques-tion, Mr. Crang. Grace never carry identity. She want nobody find her from not going to court with you. Do that later, go to court for sentence in prison. Not get caught before then."

"If she had nothing on her person, no name or address, how did the two police people get to this apartment?"

"Grace make mistake. Have ticket in her pocket. Dry cleaning. She forget ticket. Police find this morning. Go to dry-cleaning store. Get address for here."

"Cops can be resourceful sometimes."

I'd got the part right about Grace's efforts at anonymity. Probably explained why she and Steve moved out of the Lombard condo, a matter of lying low. But there was plenty I still needed to pump out of poor Steve. For a guy so recently widowered, he was a remarkably frank answerer of questions. Must be the Buda influence. Or Pest.

"Steve," I said, "you knew all along Grace's work was in ceramics?"

"Of course."

"She was getting well remunerated for the work?"

"Paid?"

"Sorry, yes, remuneration is pay."

"Million dollars."

"Jesus," I said, "she was certain about the million?"

"Paid in advance part money. Quarter million."

"Where's the quarter million now?"

"Cash money in safety deposit boxes. Many boxes. Much bills. Hundred-dollar bills. Fifty."

We had reached a crucial point in events. I needed to be clear with my next words to Steve.

"Very important, Steve," I said. "Is your name on the safety deposit boxes as well as Grace's? Do you have keys to the boxes?"

Steve nodded vigorously. "Grace and me. Both names. Grace said in case anything happen."

"To her?"

"Of course her. Nothing happen me. Not ever. Only her it happen."

"Listen to me carefully, Steve. Go to the bank this afternoon. Take all the money out of the safety deposit boxes. Don't tell the bank Grace is no longer with us. You follow me?"

"Get money."

"Right away."

"Police come back in couple hour," Steve said. "Need me to say dead person is Grace."

"Identification, right," I said. "That's routine. The money isn't routine. Get it all out before the bank learns Grace is dead. If they do, they'll want her estate probated before they'll release contents of the safety deposit boxes. You understand the problem? First, the bank holds up the release of the cash. Then the cops find out. They'll want to know where the quarter million came from. Could mean a lot of grief for you."

"Grief?"

"Financial grief I'm talking about. As opposed to death-in-the-family grief."

"Take out money."

"You got it," I said. "Speaking of money, you have any idea about the other three-quarters of a million? The rest of the money Grace was earning for the ceramics?"

"From Levin."

"You must be talking about the Levin Museum."

Steve shrugged. Hungarians really knew how to shrug. Steve's shrug conveyed complete and unquestionable cluelessness.

"A person from the Levin Museum," I said, "that was who delivered the first quarter million? And will theoretically do the same for three-quarters of a million more?"

"Levin not person?"

"She once was but no longer."

Steve nodded, thinking over his situation. Or so I assumed.

"Did Grace have a particular friend at the museum?" I asked.

Steve looked blank, an expression that seemed to come easily for him.

"Let me mention a name, Steve," I said. "Elizabeth Janetta mean anything to you?"

Steve's face brightened. "Good lady," he said.

"You've met her?"

"Not meet," Steve said. "Grace say she's good lady."

"Do you think it was Ms. Janetta gave Grace the money?"

"Could be so."

"What makes you think it's possible? Did Grace all of sudden have a quarter-million bucks one time after she got together with Elizabeth?"

"Maybe."

"Just maybe?"

"Elizabeth rich."

"I've noticed that, Steve."

"Elizabeth generous."

"That's what Grace said?"

"Many time," Steve said.

I had grown seriously tired of the increasingly monosyllabic nature of the conversation on Steve's side. My fatigue seemed the signal to wrap it up with him for the time being.

"Steve, both of us have things to do, places to go," I said. "Shall we agree to get on with our chores?"

"Get money from bank."

"Good man, Steve. But first maybe you can do something else."

"What?"

"Help me out of this chair."

Once more, a blank look crowded out everything else on Steve's face. I divined he wasn't going to be of assistance in my pickle with the chair. It was up to me all alone. I grasped both plush arms of the plush chair, and gave an almighty shove. It worked. I rose from the chair in a catapult action, just barely keeping my balance on landing.

"Steve," I said, holding out my hand to shake his, "phone me if you need a word of guidance in any area."

"Phone you?"

I got out one of my cards and handed it to him.

Steve looked at it. "Got same card from Grace," he said, handing it back to me.

"Can't have too many cards, Steve," I said. I wrote my home address on the back of the card. "Keep it."

I pushed the card into his hand and left the apartment.

Grilling Steve had been like the thing with hen's teeth. But I felt confident I'd forged ahead in the information game.

Way ahead.

27

When I got back to Major Street late in the afternoon, a large, open trailer hooked to a pickup truck sat half on the road and half on the sidewalk across the street from my house. I walked down the side alley to the backyard. The first person I ran into was the goddess of the garden.

"Hey, Kathleen," I said. "Got the slaves at their toil?"

The goddess was too busy waving her arms at four slaves to have time for an exchange with a non-gardening ninny like me. All four slaves were new faces to my eyes except for Rita, the woman of the encounter with my pants down. It probably wouldn't go over well if I mentioned the episode in front of her boss.

A wiry young guy with an Errol Flynn moustache stopped in front of me.

"I'm Duncan," he said. "We all loved the story about you in the manure without your trousers."

I sneaked a look in Kathleen's direction, me trying to appear devil-may-care. One glance, and I knew my cautious approach wasn't needed. Kathleen was having a large laugh. So was the whole crew. This was a happy bunch of slaves, worth watching in gardening action for a bit. Kathleen took the time to identify everybody, telling me all of them had skills in and out of the backyard business. A slim blond young woman named Lee taught violin and played in a band called Rival Boys. Monique was gorgeous and a fiend at pruning. As best I could make out, the slaves were at the moment mostly digging earth out of the backyard, wheelbarrowing it down the alleyway, returning with a load of fresher-looking earth.

"You understand what we're doing to your yard?" Kathleen asked me.

"Seem to be exchanging one batch of dirt for another."

"You're roughly correct. Earth in this old part of the city isn't good enough to grow as much as a weed."

"The trouble being?" I asked, not panting to find out, but interested.

"A big reason for having a backyard in the old days was for dumping stuff. Cinders from the coal furnace. Cat and dog corpses. Human waste."

"Shit?"

"My word exactly."

"You and the slaves are doing a removal of the lousy old earth?"

"Nothing decent'll grow till we replace the soil."

"I'm learning gardening's not always a glamorous pursuit."

"Wait for the beauty when the plants come to growth. Doesn't get more glamorous than that."

I went inside the house. My plan for the evening was to troll through recent events and sort out my options. Do it with a drink in my hand and a meal on the stove. But there'd be no drink until the goddess and her slaves wound up the day's slogging. This wasn't a plantation of the Old South. The master didn't sip his julep while the slaves sweated in the fields. Nosuh, boss.

Kathleen tapped on the dining room's glass door.

"Mind if I give Annie's new secateurs a testing?" she asked.

"The ferocious little weapon?"

"I'm the one who recommended she buy this brand," Kathleen said. "Want to make sure she was given the real goods."

I got the secateurs out of the big bureau that was otherwise home to dinner mats and other harmless dining implements. Kathleen took the secateurs and headed for a slumped-over bush at the back of the garden. I watched her make three or four swift passes at the bush's branches. They dropped into a tidy pile at Kathleen's feet. It was a performance not unlike a magician wielding his wand.

"Very theatrical," I told Kathleen after she came in from the garden. She gave a small bow and handed me back the secateurs.

"Special, this pair," Kathleen said, pointing at the secateurs. "They're called by-pass. The trick to using them, you have to squeeze the handles twice to get any action. Squeeze once, pause, squeeze again, and they'll cut through a redwood."

"Impressive," I said, twirling the secateurs like I had a pistol in my hand.

"Not literally a redwood," Kathleen said.

"Strong and powerful," I said. "I get the idea."

Fifteen minutes later, Kathleen and the slaves having pulled up stakes, I made a martini, hoisting my glass for the first sip to Grace's memory. Two more sips later, I phoned Annie in her suite at Columbia University and told her Grace had probably been murdered.

"I'm coming home," Annie said.

"No need," I said.

"A murderer's loose, and all you can say is no need? Honey, consider your past record. Whenever a killer's on the scene in a case even tangentially involving your good self, the killer sure as shooting finds his way to the Crang front door."

"I've learned from past lessons," I said. "Besides, look at it this way, I'm behind a different front door. No killer'll ever locate the new address."

"I'm still coming home."

"Let me explain how I'm playing it safe."

"Don't expect me to swallow whatever it is you're imagining."

"How about I swear an oath on all that's holy?"

"What could possibly be holy to you?"

I paused a beat or two. "My entire Bill Evans record collection."

"Good heavens, you're really serious."

"Okay," I said, "the gist of the oath, I promise I won't initiate any encounter with a person that promises danger."

There was quiet at Annie's end. It stretched close to thirty seconds.

"You don't suppose," I said, "this is one of those phone calls that includes unlimited free time for reasons I never understand."

"Cost of the phone is secondary right now to the decision-making process," Annie said. After a little more quiet, she said, "Okay, I trust you. I'm staying on the job down here until my plane ticket says it's time to come home."

On that note of comity and after several telephonic kisses to one another, I freshened my martini and chopped up carrots, celery, an onion and a tomato. I opened a can of sodium-free kidney beans and dumped a quarter pound of extra-lean ground beef in a frying pan. I was on my way to making a pot of chili. The Dizzy Gillespie–Charlie Parker 1945 concert at Town Hall played on the sound system, and instead of whistling while I worked, I thought about Grace and death and ceramic figures. It also occurred that I should wonder whether Grace's guarantee that she had set aside my seventy-five-thousand-dollar fee lasted beyond her demise.

By the time the chili was more than halfway to cooked, and Symphony Sid Torin doing MC work at Town Hall had introduced Sid Catlett on drums in place of Max Roach, I'd come to a conclusion about the next step in my own inquiry into Grace's murder. Tomorrow I would get together with a guy I knew from law school, a classmate named Walter Torgol. Wally was a person of unique marvels. After he finished law school, he got a medical degree. Some of us thought Wally would keep going until he was head of the World Health Organization or some such lofty organization. But his career seemed to have plateaued in the Ontario coroner's office on Grenville Street. Wally did autopsies. I wanted him to find out what he could about Grace's death. What killed her? I was sure Wally would come through for me. What the heck, he'd delivered in the past.

I ate my chili, accompanying it with a third martini, which I didn't finish. Fatigue was closing in early. I tidied the kitchen and went to bed with the new William Boyd novel. I read until eleven o'clock when I had the presence of mind to mark my place in the book and turn off the light. Then I dropped off into an immediate and deep sleep.

28

In my sleep, I thought I heard noises downstairs. I opened my eyes. It was as close to pitch-black as it gets in downtown Toronto. I blinked a couple of times and listened hard. For the moment, nothing more drifted up. I held my wristwatch close to my eyes. Almost two-thirty. Sounds returned from below. The first time, I'd supposed the noises came from Annie's office at the front. The second time, they'd changed location to the dining room at the back.

I managed to stand up without drawing any creaks from the bedroom floor. I had on my Dirk Nowitzki T-shirt and black underwear. I did a silent job of pulling on a pair of jeans. Wouldn't do to appear pantless in front of a burglar. I tiptoed down the stairs, masterful at not stepping in any spots I knew to have a propensity for groans. The burglar wasn't as fastidious. He was opening drawers as if he were alone in the house. Didn't he give a damn about the burglary victim's sensibilities? I made it all the way to the kitchen without making a peep.

The intruder was bending over a shelf in the tall antique bureau against the north wall. I recognized him right away, even from behind, even in the gloom.

"Rocky," I said in a normal speaking voice, "all you had to do was phone for an invitation."

Rocky turned toward me.

"Crang, you fuck!" he said. "Where's the little clay thing?"

I still couldn't make out Rocky's face or the expression on it, but his voice told me all I needed to know. Rocky was in a fury.

I came down the four steps from the kitchen to the dining room level. That put me not more than a couple of yards from Rocky. I felt vibes that told me I was too close to the guy.

"Let me just turn some lights on, Rocky," I said. "We'll have a drink and work this out."

"Don't jerk me around, you asshole! Give me the fucking piece of clay!"

"Not even vodka? Polish potato? You'll love it."

"The clay, asshole!"

"You don't mind my asking how'd you get in here?"

Rocky's hands shot out, grabbing me around the neck. I felt myself being slammed down on the dining room table. At least I had the reflex smarts to hold my head high enough to avoid a smack on the tabletop. That would have meant concussion for sure, undoubtedly followed by unconsciousness.

"Get off me, Rocky!" My voice came in a gurgle. Rocky would never have heard what I was begging. Rocky wouldn't care. Rocky had once again gone more than a little psycho. Probably out-of-control psycho. He was trying to get a firm enough grip on my neck to throttle me. He wasn't saying anything, but he was making scary huffing and puffing sounds. All his energies seemed to be concentrated on tightening both hands around my windpipe.

I writhed and squirmed and thumped his skull with my right fist. The fist bounced off his noggin without slowing things down by a hair. Rocky's hands were squeezing my neck. The guy had taken departure of his common sense. Maybe he was born without any. He seemed to have nothing on his mind at the moment except wiping me out.

With my left hand, I tore at Rocky's wrists. If I expected that to make him lay off, I was way out of luck. My right hand scrabbled around the table searching for a stray knife or fork. Anything that would stand in as a weapon. There was no weapon. No knife or fork.

Then my right hand landed on something far more potent than a knife or fork. My right hand touched the secateurs. Hope filled the parts of my brain that were still operative.

Rocky tightened on my throat. Despite the boost in morale I'd drawn from locating the secateurs, I was fading toward the stage just before the stage of unconsciousness. This was authentic peril. My right hand got the SOS message. The hand seized the secateurs by the grips. Hand and grips meshed just the way they were supposed to, just the way they would if I could actually see what I was doing. I was riding a tiny piece of good luck.

I aimed the secateurs' blades at Rocky's right hand, the hand that was digging most lethally into my throat. I felt the blades engage with a piece of Rocky's flesh. It was a part of his hand, but I wasn't sure whether it was a digit, a bit of wrist or what. The secateurs had a piece of Rocky in their mean little blades. I squeezed the handles for all I was worth. Nothing happened except Rocky kept pressing my neck. Jesus, I was done for. An instant came and went when I felt sure I was on the verge of giving up the ghost.

Until I remembered these were special secateurs. By-pass secateurs. They needed two squeezes. I squeezed a second time. I felt the blades drive through a piece of what I took to be bone or flesh.

Rocky screamed.

It was a very loud scream, the sound of primal pain, and it was directed full blast at my right ear. For a fraction of time, I went to black. It wasn't the scream that generated the blackness. It was the relief of Rocky's hands falling away from my throat. I could breathe again. What was it about damn Rocky? This was the second time in a week he'd robbed me of wind and breath and most of my consciousness.

"You cut off my hand, you crazy fuck!" Rocky shouted. He was sitting on the table, bent over, cradling his hand in an awkward way that I couldn't entirely make out in the darkness.

I jumped off the table and snapped on the overhead light.

"Oh, god, that's gruesome, Rocky!" I said.

It wasn't Rocky's whole hand I'd cut. Just his little finger. It dangled from the rest of his hand, not completely severed but close to it. Rocky looked at his pitiful dangling little finger and began to cry.

"Man up there, Rocky," I said. "You didn't hear me sobbing when you were wringing my neck."

"Do something! I'll die!"

"Not likely," I said. I took a closer look at his wound. "Hold the finger more or less in place till I get some ice."

Rocky's tears ran down his face. He made a blubbering sound.

I scrambled to the freezer, yanked out a tray of ice cubes, and dumped the cubes in a dishtowel. I came back to Rocky and wrapped his hand, including the helpless semi-severed little finger, in the towel of cubes. I tied the whole works in place with a piece of cord from the drawer that holds our kitchen bits and pieces.

"Keep that firm as you can stand," I told Rocky. He'd stopped blubbering, but the tears hadn't dried on his cheeks. "Doctors at the hospital'll sew the finger back on. Routine surgery. Probably do it twice a night. Very common."

Rocky resumed his blubbering. Maybe my bedside manner needed a little work. On the other hand, why should I care about this idiot who'd been in the act of obliterating me two minutes earlier?

"You park your car close to the house, Rocky?" I asked.

Through his sobs, Rocky seemed to be saying something about the Navigator out front.

I put on a pair of loafers from the downstairs closet. Went into Rocky's pants for his car keys. Then guided him to the Navigator. It occupied the same spot on Major where the gardening slaves had parked their truck and trailer the day before.

I helped Rocky into the passenger seat and sat myself behind the wheel.

"Whoa, this is high up," I said. I felt momentarily exhilarated. "Makes a guy feel like the king of all he surveys."

I drove the SUV through the side streets to Harbord and steered east toward Queen's Park. Rocky had quieted down.

"What you tell the doctors in Emergency," I said, "you were chopping onions with a very sharp knife, and your hand slipped."

Rocky grunted.

"That a yes?" I asked.

"Fucking yes."

"Ah, getting your spunk back. Good lad," I said. "If you don't have a believable story, the doctors might summon the coppers."

Rocky grunted again. I took it for agreement. I turned down Queen's Park Crescent pointed south toward hospital row on University Avenue.

"On further reflection," I said, "the chopping-onions story isn't going to work unless you tell them you're left-handed, okay, Rocky old pal?"

"I already am left-handed."

"Rocky, this heralds something good. It may be your lucky night."

An amazing number of cars for the late hour were speeding around Queen's Park. Was half of Toronto headed for the emergency wards?

"While you're in one of your rare co-operative moods," I said to Rocky, "let me ask you another question."

He grunted again.

"What's the big deal about the little clay figure?"

"You think I fucking know?"

"Let me rephrase. What's in the figure for you?"

"Two hundred thousand bucks. Would I be doing all this shit if there wasn't a big payoff? The answer to that is fucking no."

"It's Elizabeth who's paying you this astronomical sum, am I right?"

Rocky had the presence of mind to realize he might have gone too far in bringing up the subject of money. He looked like a man who had decided to clam up.

"Here's a tougher question, Rocky. Did you kill Grace?"

Outrage took its turn in Rocky's range of attitudes. "You're the third person asked me that. No, no, no, I never put a finger on Grace."

I thought of commenting on Rocky's unfortunate choice of "finger." But resisted the obvious.

"Somebody else suspects you in Grace's death?" I said.

"Goddamn Elizabeth asked me about it. So did her fuckin' partner. After all I done for the two of them."

"Her partner? Who's that?"

Once again, it dawned on Rocky he might be giving away too much.

We got a green light at College. Mount Sinai Hospital was less than a minute away.

"A more generalized question, Rocky," I said. "What is it with Elizabeth and ceramics?" I asked.

"None of your fuckin' business."

"Why's she panicking about the little piece of clay? Why send you to my place after the damn thing?"

"Because you're such an annoying asshole." Rocky's familiar rage was reasserting itself. "Elizabeth says you might get bright ideas from the fuckin' clay thing."

"Not so far I haven't."

I turned into the driveway to Mount Sinai's emergency entrance. Rocky looked up at where we were headed. His eyes opened wider, his rage fled, and he began again with the whimpers.

I stopped the Navigator outside the Emergency entrance, got out and guided Rocky to the hospital door.

"Walk right up to the front counter, Rocky," I said. "One look at your little pinky, and they'll rush you to the front of the line. But I'd quit the whimpering if I were you. Might alienate the nurses, big guy like you carrying on like the Cowardly Lion."

I nudged Rocky's back. He stumbled through the automatic door. I got back in the Navigator and found an empty parking space on the second level of the hospital's garage. By the time I stowed the car and walked back to Emergency, Rocky had disappeared.

"Gentleman just come in here with his hand in a towel?" I asked the nurse behind the counter.

"The resident's sewing him up now," the nurse said. She was middle-aged, and looked like she'd seen it all. "Are you with him?"

"Just happened to notice he dropped his keys and parking ticket," I said, holding up the ticket and keys. "He seemed in a rush."

"He'll be fine," the nurse said. "Are you a relative?"

"Just trying to help the man out."

The nurse raised her eyebrows. I had the notion she didn't believe me, but was she going to challenge my story? I was betting she would figure it wasn't worth the trouble.

"Thank you," she said after a small pause, reaching out to take the ticket and keys. "I'll see he gets these."

I gave her my best smile and left Emergency with a spring in my step.

It took me twenty minutes to walk home. My neck hurt a little, but otherwise, I felt pretty chipper for a guy who'd almost been strangled on his own dining room table.

29

When I got to the office late the next morning, about ten-thirty, still feeling A-OK with the world, a woman was waiting in the corridor. I didn't know her name, but I recognized the dimples.

Just as she said, "Good morning, Mr. Crang," I trampled all over her line, saying, "You're the housekeeper at the Janetta place."

A pause on both sides came next. Then I said, "You've got business with me? Or for me?" at the same time as the housekeeper said, "I'm Isabel MacDougall."

Both of us laughed. The laughs were companionable and kind of merry.

I unlocked the door and ushered Isabel MacDougall inside.

"Care for a coffee from my almost-new machine?" I said. This time, nobody talked over anybody else.

"Love one," she said with the faint accent. Scottish, not Irish, I gathered from her name. "And aren't those Matisse reproductions well done," she said, looking around the room.

"Lifts the mood of the working environment," I said. I occupied myself with the coffee making. Isabel took hers the way I took mine, pure black and unsweetened. She did her dimpled smile when I handed her the cup. She had on navy blue slacks, a blouse in a lighter tone of blue and a loose scarf in shades of red and yellow. The clothes seemed exactly right for a sixty-year-old woman, though she made them and herself look a decade younger.

"Those little bruises on your neck must hurt," she said.

"You should see the other guy."

"I believe I have," Isabel said. "I thought of calling him three-fingered Rocky to his face. But he wouldn't have appreciated the light approach. Never does. Besides, he's still got four fingers on the right hand. It's just that the little one's under cover."

I drank some coffee, thinking about the way I could approach the new situation Isabel MacDougall represented. "Ms. Mac-Dougall, are you an emissary from the Janetta family?"

"Call me Isabel," she said. "And, heavens, no, I'm far from an emissary."

"Going behind someone's back, are you?"

"Lou's principally. Neither Janetta has the faintest suspicion I'm here, not him and not my darling Elizabeth."

"That puts you all the way off the plantation."

"Let me start at the very beginning, Mr. Crang."

"Always a helpful approach in a narrative."

Isabel crossed her legs becomingly. She had an attractive precision in everything. Clothes, gestures, speech. "I worked for Elizabeth's family beginning when I was twenty, fresh off the boat from Dundee. In my case, it was fresh off the plane."

"Those were the Baldwins?"

"They were, on Elizabeth's mother's side. Very historic family, the Baldwins, though I imagine you know all of that."

"Father of Responsible Government."

"It was explained to me a hundred times what the phrase means, but I've never kept it in my head."

"You're not alone in that," I said.

"Anyway, I started as a maid," Isabel said. "I was live-in with the Kierans, Elizabeth's mother and father. Elizabeth was an only child. So I've known her since the day she was born. Had Elizabeth all to myself for much of the time. We were very close, sisters almost, me the much older one. It continued in the same general way after she married Janetta, and I moved with her."

"You live in at the Bridle Path house?"

"Only when they're having functions they need me to super-vise. There's one of those this Sunday, which is what I want to talk to you about. Elizabeth keeps a small suite I stay in for occa-sions like this. The rest of the time, I have a nice bungalow in Don Mills. My own home, the mortgage damn near paid off, Mr. Crang."

"You're single?"

"I have my gentleman callers. But that's got nothing to do with today's topic, the reason why I'm here in your office."

Isabel held up her empty cup. "Half again?" she said. There was enough for one full cup still hot in the coffee maker. I split it between the two of us, and asked Isabel, "You want to talk about Elizabeth's scam in the area of ceramics?"

"Now, now, Mr. Crang, scam is rather harsh."

"But you're concerned?"

Isabel took the time to get her thoughts in order.

"You have to understand the relationship between Elizabeth and her husband," she said. "The man is very possessive."

"Isn't that just the way with gangsters?"

"I wouldn't know. Lou's the only gangster I've met except for his friends and underlings.'"

"Rocky among the latter," I said.

"Thick as a plank, that one. He came to the house this morn-ing, his right hand bundled like a mummy's. Said you'd tried to kill him."

"Self-defence," I said. "Not worth getting into."

Isabel smiled. "So who's asking?"

I smiled back.

"You were saying," I said, "Mr. Janetta wants Elizabeth close and clingy?"

"I didn't put it like that, but your version's not too bad a description of their relationship. What Elizabeth wants from Lou is his respect for more than just her good looks."

"Which are considerable."

Isabel gave me a reproving stare. "That's exactly the attitude that drives Elizabeth batty. Men can't see past her beauty. You, Lou, every man she meets, they're all the same. It's only about her face and her figure. She's got a mind too, you know, a good one."

"So she's on a mission to show Lou her deep-thinking side?"

"Exactly."

"But you're not sure what the vehicle is for this display of brainpower?"

Isabel sagged a little in her chair. "No, but I'm afraid it might be something a little fishy. It may even have been a factor in one person's death."

"Grace Nguyen you're referring to?"

"Your client."

"That's why you've come to me? Because of my relationship with the late Grace?"

"Not just that," Isabel said. "I liked the cut of you when you walked into the Janetta house the other week with that load of malarkey about building something just like theirs."

"Malarkey? That's what you call it in Scotland?"

"Bullshit is what we'd call it back there."

Isabel and I laughed. Isabel's laugh stopped first. Her expression went back to the look of worry she'd been wearing through much of our conversation.

"What I need to tell you, Mr. Crang," Isabel said, "is I was on the Highbury property Monday night at about the time the young woman was killed. Probably an hour or so after that, if I understand the order of events from what the police are saying in the newspapers and on television."

"You were there for what reason?"

"To pick Grace up and drive her home. It wasn't the first time Elizabeth asked me to do it. Four or five nights in the last months, Rocky hasn't been available for one reason or another. The night of the killing, he was off with Mr. Janetta. Some business thing where Lou needed what they call muscle. So like the other times, Elizabeth phoned me at an ungodly hour, well past midnight, asking would I take my car and give Grace a lift? I did what she wanted. But this time, the poor woman, Grace, never showed up. I didn't understand the reason why until I saw it on the news last night."

"Did you know why Grace was at the Highbury house this time and all the other times you were asked to fetch her?"

"Elizabeth just said it was a matter of some discretion. That was her exact phrase every time. 'Some discretion.' I wasn't to inquire any further, and I didn't."

"What about Grace? She tell you anything about her activities?"

"When it came to conversation, Grace was a sphinx. Never a civil word. Never an uncivil word, for that matter. Not even a thank you when I'd let her off at her apartment."

"What did you see last night at 32 Highbury?"

"Not a bloody thing, that's the point. I waited, I knocked on the front door to the house, I hung about for fifteen or twenty minutes. The poor girl must've been lying in the woods, and I had no idea. I just grew irritated, and then I got out of there. Drove home in a funk."

Isabel looked down at the mouth as if everything she contemplated was dark and hopeless.

"Listen, Isabel, there's no way you could've known what'd happened to Grace," I said. It was a statement, not a question. "It's ridiculous you should blame yourself for something that was beyond your control."

"Doesn't keep me from feeling guilty, wondering whether Grace was already dead or still in the process of dying. Could I have helped her? I just don't know."

Isabel and I sat unspeaking for a minute or two, both of us thinking about her predicament. Neither she nor I could imagine a way out of her feelings of blame, no matter how unreasonable the feelings were.

I changed topics, slightly. "Have we already established that you don't know anything about Elizabeth and whatever she may be planning that involves ceramics?"

"All I know," Isabel began, then stopped. "Change that. All I suspect is that things are intended to come to a head late Sunday afternoon."

"Is this the function you mentioned?"

"That's the one."

"And you're going to tell me about it?"

"It's very different from the usual Janetta bun bash. This one's strictly Elizabeth's affair. Always it's been Lou throwing the parties, Elizabeth playing her role as the decoration on his arm. This time, she's managing the whole works, and Lou's nose is out of joint."

"What's the guest list look like?"

"Far from what's the custom. Much smaller list. And heavy on Chinese content, if you can imagine. The featured guest is a man named Wang. He and his wife and their entourage of half a dozen or so. A few of Lou's pals are invited plus somebody from the Levin. This Levin person's your ceramics representative at the party if you want to make something of that, Mr. Crang, and I'm sure you do."

"What's the name of the woman from the Levin?"

"Ah, Mr. Smarty-pants, you know it's a female because that's all the Levin hires."

"So who is she?"

"Tell you what, I'll email you the whole guest list. I've just had one quick scan of the names myself. Can't rhyme them all off right now."

"Can you fill out the details a touch more? Time of the gathering, focus, feature attraction if there is one."

Isabel said guests were invited for four-thirty Sunday afternoon. Everybody would gather for drinks on the back patio. Then they'd be ushered into the library around six. Elizabeth would make a little speech. There'd be a presentation. Isabel didn't know of what or to whom, but she thought likely the recipient was one of the Wangs, husband or wife. The affair would be catered by an unpretentious outfit Isabel regularly hired, a bunch of young culinary and serving whizzes. Isabel herself was in overall charge of party logistics, though she expected Lou to interfere with what he would call suggestions but which Isabel knew to be orders.

"And your expectation," I said when Isabel finished, "what you're asking of me, is I keep Elizabeth from getting into hot water or worse over an enterprise that neither you nor I can pinpoint with a hope of accuracy?"

"Not yet we can't," Isabel said. "But you're a clever man, so I hear, and I expect you to sort out the nature of what you call the enterprise by six o'clock on Sunday evening. Preferably earlier."

"You don't beat around the bush, Isabel."

"I'm prepared to pay whatever your fee amounts to."

"This's not a paying job," I said. "I'm as curious as you are about the scam, pardon my choice of noun."

"Mr. Crang," Isabel said, "I'm way past curiosity. I've reached full-blown panic."

"For Elizabeth?"

"For the girl I've known all my life."

I stood up. "Leave it with me," I said.

Isabel smiled a wry smile. "That's bloody well what I'm doing."

She stood up, and I asked her, "One last thing, Isabel. What make of car do you drive?"

"Make?" she said. "A two-door Toyota. Silver. Four years old. Why do you ask?"

"Just something I need to verify."

Isabel gave me a steady look while she retied her scarf.

"I always think it's a good sign," she said, "when a person pays attention to detail, as you seem to be doing."

30

As soon as Isabel left the office, I phoned I Spy Griffith and asked him about the silver Toyota.

"Oh my," I Spy said, sounding as if he was fumbling for an explanation. "You've caught me out."

"This means you remember a silver Toyota picking up Grace some nights?"

"Very, very few times. I can say that in my own defence. The silver Toyota hardly ever appeared."

"The second car just slipped your mind?" I said. "I Spy, it's no problem if all we're talking about is a little memory lapse."

"Hold on, please, Crang. I'll get my notebooks."

"You actually wrote down all of the stuff that went on at 32?"

"I like to be thorough," I Spy said, sounding wounded at my tone.

"I'm not accusing you of anything, I Spy," I said. "Just confirming what someone else told me."

"Another person kept track of things over there? That comes as a personal blow, Mr. Crang."

I'd lost control of the conversation. "I Spy, there's no one else doing your observational work. It was the driver of the Toyota who identified herself to me as the Toyota driver."

"I wish you'd keep me up to date on developments in our case," I Spy said. "And just for your future reference, I much prefer to classify what I do as analytical. Observational is far too passive in terminology."

"Sorry, I Spy."

What the hell was I apologizing for?

As soon as I got off the phone, fed up with telling I Spy I was sorry for more offences he'd completely misperceived, I left the office and went for a walk. I needed to think through the dilemmas in the damned case I was still trying to claw my way through.

I walked up to Bloor, went west a block, then north up a handsome curving street named Walmer Road. Annie and I had taken many strolls through our new neighbourhood since we moved in, but we tended to point south and east. We spent Sunday afternoons exploring the university grounds, which lay in both directions. South and east. To the north, the Annex and whatever its treasures might be were still mystery territory for both of us.

One block up Walmer brought me to a tiny parkette surrounded on all sides by cross streets, like a green island in a sea of concrete. It had three benches, minimal landscaping and the bust of a woman named Gwendolyn McEwan. It turned out the parkette was named after her. I read the McEwan mini-biography on a plaque next to the bust, and learned that the late Gwendolyn had been a poet who lived in the neighbourhood. How quaint, the city recognizing a writer of verse.

I followed the jogs in the streets north and west on Walmer and another street called Kendal until I came to a much larger park, ambitiously landscaped, flowers, trees, lot of children's play space. According to the signage, this one was named Sibelius Park. Even more quaint than Gwendolyn's parkette, here was a whole park in the middle of Toronto celebrating a composer who spent his entire life in Finland. Lucky Annex residents, culture in their face twenty-four hours a day.

I sat on the bench closest to the Sibelius bust and admired it for a minute or two before I turned my mind to my problems.

First up came the seventy-five Gs. These were turning into the least of my worries. Grace said in our last encounter she'd set aside the cash for me. Her widower, Steve the morose Hungarian, allowed as how he had access to what sounded like many more tens of thousands of Grace's dollars than my piddling seventy-five. Both Grace and Steve could have been dealing me a line of false goods. But on balance, I thought not.

That left the rest of the mess. It broke down essentially into two categories. Grace's murder and the fooling around with the ceramic figures. The murder could wait for further thought later that afternoon after Wally Torgol, my brainy pal from the morgue, brought whatever light he could shine on Grace's murder. A bright and illuminating light, I was wagering.

As for early speculation on who might have done the dirty deed, Rocky, my semi-regular sparring partner, seemed the most likely candidate. But Isabel had said Rocky was with Lou Janetta the night Grace was killed. I couldn't see Lou allowing a hit job to get anywhere close to him, not even if his role was merely as Rocky's alibi witness. Reluctantly, I ruled out Rocky unless further data came to hand.

The lovely Elizabeth Janetta didn't strike me even glancingly as a person capable of an act so final and gross as murder. That left only the third person involved in the goings-on at number 32, the mystery guy who showed up only on the occasional Monday night, the guy referred to by Rocky as Elizabeth's "partner." Maybe I should put more brainpower into pinpointing this guy's identity. If I knew who he was, I might make a case for him as the killer. For the moment, I came up short on ideas vis-à-vis fingering this elusive character.

The puzzle of the ceramic figures lent itself to more accessible sleuthing. I was already pretty sure about many aspects of the scenario. Elizabeth Janetta was for sure the mover and shaker behind the ceramics plot, the person who hired Grace to make what I figured must be a copy of *Company of Fools*. The original *Company*, the real thing in the Levin Museum, was maybe the most valued of all the ceramics world's collections of figures. And the way my deducing shaped up, Elizabeth intended to make a gift of the Grace copy to a Chinese business guy. The recipient had to be the Chinese guy Isabel talked about. Why else was Elizabeth making so much fuss about the Sunday reception at her house?

All of this wasn't bad as theories went—with the drawback, not inconsiderable, that it didn't make sense. Elizabeth wouldn't pay Grace a million bucks to make a copy that would end up as a frigging gift. Not to forget the two hundred grand she was shelling out to Rocky for his services as driver and thug. The third guy, the Monday-nights-only guy, was also no doubt in for some of Elizabeth's bucks. Why would she invest such large sums in a present that she could probably pick up for chump change in a ceramics reproduction shop?

It could be that Elizabeth had in mind conning the Chinese guy. She would sell Grace's copy to the guy, passing it off somehow as the original *Company of Fools* created by L.L. Schwartzmann in 1774 and now residing in the Levin in all its glory. But that didn't shake down as any more believable than the notion of a gift. The purchaser would presumably be paying top dollar, in the eight figures Charles had suggested. That being the case, the Chinese guy putting up the huge bucks would bring along an expert to assure him he was getting the genuine article. I couldn't imagine Grace's copy passing that kind of test.

Nothing I could think of was adding up. There must be some tidy explanation, even a messy explanation, for the events that had so far taken place in relation to *Company of Fools*. To be accurate, the events applied only to the Grace Nguyen copy of *Fools*. It was incontestable that the original languished in its handsome Levin case. Charles had been telling me a few days earlier how he had been up to the Levin's fourth floor basking in the *Fools'* beauty. He didn't question its authenticity. So, no reason to concern myself with it. Not for the time being.

I ought to aim all efforts at Grace's copy, assuming she'd finished it before her untimely demise. If I knew where it was, I might get my hands on it. Then I'd have control of the situation. Elizabeth would be at my mercy, after a fashion. I could get her to explain what was going on. With a few answers, whatever was afoot could be put to rest. No more troubles and worries, no more punchouts from Rocky, even if he was temporarily functioning on one wing.

So where was the copy? Did I have a clue or a hint? Was there a likely location? Anything?

Hot damn, there was a place to scout for the copy. Maury had mentioned it days ago, and I'd let it slide since then. But now that I revisited Maury's remark about the safe at 32 Highbury, I realized it made an obvious and logical hiding place for Grace's copycat version of *Company*.

I looked around Sibelius Park and assured myself that I had the grounds in my immediate vicinity all to myself. It wasn't security that motivated the check for possible eavesdroppers. It was good manners. I loathed cellphone users who assumed the entire world was their personal telephone booth. They talked loudly of inanities without a thought about the rights to peace and quiet of everyone within earshot.

Satisfied I wouldn't be giving offence, I punched in Maury's number on my cell.

When Maury answered, he didn't say hello. He said, "Freddie Biscuit."

"What?"

"Not a what, Crang. A who."

"Who?"

"Freddie Biscuit, the guy I told you about'll open the safe in that house out in the west end we broke into."

"That's rich, Maury. How'd you know I was phoning about the safe?"

"Retired guys like me, we like it when a conundrum comes along. I been thinking about your little piece of trouble. I planned solutions. Chose personnel."

"Conundrum? Wow, hundred-dollar word, Maury."

"I used it right?"

"Like you were a scholar," I said. "So, in the case of my personal conundrum, Freddie Biscuit is the guy?"

"Best safecracker I ever met or heard of."

"That's a hell of a recommendation. Coming from a guy who's cracked a few things in his career. Safes excepted."

"I already took him out to the Highbury house so he could look at the general layout," Maury said. "He liked the type of safe it was."

"Jesus, when was this you went out there?"

"The murder don't change nothing."

"Maury, when? Tell me when you went out."

"After the murder, but before the cops left. Which I happen to know they have now."

"Don't put me hanging out here on a limb, Maury."

"You wanna know how we went into the house with the yellow tape in the driveway and the cop car sitting out front all night, two guys in it?"

"Roughly, yeah."

"Very simple." Maury didn't sound the least smug. "Went in the back way. Walked up from the valley. Used the door to the house next to the shed you stepped in shit in."

"As easy as that?"

"My experience, cops never think about the back way in any situation, never mind what cops do on TV shows."

"And after all that, Freddie Biscuit's still on?"

"Said so, didn't I? How 'bout Friday night?"

"Perfect," I said. "Just one thing. What's it about the man's name?"

"Real name's Biscotti. People who know him kinda close call him Freddie Biscuit. But all one word's the way you pronounce it. That's for people kinda close. People really close call him Biscuit."

"What'll I call him?"

"Biscuit. Really close friend of mine's a really close friend of his."

"You two go back a way?"

"We were kids together in that reformatory used to be up in Guelph."

"One more thing," I said, "what's Biscuit charge for the night's work?"

"Bottle of Johnnie Walker Black."

"That's all?"

"Biscuit's like me. Retired. He does jobs for the fun."

"Tell him thanks."

"Tell him yourself," Maury said. "Biscuit and me'll pick you up in my car ten-thirty Friday night."

31

After Maury and I finished on the phone, I still had an hour until my sit-down with Wally Torgol from the coroner's office. What were my choices for whiling away the spare sixty minutes? I voted to get on with more of my cultural Annex tour, not knowing what culture there was still to be had. Or where.

Following blind instinct, I walked east from Sibelius Park along Bernard Avenue to Spadina, carried on another block to Madison Avenue, turned south down Madison. Presto, in practically an instant, I entered architectural nirvana.

More than a few of the street's houses were magnificent, sporting their three storeys and their stone of a deep reddish colour. For people of my generation, the word "magnificent" carried the same message as "awesome" did for today's kids. Except we weren't as free and careless with our word. Were we?

"Magnificent" was *le mot juste* for the Madison Avenue homes. I knew they'd been designed by a guy named E.J. Lennox or, in some cases, by Lennox copycats. Annie and I had gone to an exhibition about Lennox's work at the Toronto Archives over on Spadina a month earlier. Lennox designed Old City Hall, speaking of magnificent, in the 1880s. But he warmed up for the big job by designing four or five Annex houses, most of them on Madison Avenue. Somebody named his style Richardsonian-Romanesque.

Judging from all evidence—Old City Hall, the houses I was now looking at with great respect—the style balanced power and grace. Made a heck of a beautiful bunch of buildings. Awesome even.

I was enjoying myself on Madison until I checked my watch. How time flew when I was having fun. The dallying had put me overdue for Wally Torgol. I trotted down Madison at good speed to Bloor, turned west and proceeded at the same clip till I came to By the Way. Wally was sitting on the patio.

"You're in luck, Crang," he said after we shook hands.

"Something I'm in the market for. Especially these days."

"The murder throwing you for a loop, the dead woman on Highbury?"

"Do I get the feeling it might not be so bothersome after you and I finish talking?"

There was nothing high style about By the Way's patio. It was crammed into a space more suited for Lilliputians than normal-sized people like Wally and me. The tables and chairs were made of metal, and tended to tilt threateningly. It was a place where I sensed nobody could be trusted to make a decent martini. But on the plus side, the waitresses were sparkly; awnings shielded customers from the sun; and the view was of the action along Bloor among the Annex's colourful residents.

I checked with Wally about his preferences in refreshments, then ordered glasses of red wine and a plate of pita and hummus to nibble on. By the Way made a specialty of what it called Mediterranean dishes. I was willing to take their word for it.

"What I mean about luck, I did the autopsy on the woman myself," Wally said. "Luck of the draw and lucky for you, I happened to be next up when the body came in."

"I'll drink to that," I said. Wally and I tapped our wineglasses.

"You're defending the accused person in this one, that's your concern?" Wally said.

"Nobody's been charged yet as far as I know," I said. "Anyway, my client was the dead woman."

"Too bad."

"Too bad what? The woman died?"

Wally shook his head. "Too bad the accused isn't your client. If he was, you'd look like a hero in the courtroom."

"You think the Crown can't make a case?"

"Not on first-degree murder," Wally said. "Not on second either. The evidence looks to me like the whole thing was an accident. A guy threw a punch in anger, and it went wrong."

"No premeditation, no intent?"

"That'd be impossible. Not to mention unprovable. This is for real, Crang, not just me sitting here speculating."

Wally helped himself to a small piece of pita, which he dunked delicately in the hummus. I liked Wally. He was an alert, organized, unassuming guy. For all the brains he had, more than almost everybody I knew in the law business, he never took himself seriously. He looked at everything with a smile on his face.

"What was the murder weapon?" I asked. "I heard she caught a terrific blow in the face."

"A human hand," Wally said. "That was your weapon."

"A punch is what killed Grace? But a lot of punches, right? A blizzard of roundhouse rights? Killer goes berserk and keeps throwing the lefts and rights?"

Wally held up his index finger. "One fist, one punch," he said. "One fortunate punch, if I could put it that way, though I don't imagine the victim would care for the phrasing. She'd call it unfortunate. So would the puncher if my theory's correct. And I'm pretty confident it is."

"Your theory being the guy lost his temper, smacked Grace in the face, and the punch landed just so? Happened to kill Grace?"

"That's about it. Simplistic, but accurate in the essentials. What happened, behind the nose, the olfactory mucosa—"

I interrupted Wally. "Spare me anything technical. I'll never be arguing the case in court. So it's not necessary I should get the deep stuff down pat. All I want to know is enough to figure out what people shape up as possible guilty parties. You know, suspects."

"Crang, this is going to take away half the fun for me, man. Can't I just show off for you a little bit?"

"Fifty-dollar medical phrases would be wasted on me, Wally. I already know you're the superhero of the crime lab. Save the good stuff for a fresh audience. People in the courtroom'll be dazzled when the Crown puts you in the witness box."

Wally gave an aw-shucks shake of his head.

"Whatever," he said. "In non-technical words of one syllable where that's possible, the victim and the assailant were standing so they were facing one another on a street or a driveway. Pavement underfoot anyway."

"Not in a woods? Not in the place Grace ended up?"

"The guy dragged her there, that's clear enough. But it comes later."

"Okay."

"Don't be so impatient, Crang. Throws me off my rhythm."

I held my hands up in surrender.

"The two of them are having an argument," Wally said. "Face to face. Grace is pointed a little to her own left. So when the assailant gets angry, Grace is more directly in the path of the assailant's right fist when he lets fly with a punch. Did I mention this assailant was taller than Grace?"

"Not yet."

"Well, he was. Grace was five feet, five inches. The guy was damn near six feet. Maybe an inch over but no more. The height difference meant Grace was looking up. Not a lot but enough to matter. The guy fires his punch. It's part straight right, but it necessarily follows a somewhat downward path on account of his superior height. The punch lands square."

"On what?"

"The nose," Wally said. "That's the fatal detail. The fist drives into Grace's nose, and her fate is sealed."

"This is dramatic stuff, Wally. And tragic."

"Since you don't want medical terms and anatomical exactness, I'll just tell you a bone from Grace's nose got knocked loose and drilled into her brain. At that moment, Grace's time on this earth came to an end."

"Complete fluke."

"Mike Tyson himself couldn't have planned the punch. One million boxers throwing one million punches would have no hope of duplicating a blow like this one. An accident totally. The assailant must've freaked."

Wally stopped the explanation long enough to ask if I wanted to split a second glass of red wine with him. "I got to take it easy on the alcohol," he said. "Keep my mind clear for tonight's Tafelmusik concert."

"For what?"

"At that big church right over here." The church Wally was pointing at was on the south side of Bloor a block east of where we were sitting. "You know about Tafelmusik?"

"Chamber group, I think maybe? Never heard them play myself."

"Started up performing right here in the Annex about thirty years ago," Wally said. "Fairly small orchestra, but it specializes in baroque music. Mozart, Handel, plus a lot of period composers nobody ever hears much of today if it weren't for Tafelmusik."

"You're going to tell me it's world class."

"I wasn't," Wally said. "But it is."

"And it's a product of the good old Annex?"

"No reason not to be proud of Tafelmusik."

"I imagine not," I said. "And it's okay with me about splitting the second glass of wine."

"So, to resume with my explanation, the result is Grace is dead," Wally said. "She's lying on a street or a driveway. I think driveway myself. I told the detectives on the case they should look carefully on that long drive up to the house at number 32.

Haven't found anything so far. No blood or other traces of the victim."

"After the punch, the assailant drags the body into the woods?"

"Lot of evidence of that. Heels of Grace's feet making a sort of path through the dirt and twigs and other lower-level flora. The guy gripped her under the arms and just yanked her along."

"In a panic?"

"Definitely in no condition to think things through, this guy."

Wally took a healthy swallow of wine from his half glass.

"Everything I can read about the situation in the available evidence," he said, "points to haste and carelessness. Guy couldn't put his head around what he'd got himself into. What a terrible thing he'd done."

I had a sip from my own glass, and thought about Wally's breakdown of the killing.

"One more thing you'll want to know."

"Yeah?"

"The deceased, Grace, she was pregnant."

The news came as a mini-bombshell, but I couldn't think of any influence it had on Grace's work for Elizabeth Janetta.

"How much pregnant, Wally?" I asked.

"Not a whole lot in terms of time. Around two months."

"Her husband doesn't appear to be aware of a pregnancy."

"Really," Wally said. He stood up. "Now I got to be on my way," he said. "Tafelmusik, you know."

"You go all the way home, wherever that is, grab something to eat, and come back to practically the same spot? That's a gruelling timetable, Wally."

"Not a problem. We live up the street right here on Brunswick."

"You're an Annex person?"

I felt a sense of dismay. I think my jaw dropped. The dismay must have been on full display because Wally picked up on it. And promptly misinterpreted it.

"Hey, listen," he said, full of concern, "did I let you down on this Grace thing? You're suddenly looking a little flat. You need more from me?"

"Not for a second am I disappointed, Wally." I was scrambling to cover my tracks. "On autopsies, you're aces by me. Nobody better at interpreting the messages a dead body leaves behind."

Wally seemed mollified. He gathered his things and left the patio. I watched him turn up Brunswick and stride deeper into his neighbourhood. Into the Annex.

After a few minutes of contemplation, I paid the bill and walked home. Wally had gone north. I went south. First thing I did in the house was phone Annie in New York.

"We should call off the war we're waging with the Annex," I said. "It's a sure loser."

"But they're our mortal enemy, sweetie."

"Doesn't matter," I said. "What I'm surmising from observations, people in the Annex haven't noticed they're even in a skirmish with the pitiful crowd below Bloor."

Annie listened patiently, adding nothing to the chat except a couple of uh-huhs. It finally came through to me she had other fish to fry, conversationally speaking. She said she'd just received by email the goddess of the garden's plan for our backyard.

"Fabulous, Crang, honestly. With our garden, Kathleen's emphasizing structural plants."

"Right away, you've got me stumped."

"Structural means trees and shrubs. All of them native."

"A patriotic garden?"

"That's a way of explaining it, I suppose," Annie said. "It's only natural to grow things native to the region in whatever region a person lives. Kathleen's allowing us one Japanese maple."

"The Japanese maple is native? Despite the name."

"Honey, think of it this way, we're going to be thrilled having such beauty at our back door."

"You can tell all this just from a drawing?"

"Ah, but Crang," Annie said, "I've been in Kathleen's own garden. I've walked through it with her, a garden that reflects what she's making for us. It's a work of art, her place. Ours'll be the same, except on a lot smaller scale. Magnificent, you'll say about ours."

"Magnificent?" I said. "That's something I can relate to."

After Annie told me that the goddess and her slaves would install our garden the following Tuesday, I hung up and made a dinner out of leftover chili. I read more William Boyd and was just dozing off when damn Rocky snapped me awake. Not the physical Rocky, but a memory from Rocky. The son of a bitch never answered my question about how he broke into our house the night before.

I went downstairs and toured the place, switching on all the lights as I proceeded. No windows were broken or even seemed tampered with. I got the flashlight and shone it up close at the lock on the front door. The light didn't reveal scratches or anything else I might interpret as an indicator of lock picking. I went into the dining room to do the same check on the door into the garden. When I put my hand on the inside doorknob and turned it, the door opened without me touching the lock. The damn door hadn't been locked. I hadn't touched it after I got home that afternoon from the meeting with Wally. Had I left it unlocked the whole time since yesterday? Unlocked last night, all day today, right up until this moment? I felt pretty certain the pitiful answer was yes. Rocky hadn't needed to break in. He could just walk in. I'd practically ushered Rocky into the house. This was a serious goof. Now, as I locked the door, I was thinking metaphors about locking barn doors after the horses had left.

I got back in bed, and took a long time to fall asleep.

32

The first thing I couldn't help noticing about Biscuit the safe-cracking guy was that he belonged among the little people. He was sitting in the front passenger seat of Maury's big old Cadillac when the two of them pulled up to my house at the appointed hour of 10:30 p.m. Friday. Biscuit's head barely cleared the dashboard.

I got in the back, carrying a liquor store brown paper bag. It held a bottle of Johnnie Walker Black Label.

"Crang, this here's Biscuit," Maury said. "Biscuit, want you to meet Crang the mouthpiece."

Biscuit stretched to reach his hand over the back of his seat, and we shook hands. My hand came near to lapping his a couple of times.

"You're thinking about the size of my hand," Biscuit said to me. "I'm right?"

"No offence intended," I said.

"None taken," Biscuit said.

Biscuit was a dapper little guy from what I was able to make out in the Caddie's semi-gloom. Tidy moustache, full head of dark hair combed just so. He had on a dark jacket, light-coloured shirt and striped tie. The colours I couldn't be sure about.

"It was my size determined my path in life," Biscuit said.

"Biscuit's of the subculture," Maury said. "Goes without saying."

"I knew I preferred the subculture over the dominant culture from when I was a child," Biscuit said, addressing his remarks to me.

"What's your choice gonna be if you're in reform school at age fifteen?" Maury said.

"Really, Maury, a little respect," Biscuit said, sounding the soul of patience. "Let me tell the gentleman my life story the way I want to tell it."

"*Reader's Digest* version, for crissake," Maury said. "Otherwise I'm turning on my CD player. Got beboppers on there, drown you out. Art Blakey and the Jazz Messengers."

"As a child," Biscuit said, "I was very good at arithmetic."

"The couple of years you went to school," Maury said.

"It's true, Mr. Crang," Biscuit said, "my formal education was brief, but I gravitated to anything mechanical. If it involved numbers, I had the answers."

"What inclined you to the subculture, if I may ask?" I said.

"It was genetic."

"His old man made a grand tour of the country's prisons," Maury said. "An inside view at every stop."

"As Maury implies," Biscuit said, "my acquaintanceship with my father the bank robber was fleeting. But his example taught me a lesson. Namely, if you join the subculture, choose an activity that promises the least exposure to risk of apprehension. That's especially significant for someone of my stature, unfitted by nature for muscular undertakings."

"Very sensible," I said.

"My career as what is referred to in popular argot as a safe-cracker reflects my mechanical bent. But it also grew out of my desire to avoid incarceration. Safecracking is largely carried on behind the scenes and out of sight of the authorities."

I said, "Have you been successful at staying out of the law's grasp?"

"Largely."

"Tell Crang about out west," Maury said.

"I did a nickel in the B.C. pen," Biscuit said. "Quite a taxing interlude in my life, but the experience provided me with another valuable lesson."

"Which was?"

"Never venture far from home. Don't go where you're unfamiliar with the terrain and the methods of police enforcement."

"Toronto's your natural stomping grounds?"

"Should never have left."

Maury said, "Enough autobiography, Biscuit."

Art Blakey and the Jazz Messengers blasted from the speakers. They weren't bad. Sounded to me like Horace Silver on piano, Lee Morgan on trumpet. I didn't know the tenor saxophone. They played us all the way to Highbury Road.

Maury turned the music off and coasted past number 32. No police cars were in evidence. The yellow crime scene tape had been taken down.

"You tell the peeping guy we're gonna be out here?" Maury said to me.

"I Spy's been feeling hard done by lately," I said. "But, yeah, I let him know. He ought to be in place at one of his windows."

Maury made two right turns and steered down a hill that ended on the edge of a park behind the backyards of the Highbury houses. He pulled the car into a relatively isolated area, and all of us got out. Biscuit was just about five feet. He carried in one hand the kind of black bag doctors on calls are never seen without. Everything about Biscuit was stylish except for the rubber boots on his feet. I hadn't a doubt he normally wore shined oxfords.

"These are to accommodate the terrain," Biscuit said, pointing to the rubber boots. They were red, and looked like Biscuit had bought them in the children's department.

Maury led us in single file up a rough path. It wasn't muddy enough to call for rubber boots, but Biscuit seemed happy with his choice in footwear. The path ended in number 32's backyard.

"Somebody's been taking this route into the place the last weeks," Maury said. "Enough times to make the path."

"I'm betting it was the third guy," I said. "The one who came Monday nights only."

Maury picked the lock on the back door, and the three of us assembled in front of the safe. It sat in what once must have been a cupboard on the short staircase up to the kitchen. The safe was black, squarish in shape, old and cumbersome looking. Biscuit opened his bag. He took out a flashlight, a small notebook and a doctor's stethoscope. He handed me the flashlight.

"If you would oblige me, Mr. Crang," he said. "Hold the light on the safe's dials."

"My debut at safecracking," I said.

"Won't be much of a lesson in this one, if I've read it correctly."

Biscuit leafed through his notebook. From the wear of the book's cover and rumpled condition of the pages, I'd say he had given it the leafing treatment several hundred times before.

"What I deduce," Biscuit said, "this safe's combination is what we call in the profession a tryout job. Manufacturer that made the safe sold it with a combination they already set. The reason being so the purchaser could go in there and set his own combination. But most people never got around to doing that. Manufacturer's combination stayed operative. I got a list in my notebook here of every manufacturer's tryout number. I'm betting it'll work this time. That's judging from the looks of this old safe."

Biscuit spun the dials, the stethoscope pressed to the safe in the close vicinity of the dial spinning. Biscuit had pretty hands, his motions with them dainty and precise. I could imagine his style holding a cup of tea, his pinky figure crooked in the air separate from the other fingers. He nodded as he spun the dials and listened through the stethoscope to the tumbling of the combination numbers. Or at least that was how I pictured the internal process. Biscuit was all silence and concentration.

"I believe my supposition was correct," he said, turning to speak to me.

He pulled at the safe's door. It swung open.

"Shine the flashlight upward a trifle, Mr. Crang," Biscuit said.

I did what I was told. The flashlight's beam aimed directly into the safe's interior.

"Oh my," Biscuit said, "this is unfortunate."

The safe was empty.

"Win some, Crang, lose some," Maury said behind me.

"What did you expect to find?" Biscuit said.

I felt too deflated to answer right away. I'd allowed my optimism to outpace reality, and now I was paying the penalty. Or something clichéish like that. My hopes were dashed.

"Some porcelain figures," I said. "That's what I was expecting. Relatively small figures."

Biscuit ducked his head partway into the safe, the top of his head brushing the safe's ceiling. "If it's any consolation," he said, "something very like small porcelain figures might have been in here recently. I'm supposing that from the state of the light dust on the safe's bottom level."

"Could be it's a case of we got here a day late," Maury said.

"Thanks, guys," I said. "I'm beginning to cheer up."

"You're on the right track, it might appear, Mr. Crang," Biscuit said.

"Okay, gentlemen, enough with the optimism," I said.

My cellphone went off in my pocket.

"I trust this's not bad news," Biscuit said. He got very speedy about tidying up his work, stowing his implements of the trade in the doctor's bag.

I checked the cell's screen and answered.

"Yes, I Spy," I said into the phone.

"Did I understand you correctly, Crang?" I Spy sounded crisp. "You are going into 32 tonight with your other friends?"

"We're in, I Spy," I said. "Just preparing to take our leave. Empty-handed."

"How could it be you're in there?" I Spy sounded outraged. "I've not budged from my post in two hours. Haven't seen a thing over at 32."

"Back way, I Spy. We came up a path behind the houses on this side."

"Nobody keeps me informed," I Spy said. He hung up in what I took to be a show of pique.

Biscuit finished his tidying, and within minutes, our little troupe was back at Maury's Caddie. Nobody said much on the drive home. Maury played no bebop. Under better circumstances, I would have invited the two gents in for a celebratory beverage. But on this night, I settled for handing Biscuit the bottle of Johnnie Walker Black he'd earned. The three of us shook hands all around, and I went into my house alone.

It'd been a bum couple of days. The copy Grace Nguyen had made of *Company of Fools* wasn't where I thought it would be, and Isabel MacDougall, the Janetta housekeeper, hadn't emailed me the copy she'd promised of Sunday's guest list for the Janetta reception. I'd sent Isabel two polite emails asking what the holdup was, but neither drew any action. It was true, much of my deducing about the case was theoretical, maybe even fanciful, but I still thought I was headed on the right path. It was circumstances that were running against me. Not theories.

I made myself a vodka on the rocks, a pure and bracing drink. A couple of swallows, and I got on my computer and composed a third inquiring email to Isabel. This one wasn't polite. I took another large sip from my glass and let the vodka run down my throat, straight into the old bloodstream. For a moment, I felt reinvigorated if not exhilarated. In that moment, I pressed the send button on my computer. The not-polite email was zinging its way to Isabel.

I leaned back in the chair. Was there anything else I could do to rescue the investigative process?

A good sleep might help. I went upstairs to try it out.

33

In the morning, an email from Isabel waited on my computer. An attachment came with it. Sent 3:41 a.m., I noticed. Was something worrisome keeping Isabel up nights? Or did she naturally gravitate to late hours?

The email said:

I had second thoughts about handing over the guest list. Now I've had third thoughts. Herewith the list. See what you can do about not letting my dear Elizabeth get in any deeper than I think she already is. Yours, Isabel.

I felt a small surge of fresh hope. Maybe the list would get my sleuthing cranked again.

I brought up the attachment, printed it out and set about the business of studying the list over a steaming hot cup of Kenyan.

It had twenty-one names. The first eight were Chinese, leading off with the Wang husband and wife. Their given names were Elvis and Trixi. Something meaningful seemed to have been lost in the names' translation from Chinese to English. Or maybe Mr. and Mrs. Wang actually chose these inelegant monikers for use when mingling in North American circles. For all I knew, the Wangs might have a staff person assigned full-time to cooking up names in all of the world's non-Chinese languages. But, come on, Trixi? Elvis's name came with its own history, even if it spoke to narrow-minded me of music the world could have done with-out. But "Elvis" at least had the appeal of striking a chord in my memory. The memory was recent, not old-timey. Very recent.

I hustled outside to the recycling blue bin, and shuffled stuff around until I found the business section of Thursday's *Globe*. Back at the dining room table, I topped up my coffee cup and turned through the business pages until I spotted the short piece I remembered noticing about Elvis Wang's mission to Canada. He was a billionaire. "Said to be the fifth- or sixth-richest man in all China," I read. According to the article, the Wang multi-fortune came from Internet technology. I was never sure what that embraced, the damned term "Internet technology."

"Mr. Wang," the article told me, "owns a piece of almost every-thing IT-related among China's teeming billions." Not the usual restrained *Globe* phrasing, but there was no mistaking the meaning as far as my sleuthing was concerned. Elvis was such an obscenely rich guy that it would cost him comparative chicken feed to snap up twenty-seven ancient pieces of clay priced at a few million smackers for the lot.

As the *Globe* went on to report, Elvis Wang was presently in our fair land for a six-day dash of meetings with the titans of Canadian banking, industry and politics. The prime minister was sparing a half hour for Elvis on Monday before he and his gang winged home. But as a sideline to the tour, I was figuring, Wang intended to dabble in illicit porcelain figures.

I went back to the guest list. It was no problem classifying the rest of the Chinese names. Had to be Elvis's entourage. Advisers, translators, gofers. Everybody in the entourage, Trixi aside, was a guy. Farther down the list were some Italian-Canadian names. I'd say these were Lou Janetta's best buds plus spouses. That left the bottom name on the list. An eye-opener. It opened my eyes as wide as they could get. Hugette Jennings.

She was the young woman I'd recently met at the Levin. The museum's deputy security person. What was she doing on a list otherwise made up of her betters and superiors? No question, she had to be Elizabeth Janetta's guest. But why was a Levin employee invited to the gathering at all? If my theory was right, Elizabeth was in the act of scamming the Levin big time. For what reason was she including among her guests somebody who worked at the Levin? Hugette would be a witness, witting or unwitting, to Elizabeth's piece of skullduggery. And not just an ordinary Levin employee. She was a security person. But was it possible she was also a scammer? In on the deal with Ms. Janetta? This needed research, putting the situation mildly.

I sipped some coffee. It was cold. I had two choices. Either hang around the house long enough to make fresh coffee or hustle up the street forthwith, and bring Charles the neighbour further into my confidence vis-à-vis the Levin. I weighed the alternatives. I needed to share the load of the whole boondoggle with somebody who was savvy to the Levin and its functioning. Charles was the only person I knew who had the credentials. I considered the decision for another few seconds. It wasn't much of a choice. I dropped the idea of the fresh coffee, put on my Nikes and skedaddled in the direction of Charles's house.

Charles was in his front yard, lounging on the iron bench, holding in his hand an industrial-sized coffee container.

"Crang, my good fellow," he said, holding up the metal thing. "Join me for a cup?"

"Not that humungous, Charles. But, yes, coffee, thanks."

I sat on one end of the iron bench while Charles wasted no time completing his run for the coffee. He handed me a conventionally-sized mug. It was an attractive green in colour, but the handle of the thing looked askew, and the shape of the bottom was none too flat.

"One I made myself," he said, nodding at the wobbly mug. "In my own ceramics period."

I tasted the coffee. "Sensational," I said, meaning the coffee, not the mug. "What's the brand?"

"Sumatra, old chap."

"I may have to rethink my coffee future. This edges out Kenyan, I'm thinking."

Charles smiled. "You've come with a paper in your hand," he said, pointing a finger at the guest list.

"It needs your keen eye and keener brain," I said.

I told him Elizabeth Janetta was throwing a party tomorrow afternoon, though I held back on what I expected to take place at it.

"These," I said, handing Charles the piece of paper, "are the guests."

"Ah, the Wang chappie," he said immediately.

"He's crossed your path?"

"His lady wife visited the museum yesterday."

"Trixi."

"Spelled quixotically," Charles said.

"No 'e' on the end."

"Unfortunate name under any circumstances."

"Was Trixi at the Levin, do you think, to check out *Company of Fools* in particular?"

"No idea, old lad," Charles said. "I was stuck downstairs on tickets. Melissa said she was generally keen on ceramics, the Wang memsahib was. And very knowledgable, according to Melissa."

"Melissa is who?"

"Top dog at the museum," Charles said. "Lovely person. Melissa Novak, our director."

"Ms. Wang got special treatment, did she?"

"One assumes as much, old bean."

"The plot thickens."

Charles sat back on his half of the iron bench, leaving me to turn awkwardly if I wanted to address him directly.

"I can tell you're just busting with something newsy, Crang, me old lad," Charles said. "If your aim has been to prick my curiosity, you've scored resoundingly."

I told him my whole story, some of it fact, some conjecture. I talked about Grace Nguyen's role as the creator of a *Company of Fools* copy, all twenty-seven pieces. I put Elizabeth into the picture as the mastermind, Rocky as chauffeur and assassin, the phantom third guy as I didn't know what. I wound up with a description of Elizabeth's scheme to peddle the copies to Elvis Wang as the real thing.

"Good lord, man, we must convey this tomfoolery to Melissa," Charles said. "Without delay. I'm gobsmacked. Elizabeth Janetta, really, I don't understand the woman."

I waited a beat or two. Then I said, "You finished being indignant, Charles?"

"Not nearly."

"Because I changed my mind this morning about the dimensions of what's afoot."

"By jove, you're full of surprises, Crang. Get along with the rest of the story, old fellow. Riveting. But is it possibly far-fetched?"

"What I think now, the updated version, Elizabeth's not peddling Grace Nguyen's copy of *Company of Fools* to Wang. No, she's dealing the real and original set of ceramic pieces. That's what she's got in process, and the thing that enables the transaction is she's switching the Nguyen copies for the originals in the display case at the Levin."

Charles straightened up on his half of the bench. He looked like he might do one of his splutters. "Sounds preposterous," he said. But he didn't splutter. He just continued with his concerned demeanour. "Still possible, I will concede, old sport," he said. "By gad, this is devious beyond measure, if you've got it right."

"Before we go further," I said, "let me redirect your attention to the guest list. Check out the name at the bottom."

Charles turned back to the list. "I'm damned. Hugette Jennings? I never would have thought she and Elizabeth were best pals. Mind you, I'm not intimate with either of them. But around the museum several days a week, as I am, we volunteers get gossiping, try to keep abreast of Levin politics and intra-office feelings, romantic liaisons and so on. I have to say none of us ever paired these two off as palsy at any level, old fellow."

"What sort of person is Hugette?" I said. "How did she get the Levin security job?"

"That part's vastly gripping, if I do say so. And all of us volunteers say it all the time. Hugette is much, much overqualified for the security job. She happens to have a very good MFA from York University. Three years back, she applied for a curator's opening at the Levin. Failed to make the cut, she did. Very downhearted in the result, I'm told. Begged for any job, as long as it was at the Levin, and got offered the security appointment. Very demeaning experience for her, I should think. Nevertheless, she's hung on all this time, hoping for a second shot at curating. But it's just never happened for poor sad Hugette."

"She's bitter?" I said.

"Who knows?" Charles said. "She keeps herself to herself. God knows she's cranky much of the time. One doesn't want to cross Hugette. Never, never, never."

"That could be motivation."

"For what?"

"For throwing in with Elizabeth's scam."

"Revenge you mean?" Charles said. "And a cash payoff from Elizabeth at the same time?"

"A persuasive combination."

I finished the last of my coffee, stood up and tried to balance the mug on the iron bench. It insisted on tipping over.

"Got a few minutes right now?" I said to Charles. "We might check *Company of Fools* at the museum."

"See if the one on display is real or fake?" Charles said. "Right you are. It'll bring us up to date. Give us the ultimate proof perhaps. But I'll tell you, Crang old fellow, we mustn't get carried away without some powerful backup evidence."

"You're not as convinced of what I'm saying as you seemed to be a few minutes ago?"

"Don't want to go off half-cocked, old chap. My wife accuses me of doing that too often. Tendency to sudden enthusiasms, that sort of thing. Followed by falls to earth just as suddenly. But by all means let us get going to the Levin. See if I can't make up my mind."

At the Levin, the guy manning the counter waved Charles through free of charge, one volunteer to another, but he hit me up for the regular eight bucks. We took the elevator to the fourth floor, and after no more than two minutes of hovering over the *Company of Fools* exhibit, Charles pronounced what we were examining was the intact original.

"Tell you what to keep your eye out for, old trout," he said. "Certain lines and creases in the figures. Look there at the jester with the pig face, he's got a pronounced marking down his left torso. Notice that? Nothing untoward about it. Wrinkling, one might call it. The wrinkling's just a product of the figure's advanced age. It happens to porcelain just as it happens to us *Homo sapiens*. With the caveat that the porcelain never dies. Not yet at any rate, not between 1774 and now."

"I'm following," I said, not sure whether I was happy the figures hadn't been switched for fakes. I still thought my theory was solid. It was just that the moment when it was borne out by events hadn't arrived yet. There were still more than twenty-four hours to go before Elizabeth's party for the Wangs.

"Something else in identification is specific to *Fools*," Charles said. "Focus on the jester with the giraffe face. Got that, old sport?"

"Far right in the first row."

"Concentrate on the area just above the beast's left eye. See that in the forehead?"

"The gouge?"

"Not quite that bad, do you think?" Charles said. "Gouge-like perhaps. It shouldn't be mistaken as a defect in the ceramist's work. The indentation resulted from someone dropping the piece or otherwise mishandling it. Probably happened in the late nineteenth century. Ever since, the gouge, as you refer to it, has identified the giraffe among the ceramic cognoscenti. I have my doubts that a copyist, your Grace or anyone else, would include it in their attempt at forgery."

"Good to know," I said.

Charles led the way to seats on the bench across from the cabinet.

"So now what, Crang, my old spinner of suspense?" he said.

"What I'm talking about, the swiping of a work of great ceramic art, all for the benefit of a rich man," I said, "it's common enough in the world of the visual arts in general?"

"Indeed it is," Charles said. "According to the literature, rich collectors do it all the time. Bastards that they are, these wealthy laddies hire professional thieves to commit designated burglaries. Man wants a Monet? Thief's only question is, how big a Monet? He breaks into a gallery in, say, Barcelona, whose only valuable painting on offer is the aforesaid Monet. Next thing anyone knows, or rather I should say, the next thing no one knows, the priceless work is hanging on some sodding selfish idiot's drawing room wall in Mayfair or Beverly Hills or Tokyo."

"So the case I'm speaking of, the slippery stuff with Elizabeth and Elvis, it's a variation on an established crime in the world of art?"

"One could say."

"I just did."

"Hmm, yes, old bean."

"If Elvis is dealing with Elizabeth for *Company of Fools*," I said, "then he's home free as soon as he gets his hands on the collection. No Canadian authority, the customs or security people or whoever, is going to search a rich guy like him and his party. He takes *Company* home, and forever after, he displays it to nobody except his very best friends just like your guy with the Monet. Same thing. Only difference is, given China's teeming billions, Elvis's best friends may run to a couple thousand people."

Charles's expression gave away his doubts.

"What's wrong with my theory, Charles?" I said. "The substitution at the Levin of the Grace copy for the real thing only needs to hold up for a day or two. Long enough for Elvis to clear out of Canada. After that, nobody'll have a clue where the original has got to."

Charles didn't look any more reassured.

"What are you thinking, Charles?" I said.

"I'm not turning my back on you, old chap. But bear with me if I withhold my final judgment."

"Withhold until when? What more do I have to produce if I want you all the way on side?"

"Why not we try this, old boy? You take a watching brief on *Company of Fools* over there, and if something more evidentiary comes to your eye, summon me post-haste. I'll be at your side in a flash. Supportive all the way."

"But until then," I said, "you'll sit on the fence?"

"There remains room for query," Charles said. "Put another way, I wouldn't feel steady on my ground if I trotted along to Melissa Novak at this moment. Therein lies the ultimate test. What would Melissa say to the story of Elizabeth, *Company of Fools* and so forth? As things stand, if I related our fears to her, she might kick me in the hindquarters."

"It's a smoking gun that's lacking?"

"I myself am tilting in your favour," Charles said. "But I need a smidgeon more to win over the top Levin crowd."

"Especially Melissa."

"Quite so, old chap."

"I'll be back to you, Charles," I said. "Count on it."

34

Across the street from the Levin stood a brick business building, four storeys high, the same height as the museum. The building had an Italian restaurant called Bartello's on the ground floor. It was there, at Bartello's, eight hours after my conversation with Charles in front of the *Company of Fools* display, that I sat down to dinner all by myself.

I'd reserved a table earlier in the afternoon, managing to score one in the window. It gave me a clear view of the museum, at least of its front part. My purpose in coming to the restaurant was unclear even to me. Partly, it was to work on Charles's notion of a watching brief. Partly, I was drawn to a spot within spying distance of the scene of the crime, the final swiping part of the crime, the actual removal of *Company* from the museum, if it in fact happened. Or maybe I just thought it was time for action of some sort. Or I was curious. I was restless. I was sick of being alone in the house without Annie. If I tried a little harder, I could come up with lots more excuses to be dining *seulement* on a Saturday night in a restaurant I'd never been in before. Never even read a review of the place's cuisine.

I recognized that Bartello's had one thing going for it even before I sat down. There was no music on the sound system. Maybe there was no sound system. Whatever the reason, no intrusive noises drove me crazy, just patrons chatting with one another. I hated the invasion of thumping beats and banal melodies, a female singer screeching the high notes, a male singer hectoring in the hip-hop mode. No thanks, not when all a guy wanted was a meal in aural tranquility.

The waiter was a pleasant-looking young guy with slicked-back hair. He said good evening, addressed me as sir and didn't offer his first name. Was I in restaurant heaven or what? I ordered a vodka on the rocks.

"Stoli be satisfactory, sir?" the dark-haired waiter said.

"No objections from me," I said. "And hold the lemon slice."

He brought the drink without the slice and with just the right number of ice cubes. I was on a roll with this guy. He asked if I cared to order or should he return? I said I was in no hurry. He went away.

I sipped from my vodka and looked across College Street at the Levin. The museum had cleared out of patrons at five o'clock, and there was now no movement in or out of the front door. Employees used the back door for their own comings and goings, no doubt because the Levin provided free parking in the rear. No employees were presently in view, though I expected to catch glimpses now and again of Hugette, the security person. Once every hour, Charles had said, Hugette made her rounds through each of the four floors.

It was easy for me or any other interested party to see into the Levin since all the exterior walls were made of glass. It was still mostly daylight as I worked on the vodka, but I could tell that the interior lights were on throughout the building. If I wanted an even more intimate view of the museum from my table in Bartello's window, I could take Annie's opera glasses out of my jacket pocket. But not right then. I didn't want to identify myself so early as a weirdo.

The slick-haired waiter returned, and I ordered a green salad to start, vinaigrette dressing, followed by veal paillard with a side order of pasta in a light tomato sauce. The salad arrived soon after I ordered. It had a lot of onions in it. That was okay by me, and it was while I was working on the salad that I got the first reward for my spying.

Walking along the south side of College, moving east to west, was none other than Hugette of the security squad. Hugette moved crisply and purposefully, nothing girly about her stride. Since she was on foot, I reached the immediate conclusion she owned no automobile. She probably got herself to work by way of the Bathurst streetcar, a couple of blocks to the east. Or maybe she'd just got off the College car. Either way, I saw her as a suburbs person. Couldn't afford the higher rents of Kensington Market or any of the more funky neighbourhoods handy to the Levin. She commuted by public transit. Hugette's working hours were nine at night to six in the morning. Her shift was about to begin.

I watched as she cut down a side street flanking the Levin, no doubt headed for the employee entrance around back. Something about Hugette stirred small signs of recognition in the deeper recesses of my busy little brain, but I couldn't quite pull them to the surface. I let the small signs go for the time being. Hugette had on a white T-shirt with some picture or symbol I couldn't make out on the front. She wore black jeans and a black vest hung loosely, thereby covering much of the T-shirt decor. She had on black gloves. What were they all about in this warm weather? A fashion statement? I supposed so. I watched a bit longer, pondering on something about her stride. What was different about it? Something struck me as odd. It was her hands, that was it. She held them out from her body as if they were separate entities and had to be treated gingerly. Something along those lines. I kept my eyes on Hugette until she was out of sight. Then I turned back to my salad. I knew I'd catch glimpses of Hugette a few more times that evening.

My veal paillard was gorgeously cooked and presented. I told the nice waiter how pleased I was. The pasta was straight-ahead spaghetti, done al dente. Everything was as I liked it. How unique an eating experience was this? Very, I decided.

I was just polishing off the veal when I spotted Hugette starting on her first all-building security check of the night. She emerged into my view from the fourth-floor hallway, presumably from the room where she watched the video coverage of all the Levin floors. She rode the elevator to the first floor and began her sweeps of each floor in turn, moving upward, first floor to fourth. She seemed thorough about the job, not rushing but not dawdling either. God knows what she had to look for. Lurking burglars? Possible, but very unlikely. In movies, sure. In real life, not so much.

Hugette spent about five minutes on each floor, walking up the stairs to move from one floor to the next. She paused for any length of time only on the fourth. I knew what she was examining. *Company of Fools.* Ah, yes, I imagined, the plot was growing thicker by the instant. Hugette finished her floor-to-floor check, and disappeared into her cubbyhole of video screens.

I ordered a tarte au citron, though it wasn't called that in Italian. I knew French better than Italian. The waiter didn't seem to mind what I called it. His accent was strictly southern Ontario. While I ate the tarte—it was scrumptious—I thought about my stirrings of recognition of something or other in Hugette, failing once again to pin them down. She had still been wearing the black gloves, but my stirrings, whatever they dealt with, concerned much more than that.

The waiter asked if I wanted coffee. I said, an espresso, please. But I told him to hold my order until I returned. I said I was headed out to do an errand. I handed him my Visa card.

"An article of good faith," I said.

"Not necessary, sir," he said, handing the card back to me.

Both of us smiled, and I walked out of the restaurant and into the small entrance hall between College Street and Bartello's front door. To the right was an elevator to the floors above the restaurant. I got on, and pressed the button for the fourth. I was interested in finding a more generally advantageous viewing spot than Bartello's front window.

The entire fourth was given over to one business, something called Smith/Wave Graphics. What did a company with a name like that offer the world? Probably IT related. Elvis Wang might want a piece. I tried the double door to Smith/Wave. Locked, as expected. At one end of the corridor between Smith/Wave and the elevator was a single door. I walked down and tried it. The door opened into a clean and tidy washroom. It had a toilet stall but no urinals. Two wash basins and a long mirror above them. The washroom was clearly intended for both genders among Smith/Wave employees. Best of all, as far as I was concerned, it faced south across to the Levin.

The only problem was the opaque pebbled window. It seemed not to have been opened in decades, and I couldn't at first budge it. This was going to take an effort. Not since I hoisted myself out of Steve Lazslo's incredible sinking armchair did I require the use of so much of my own muscle. I pushed and strained and heaved. Movement in the dratted window didn't come slowly or by increments. The lifting movement was rapid and all of a sudden. The window shot upward. I was so surprised that for one terrible sinking moment I felt as if I might plummet through the open window to the sidewalk four storeys below.

I was slightly sweaty, not to mention huffing and puffing. I leaned against the wall and waited for the recuperative process to set in. All the while, as my breathing and the rest of my bodily functioning returned to normal, I kept my eyes on the Levin. According to my timing, Hugette was due to make her second inspection tour about now. A couple of minutes crawled by, and, right on schedule, Hugette stepped onstage.

I got out Annie's opera glasses and took forever to bring them into focus. I was terrible with binoculars of any size. They refused to respond to my twiddling and tweaking. Eventually, half a lifetime it seemed, I had the damned things more or less in focus and more or less trained on Hugette. She was finishing up on the first floor and approaching the stairs to the second. The stairs meant she was out of sight for a minute or two. But soon enough, she emerged on the second floor, and I followed her for the floor's entire sweep. It went the same for the third and fourth, my eyes trained on Hugette's tall, slim, athletic form, the honker of a nose and the general contours of her head and body. By the time she finished her rounds, I'd recovered from my brain's remote chambers the judgment the brain had intuited more than an hour earlier when Hugette first appeared on College Street.

I put the opera glasses back in my pocket, got out my cell and called I Spy Griffith.

"I need you, I Spy," I said when he answered.

"How refreshing, Mr. Crang," he said. "No longer freezing me out? Is that your meaning?"

"Urgent piece of identification," I said, skating past I Spy's ridiculous grievance. "Only you can handle it."

"Really?" I Spy sounded flattered. "Well, well. You're coming out here?"

"You're coming to me, I Spy. At the Levin Museum. Within the hour. We'll meet in the restaurant across the street from the museum. Bartello's."

"I haven't been downtown in an age," I Spy said, his voice giving away a bad case of nerves. "I never take the car out at night under any circumstances. I've no idea where to find the Levin."

Jesus, the guy was in total panic.

"I'll call you a cab, I Spy. Beck. A car'll be at your place in fifteen minutes tops."

"Is it safe downtown?"

"Ask your driver to lock all the doors."

I clicked off and called Beck. I ordered a cab for I Spy and told Beck to put the ride on my account. The dispatcher said the cab would be at I Spy's in fifteen minutes. They always say fifteen minutes. I went back downstairs and signalled to the waiter that I was ready for my espresso.

Thirty-five minutes later, I Spy stepped warily into Bartello's. He had dressed for the occasion. Suit, white shirt and striped tie.

"Good man, I Spy," I said, shaking his hand. "You'd like a coffee maybe? Grappa? We've got twenty minutes till showtime."

"Neither, Mr. Crang. Just being downtown like this is making my adrenalin go mad. I'm not accustomed to leaving the Kingsway."

"Whatever you say, I Spy. Let's do a rehearsal up at action central."

"Action?" I Spy said. The poor man was petrified.

I patted him on the back. "Action of the passive sort, if you get my meaning."

We rode up the elevator to the fourth floor, and I guided I Spy into the darkened washroom.

"Is this legal, Mr. Crang?" he asked.

"Breaking and entering a private washroom maybe."

"Oh dear god!"

I gave him another back pat. "Just a piece of legal humour, I Spy."

"Could we at least have some light?" he said. He reached over to the wall switch and turned it on.

I turned it off. "Think of this as an undercover job, I Spy."

I led him to the window and aimed him at the Levin across the street. "That's our point of interest over there, I Spy. We're watching for the security person. I want you to examine that person. Use these opera glasses as your visual aid. Do an identification. Got all that?"

We rehearsed for ten more minutes. Just as I finished with all the instructions I could think of, good old on-time Hugette stepped into sight on the fourth floor. Ready for her next round of inspection.

"There's our target, I Spy. Do your stuff."

I Spy wasted no time. "That's he!" he said almost immediately. His voice had shed the fear and trembling it'd been lugging around all evening. "That's the man from Mondays at 32 Highbury! No doubt about it! There he is!"

"I Spy," I said, "you haven't used the opera glasses."

I Spy turned to me. "I don't need any visual aids. I can see plainly enough that you've found the third person."

"Just give it one more shot. With the glasses this time."

"If you insist." I Spy turned back to the view across the street, this time raising Annie's opera glasses to his eyes.

"Yes, yes," he said, "there he goes. He's on the third floor now. Crossing the floor. Inspecting. Yes, yes . . ."

I Spy's voice slowed its excited pace. "Oh, oh, oh. My goodness gracious. It's the correct man all right, but he's not a he at all, is he? I mean, is she? I am absolutely floored. It never entered my mind that the person was anything except male. Well, she does have male aspects in her appearance. I say that as no excuse, but as a partial explanation for my rather fundamental error. Her figure is a long way short of Rubenesque."

"Flat as a board, as we'd say when we were callow and sexist adolescents."

"You might have said it, Mr. Crang. I didn't," I Spy said. He had regained the waspish side of his personality.

"The important question," I said, "is the young woman over there, name of Hugette Jennings, the person you saw on Monday nights?"

"Not a fraction of doubt in my mind."

"Just one thing more, I Spy. Do you notice something odd about Hugette's hands? Apart from the gloves. She holds her hands kind of gingerly? Away from the body? You see that? Or is it my imagination?"

I Spy got back on the opera glasses. He did another minute of observation, ending only when Hugette finished her rounds.

"Not both hands, Mr. Crang," I Spy said. "She's favouring one hand only. The right. The left is more or less mimicking the right."

"You're a very precise man, I Spy."

"Are her hands important to our case?"

"Might be."

I put the opera glasses back in my pocket and escorted I Spy out of the washroom.

"Grand piece of work, I Spy," I said in the elevator. "A thousand thanks."

The two of us shook hands and stepped back into Bartello's. I Spy again turned down offers of refreshment. I asked the maître d' to call him a Beck cab on my account, and I Spy left. I ordered a grappa from the dark-haired waiter. When it came, I raised my glass in a silent toast to the evening's work.

It may have been a smallish step, identifying Hugette. But it buoyed my optimism to previously unattainable heights. Maybe the thing was going to have a decent ending after all. For certain, what we'd done this night, I Spy and I, was to definitively hook Hugette into the scheme. She was the inside contact. She represented the most logical person to make the switch, as I imagined it. She'd remove the real figures from the *Company of Fools* exhibit and substitute Grace's copies. Maybe she'd already done it, but that was doubtful. She'd probably pull off the switch in the dimmer hours of the night, somewhere around 3 or 4 a.m. Then she'd get the real *Company of Fools* up to Elizabeth Janetta's house. Maybe Elizabeth would drive down and fetch her and the goods. Or maybe Rocky would handle the fetching. He could drive without active participation from the little finger of his right hand.

I was drinking the grappa, partly because I enjoyed the taste and partly because the drink smoothed the way while I pondered a big question on my mind. What was my next step? I had choices. I could take Charles's notion of the watching brief literally and stay on duty until something else happened across the street. Somehow that didn't appeal. It would involve watching the Levin and hoping I was in position to spot the actual substitution of the real *Company of Fools* for the fake.

Jesus, I could be holding the fort all night. Bartello's would close, and I'd have no retreat except to the washroom outside the offices of Smith/Wave Graphics. Even then, I wasn't guaranteed of witnessing anything criminal or incriminating. This struck me as a lousy prospect.

Or I could go home, catch a few hours' sleep and return Sunday morning at eleven when the Levin opened. I'd be fresh, on top of my game, ready to deal with whatever events I was presented with. Good thinking, I thought, damn good thinking.

I paid the bill, left a very large tip for the obliging waiter and strolled home. As I walked, I whistled a happy tune. It was "Take the 'A' Train." I still couldn't get it right.

35

When I arrived at the Levin next morning, it was ten minutes to eleven, and I was the third person in line. When the doors opened, I was the twelfth person into the museum. A bunch of eager beavers farther back in the line had jockeyed me out of position. Who said ceramics was a genteel pursuit?

The fuss at the door didn't deflect me from my plan of action. I beat the eager beavers to the elevator and rode alone to the fourth floor. I was the only person on the floor and pointed myself directly to *Company of Fools*.

The first figure I looked for was the jester with the giraffe's face. He was in the front row, far right. This giraffe, the one I was concentrating on, had a smooth forehead. There was no gouge over the left eye. No other blemish, for that matter. The giraffe-faced fellow was manifestly a copy. A fake. An imitation. A figure not by L.L. Schwartzmann but by G. Nguyen.

I checked out the rest of the figures. Every single jester was free of creases, wrinkles, lines and other signs of great age. They were smooth and unrumpled. They looked brand new. Copies, the entire lineup. The switch had been made, Grace's copies for the originals.

I pulled out my cell and began to tap in Charles's number.

Someone thumped me on the shoulder.

"Can't you read, buddy?" a young guy was saying to me. I

recognized him, one of the eager beavers who'd elbowed past me at the door. The young guy was pointing his index finger at the sign on the wall warning patrons not to use electronic devices in the museum.

I folded my cell, galloped down four flights and out the front door. I started all over again with the call to Charles.

"Red alert, Charles," I said when he came on the line. "I'm at the museum, me and the copies of *Company of Fools*. Not an original left."

"By jove," Charles said. "I'll be there in two shakes of a pig's leg."

"Does that mean in a hurry?"

"Faster than Speedy Gonzales, old bean."

"Ah, that resonates."

When Charles arrived ten minutes later, we met at the *Company of Fools* cabinet.

"I have a plan," I said.

"One's needed, my lad," Charles said, examining the fake *Company*. "These are copies, without a suspicion of a doubt."

"Can you easily reach your director?"

"Against just such an eventuality as this," Charles said, "I informed myself of Melissa's whereabouts last night. She's at her cottage, old sport."

"That better not be in Algonquin Park."

Charles shook his head. "Relatively nearby. On Lake Simcoe. She can be down here in an hour of easy driving on a Sunday midday like this."

"Your assignment is to get her moving," I said. "Mine's the tricky part. I'm going to infiltrate the Janetta residence. From there—get this, Charles—I'm going to digitally shoot live footage of *Company of Fools* in situ, and beam it back to you and Melissa. That gives you Levin people ongoing evidence of the heist when it reaches its penultimate stage. How's that strike you for a brainstorm?"

"Brilliant, old boy."

"There remains one complication," I said. "I'm hopeless, digitally speaking."

"No fear," Charles said. "In my retirement, I've made myself a veritable Steve Jobs, may he rest in peace."

"Do I take it you've been more successful with iPhones than with ceramics?"

"By several leagues," Charles said. "I'll provide the equipment and a crash course. Amazing how basic it is, my lad."

Charles had left his car parked on College Street. He whizzed us back to Major where he went to his house to round up the digital stuff and phone Melissa Novak, and I went to my house to ring Isabel MacDougall.

I caught Isabel at her bungalow in North York.

"I'm just deciding what I ought to wear for supervising Elizabeth's party," she said on the phone.

"My very reason for calling," I said. "I need to get into the party, and I know how we'll manage the sneaky part of the job."

"One thing at a time, Crang. Why the party and why you?"

"As far as you're concerned," I said, "a key result of my infiltration will be the saving of Elizabeth from herself. To a degree anyway. Don't want to exaggerate the results I'm expecting."

For a moment, no response came down the line from Isabel's end.

"You've not got anything violent in mind?" she said at last. "Nothing destructive?"

"Shooting film is as rowdy as I intend to get."

"I'm the person who approached you," she said, speaking slowly and thoughtfully. "Not the other way around."

"All true."

"So it seems only right I should help you," Isabel said. "And I will. Okay, now tell me the sneaky part."

"I'm going to pretend I'm part of your catering team."

Isabel laughed. "You're old enough to be these kids' father," she said. Then she paused. "But you might just pass scrutiny for an hour or so. Your face is wrinkle free. Got all your hair. No gut that I noticed."

"None's there to notice."

"You need an outfit. Black trousers. Practically black everything, shoes, socks, bow tie. White shirt, long sleeves and no French cuffs. No cufflinks, I'm saying. No jewellery of any intrusive kind."

"Check, check, double check. I have all those in my wardrobe."

"Then you better get a move on. Be at the Janetta house by two o'clock. Soon as you arrive, I'll tuck you away in my room. No sense letting you do prep in the kitchen with the others. That'd blow your disguise practically before you got into character."

After Isabel and I finished on the phone, I assembled the afternoon's outfit and put it on. Not bad, I thought. Studying myself in the mirror, I felt a zing of youth.

The doorbell rang. I went down and let Charles in. He said Melissa would be hitting the road for the city any minute now, and he had brought with him an iPhone and an arrangement of tiny earphones and a little mic attachment.

"Hook these up just so, Crang old fellow," Charles said, fitting a jack into the iPhone. "Simple as pie. When you're filming, you aim the iPhone as I'm showing you. But first you plug the earphone-mic arrangement into the iPhone. See what I'm doing here? This is the right way to do it. You're getting the hang of things, old bean?"

"Getting it, yeah," I said, though I had misgivings.

"The film is going to appear on my computer," Charles said. "Simultaneously, you'll communicate with Melissa and me by way of the mic setup. We'll be watching my computer screen at her office or whatever secure location she designates. Beauty of a setup, isn't it just?"

"It is," I said, trying to keep my doubts at bay. "Concealing the equipment on my person might give me some grief."

I put the iPhone in one pants pocket and the microphone arrangement in the other.

"Rather breaks the line of your costume, old chap," Charles said.

"Can't be helped," I said, giving my pants a small hitch. "Now I gotta go. Tune in to catch my show on your computer at four-thirty, round about then. After that, it's up to Melissa to call the shots."

"Good, good, old lad."

"By the way," I said, "I don't recommend summoning the cops."

"That's Melissa's view. If word of this rot about our losing *Company of Fools* leaked out, it would make the Levin a laughing-stock."

"Gotta go," I repeated.

I climbed into the Mercedes and drove north to the Bridle Path. It was a gorgeous Toronto summer day. Shame to be spending it indoors. But I was operating in a worthy cause. Worthy? Really? Yeah, I thought so, though Annie might not agree with that part of the definition. Not all of it anyway.

36

Since I didn't want to leave my car so close to the Janetta spread that Rocky or somebody else sinister could spot it in the neighbourhood, I parked a long block from the house and walked the rest of the way. Isabel was standing on the porch. When she spotted me, she made hurry-up motions in my direction. I did as I was told.

"The catering kids got here long ago," Isabel said. "The Janettas are still in their bedroom, and the mister's heavies are sitting on the back patio swapping tales of murder or whatever those dreadful people do."

"Heavies at a party?"

"You don't think Lou opens his door to strangers without his personal muscle standing by, do you?"

"Including crazy Rocky?"

"Inevitably."

Isabel pulled me into the house and pushed a medium-sized platter into my hands. The platter held a dozen crackers with gravlax on them, topped by a dab of white sauce of some kind and a tiny piece of dill.

"Carry this at all times," Isabel said. "If a waiter's holding a platter, guests look mostly at the platter, not the waiter. See what I'm getting at? The platter'll help with your disguise."

"I can manage that."

"One more thing, Crang," Isabel said. "Why're your pants bulging? Most unbecoming, my friend."

"That's essential equipment in my pockets."

Isabel shook her head. I couldn't tell whether she was amused or alarmed.

"Follow me," she said. "Closely."

We marched in smart order along the wide main hall and into the kitchen. One pert blonde in a similar outfit to mine gave me a smile and a raised eyebrow. I smiled back and stayed on the move in Isabel's wake.

We went up a flight of back stairs, halted at the top while Isabel looked each way along the corridor, signalled me to proceed, and we concluded the hike with a sharp turn into the first bedroom on the left. It was Isabel's quarters for sleepovers with the Janettas. The room looked characterless, more like a very expensive hotel room than anything personal.

"You'll stay here until I come for you," Isabel said.

"And do what while I wait?"

"Anything you like. Read *Vanity Fair*. The new issue's on the bed."

"Geez, Isabel, I could've stayed home and done that."

"Don't be smart with me, Crang," Isabel said, a bit of acid in her voice. "I'm far out on a limb on this little enterprise, you must realize."

I raised my hand in a forgive-me gesture. "Just tell me this, Isabel, where's the *Company of Fools* right this minute?"

"That's the ceramic thingamabob?"

"Worth a few million."

"Aptly named it is," Isabel said, "given its presence in this house."

"People a little hairy around here?"

"Rocky's just one mean look from the looney bin. Elizabeth's bouncing off walls she's so excited. And the mister's eating nails in frustration."

"Okay, I've got the principal characters down pat. Now where's *Company of Fools*?"

"Set up grandly on a table in the library. Under lock and key."

"Tell me about the library."

"Practically the size of a tennis court," Isabel said. "Room for the guests and acres of space left over."

"So what's the delay in me getting in there?"

"The lock and key I mentioned?" Isabel said. "Elizabeth's holding on tight to the only two keys. She's not of a mood to give them up, not even to me. Perhaps I should say especially to me. But I'm working on it."

I put my hands on Isabel's shoulders and gave her my most soulful look. "We've just got one shot at this, kid."

Isabel patted one of my hands. "Isn't that a bit melodramatic?'" she said.

"Sorry," I said, shaking my head a little. "I've been known to get that way."

Isabel and I hugged, and she left. I read some *Vanity Fair*, an article about the richest woman in Dubai. The description of her jewellery and gowns and furs made me feel itchy. Vaguely, in the background, I heard the sounds of people arriving, doors slamming, laughter in two languages. The Chinese had assembled, and so, I guessed, had Lou's pals. I felt cool with what lay ahead, but the next piece in *Vanity Fair* wasn't any improvement over the first. This one was about Wall Street guys who'd emerged from the recession with more billions than they had when the market crashed. The damn magazine was making me edgy.

The bedroom door opened. Isabel stepped in, giving me a close once-over.

"Getting anxious, are we?" she said.

"Not on account of what you probably think brought on my case of the fidgets."

Isabel had a big smile on her face. She dangled a key in front of me.

"That's to the library?" I said.

"Worked some magic to get it."

"Which kind?"

"The old reliable falsehood. I told Elizabeth I'd been disapproving for months, not knowing what she was doing in such secrecy. But now that I'd actually seen the ceramics, I felt nothing except admiration for her accomplishment. I practically gagged on the words, but they got me the key."

"So we're set to roll for the library?"

"Time is more precious than ever, laddie. The Chinese want to be in and out of here ahead of previous scheduling."

Isabel moved into the corridor. I did too. She looked back at me.

"Where's your platter?" she said.

I ducked back into the bedroom for the platter, and we set off.

Halfway down the stairs, we met a guy coming up, a tough-looking customer in a black suit and white shirt. He had thug written all over his kisser.

"What're you doin' upstairs?" he asked me.

"Care for a gravlax, sir?" I said, holding the platter out to the guy. "Quite delicious."

"Looks like smoked salmon to me," he said, staring at the platter.

"A Nordic variation," I said. "You might enjoy it, sir."

"I don't eat nothing foreign," he said.

This guy and Maury Samuels would get on like gangbusters.

"He's with me, Spike," Isabel said to the heavy.

Spike grunted. I couldn't help noticing the guy seemed to be wearing a worried expression.

"The boss up here, Isabel?" he said. "I needa see him."

"Could be in the bedroom," Isabel said. "I've been too busy to keep track of him. He could just as likely be on the patio."

Spike grunted again, and Isabel and I resumed our trek to the library.

"Who assigns the names around here?" I asked. "First Rocky, now Spike. Sounds like a 1940s movie. Warner Brothers."

"In Spike's case, consider the alternative," Isabel said. "His real name is Percy Colombo."

"Not a good name for the hoodlum image," I said. "Percy."

Isabel and I reached the library without further socializing. She unlocked the door, and we stepped into the biggest damn library I'd ever seen outside of the British Museum. Except there wasn't a single book in sight. The room was more for the display of visual stuff. Porcelain doodads and knick-knacks of all sorts. All the room's curtains, which were black, had been closed. The lamps and other lights were switched on. *Company of Fools*, arrayed on a black tablecloth that draped to the floor, dominated the room. The table it sat on was situated at what would be centre stage, maybe a little to the right. Farther back, closer to the near wall and facing in the direction of the display, were two tables holding rows of champagne glasses. Behind the tables stood silver buckets of ice, a bottle of Dom Perignon in each.

"I'll lock you in, Crang," Isabel said. "About a half hour from now, everybody's going to shift from the patio to here for the formal festivities. I'll be back five minutes before that."

Isabel left.

I got the communication equipment out of my pants pockets. The mic fixed easily into the iPhone, and I was set to start filming in jig time.

Somebody in the hall outside stuck a key in the library door. It was way too soon for Isabel's return. Had to be Elizabeth out there, the only other person with a key. I made a swift cataloguing of the room. There was a door in the right wall. Maybe a bathroom behind the door. But it was too far away for me to reach in time. I got down on my hands and knees and scrambled under the black tablecloth on the table holding *Company of Fools*. I could hear the library door opening and closing.

Two voices began to speak above me. I detected pretty quickly that the voices belonged to Elizabeth and Lou.

"I want you to see *Company*, just you and me alone together," Elizabeth said. Her voice sounded more breathless than it did the one time I'd talked to her.

"I appreciate it, sweetheart," Lou said. He sounded calm and measured, his usual restrained but dangerous self. "These pieces of pottery are what you been messing around with all this time? Me wondering what the hell was up?"

"*Company of Fools*, they're called, and they're priceless, Lou. I've made the deal of a lifetime, honestly. You're gonna be so proud of me."

"I already am proud of you, baby."

This was embarrassing, me eavesdropping on a private husband-and-wife conversation. But it couldn't be helped. My situation on the floor was painful in the physical sense as well as the psychological. In the haste to duck under the table, I'd landed on my left side with the leg at an angle a leg wasn't supposed to be capable of. It was developing a cramp, not a gradual process but a swift seizing up.

"You're selling these ceramic pieces to the Chinese guy out there on the patio?" Lou was saying.

"Elvis's a billionaire, Lou." Elizabeth was very excited. Bouncing off walls indeed.

"What's he paying, you don't mind me asking?"

"Fourteen million, Lou."

Lou made whistling sounds. "Kee-rist, I'm impressed. I mean really impressed, sweetheart. What're your expenses?"

"About four million."

"You're clearing ten million? I never had a one-off deal like that in my life."

"Plus, I come out of it with a house in the Kingsway I can sell for a couple million."

The pain was morphing up my left leg, calf to thigh. I didn't know how much more of this I could stand.

"Let me ask about the possible downsides," Lou was saying, not sounding critical, just curious, talking like one businessperson to another. "That idiot Rocky let it drop you got a dead girl in all this."

"Oh, Louis," Elizabeth said. She sounded a little false to my ears, but who could tell? "Grace's death is shocking," Elizabeth said, "but I'm sure the police'll find it was random. A drug addict went off his head or something unforeseeable like that."

"Yeah, it happens," Lou said. "What about the Nosy Parker lawyer?"

"What Nosy Parker lawyer?"

"Guy by the name of Crang."

This was too much. They were talking about me, and I was listening? I read a scene like that in a novel once. A Brian Moore book, I think it was. The character in the book was an Irish schoolteacher, he was in a cubicle in the teachers' can, and he overheard two other teachers at the wash basins slamming him. The two other guys didn't know the main character was even in the room. The whole deal didn't turn out well for the cubicle guy.

"Rocky says he's got Crang under control," Elizabeth said.

Oh yeah? He's got me under control? Well, which one of us was currently getting by with only one operational pinky?

"My opinion," Lou said, "Rocky gets in the first shot but he's the one ends up on his ass every time he takes a run at Crang."

Well, well, so far I was making out better than Brian Moore's guy in the cubicle.

"One more thing," Lou said, "what's the girl doing at the party?"

"Which girl are you talking about, sweetheart?"

"The one got the gloves on. Shakes hands with her left."

"Hugette you mean," Elizabeth said. "Lou darling, without Hugette, I never would have been successful in this deal with Elvis."

Somebody rapped on the library door, then opened it.

"I've been looking high and low for you two." It was Isabel's voice. I took advantage of the interruption to roll cautiously over on my back. My left leg had gone numb, thigh to toes. I might never walk again unaided.

"The Chinese interpreter just told me they have to be out of here with the ceramic stuff inside twenty minutes," Isabel said. "I just wanted to tell you."

"That'll work fine, Isabel," Elizabeth said.

"Let me ask you something, Isabel," Lou said. "How'd that platter of gravlax get in here?"

Jesus, I'd left the damn thing in clear view.

"So that's where it got to," Isabel said. Her voice sounded unnaturally high. "I wondered how I'd misplaced it."

"Not like you, Isabel, I gotta say," Lou said. "Forgetting things."

"I'll just take it with me," Isabel said, still talking in the high voice.

"Never mind," Lou said. "Maybe I'll have some."

"I'll get the catering staff organized," Isabel said.

Her voice was followed by silence. Presumably Isabel had left. But Elizabeth and Lou weren't talking. Had they departed too? I didn't hear the library door open and close a second time. I was still lying flat on my back. I reached my hand out and risked raising the cloth an inch or two. Right in front of my eyes, almost close enough for me to reach out and touch, were a pair of female legs and a pair of male legs. From my limited view, the arrangement of limbs suggested a couple kissing. I dropped the curtain. There was only so much invading of privacy I could stand.

I lay back and contemplated my aching left leg. The pain had passed into the extremely intense stage.

"Let's get the people ready for the presentation," Elizabeth said in a low sexy voice.

"This here right now, you and me," Lou said, "to be continued in the bedroom."

That was a criminal kingpin's idea of sweet talk? Lou's line ranked right up there with Jimmy Cagney smacking his girlfriend's face with a sliced grapefruit.

"Later on," Elizabeth said. She appeared not to share my view of Lou's seducing technique.

The two of them crossed the floor to the door. I heard it open, and felt a long sigh of relief working its way through my system. The relief didn't last long.

"Boss, I been looking for you," another man's voice said at the open library door. "This's serious."

I recognized the voice. It belonged to Percy Colombo aka Spike.

"You go ahead, Elizabeth," Lou said to his wife.

"Don't be long, sweetheart," she said.

The library door closed, leaving Lou and Spike still in the library. Damn, I was running short on time. Were these people never going to vacate the friggin' room?

"What's serious?" Lou said. He and Spike stayed over by the door for their chat.

"Okay, I delivered all the horse to different customers this afternoon," Spike said. His voice sounded anxious. "Except the two kilos for the Three Amigos. They told me, sorry, their money's been delayed. They'll be getting it at eleven tonight. What they wanted to know, could I trust them for the cash until then?"

"Spikey," Lou said, the old familiar menace making its way closer to the surface, "tell me you didn't leave the two kilos with those guys."

"No way, boss," Spike said. "No money, no horse. It's still in the car."

"So far, you're doing okay. What're you worried about?"

I actually understood what the two guys were talking about. It seems Spike was distributing Lou's heroin around town, and the Three Amigos, which was a Mexican restaurant on Dundas near

Shaw, was one of their customers. The Amigos were buying two kilos from Lou, then presumably peddling the heroin to their clientele of addicts in gram lots. A thousand grams in a kilo . . . That could add up to a tidy sum depending on what they charged per gram. I hadn't a clue about prices.

"They buy from us at three hundred and thirty bucks a gram," Lou said. "Probably sell for four hundred."

Thanks, Lou. Nice to know exactly the current prices in his heroin business. But would he please stop with the financial seminar and get back to his guests.

"So what am I missing here, Spike?" Lou was saying. "What's happening that's serious, apart from you won't get the money from those guys until eleven?"

"Well, see, boss," Spike was almost stumbling over his words, "I stepped on the gas to get back here from the Amigos because you said it was important I should be on duty with the other guys at the party."

"And the car's out front with the horse in it even though you know it's a strict rule drugs are never to be in the vicinity of my house?"

Lou sounded like he needed all his steely resolve to avoid flying off the handle.

"Boss," Spike said, a little quake in his voice, "I hadda make a decision."

"What car you using?" Lou asked after a short delay. From the changing sound levels of his voice, he must have been walking around the room, probably thinking through the heroin delivery problem.

"The Volvo," Spike said.

"Horse's under the matting in the back?"

"Just like you want."

"You think the Amigos are square about having the money at eleven?"

"In all the time I been delivering to them," Spike said, "two years, something like that, this's the first time a delay or anything else I didn't like has come up."

"I know," Lou said. "They've been reliable."

All right already, would the man just make a decision. My left leg was aching, my patience was running low, I needed to plug in my setup to Charles and Melissa. If I didn't start shooting digital awfully damn soon, my plan was down the crapper.

"Here's what you do," Lou said to Spike. "Stick around here another hour till the ceremony ends, whatever the hell it is, and people clear out. Then take the Volvo to your place. Leave it in the garage for a couple hours, and at eleven, you drive to Three Amigos for the payoff. Soon as you got the money, phone my cell."

"Thanks, boss," Spike said in a warm tone.

A few moments of silence followed Spike's heartfelt piece of gratitude. What the hell were the two guys doing now? Giving one another the secret drug dealer handshake?

Then the door opened and closed. I waited, and I concentrated on listening for the continuing presence of human beings still in the room, apart from myself. I didn't hear a thing, not an intake of breath, not a rustle of clothing. At last, finally, I was alone, all by myself in the big old library.

The process of getting out from under the table was labour intensive. My leg was killing me. But I had no time to attend to ailments. I put together the iPhone setup, plugged in the mic and the tiny earphones. Once the parts seemed in place, I tapped in Charles's number.

He came on the line instantly.

"Crang, old chap," he said, "we've been terribly worried. You're in place, are you?"

"Time is of the essence, Charles."

"All set at this end," Charles said. "We're in Melissa's office. Six of us, Melissa, four members of the Levin board and myself.

Ready when you are, old bean. You're on speakerphone."

"This is Melissa Novak, Mr. Crang." She had a deep and breathy voice, like a younger Lauren Bacall. "We're so grateful to you."

"Nothing to it," I said.

There was a pause until I said, "I've got the camera going. I think. Receiving now, Charles?"

"You need to press the on button, Crang old lad."

"Sorry." I pressed the button.

"Now we're receiving, Crang," Charles said. "But the shot we're getting on the screen is of your foot, I believe. Raise the iPhone a notch, would you?"

I did as Charles instructed.

"Trifle too high," Charles said. "We've getting an impressive view of the ceiling."

I made more adjustments, and was rewarded with a chorus of shocked ohhhs and ahhhs at the other end.

"I'm showing *Company of Fools* now?" I said.

"Jolly right, old boy," Charles said. "But we would benefit from some tighter focusing."

I made scrolling movements with my thumb, and at the same time I adjusted the angle of the iPhone. I hadn't the faintest idea whether I was helping or harming the receiving process in Melissa's office.

Much louder ohhhs came over the line, plus one female voice saying, "I never trusted that Janetta woman." I gathered I'd done something right.

"Getting the good stuff, Charles?" I said.

"Very nice indeed," Charles said. "Now see if you can give us a close-up of the giraffe's face, old boyo. That'll clinch the case. Ultimate proof it's the original *Company* at the Janetta mansion."

Now that I was getting the hang of the gizmos, it wasn't much trouble to zoom in on Mr. Giraffe.

I heard Charles's voice through my earphones, but he wasn't speaking to me. "Melissa, my dear," he said, "do we have what Crang calls the smoking gun?"

"I should think so," Melissa said in her smoky tones. Then she spoke more loudly for my benefit. "Mr. Crang, we're coming out to the Janetta house, all of us here in the office. It's time to reclaim the Levin's treasure."

"The sooner the better," I said. "Wang and his people are speeding up the climax to the deal."

"Over and out for the moment, Crang old friend," Charles said.

I was sweating. It felt like a mighty strain to handle the filming and all the other technological stuff. My left leg wasn't helping the efforts. It ached like crazy.

I was folding up the mic and earphones, getting things tidied, when I heard once again the infernal sound of a key being inserted in the library lock.

Even with the left leg threatening to crumple under me, I took a half-dozen bounds across the library toward a chair against the wall on my left. It was an armchair done in crimson and gold fabric, an ugly damn thing. I jammed the equipment, iPhone and all, under the chair's seat pillow.

That done, the incriminating stuff out of sight, I picked up the platter of gravlax, put on my bland server's smile and turned to face the opening door.

37

Isabel was the first person through the door, moving under a good head of steam. Following her was the catering staff, five fresh and shiny young people, three men, two women.

"You there," Isabel barked at me, "you work on the champagne with Becky."

Becky turned out to be the blonde who'd given me the raised eyebrow in the kitchen. She reached out to shake my hand and flashed another arch of the eyebrow.

"How long've you been passing around that gravlax?" Becky asked. "Looks like it's getting, you know, gamey."

"You think it might poison the guests?"

"One guy here I wouldn't mind poisoning."

"Let me guess," I said. "A man with his arm in a sling?"

Becky smiled. "He's been trying to feel me up all afternoon. With his functioning hand."

"Say no more," I said. "He's as good as eliminated."

Becky laughed, and we got down to the business of popping champagne corks.

"There something wrong with your leg?" Becky said.

"Combat wound."

"I'm beginning to get the idea you're a dangerous guy," Becky said.

The room was filling in a hurry, led by the Chinese contingent. Elvis Wang was a different type than I expected. Younger, late thirties at the most, and handsome with a movie-star flash. His wife, Trixi, was the same, young and attractive. She had a cute smile and a tidy figure.

There were six other Chinese guys. The only one whose role seemed obvious was the interpreter. He was a busy little bee, buzzing around Elvis and Trixi who seemed to need his services nonstop. Lou's personal guests were doing a lot of nodding and smiling at the Wangs and the interpreter. The Lou friends, wearing lightweight summer suits in conservative shades, were smiley but hard, the wives looking almost as sleek and tough as the men. The bodyguards, four guys including Spike and three others from the same mould, ranged around the room, mostly to my right. Rocky in his sling was there too, the only heavy to my left. He was standing with Hugette who once again included gloves as part of her dress ensemble. These ones were white leather, fitting loosely. I concentrated on staying to Becky's right side, using her to block Rocky's view of me. He was bound to spot me sometime in the afternoon. All I wanted was to delay the inevitable till a point in the proceedings when I wouldn't care whether he recognized me or not.

Elizabeth and Lou were last into the room. Lou wore a summery sports jacket and trousers in two different hues of light and dark blue, no tie included in the ensemble. Elizabeth had on a simple white dress, form-fitting and ending just above her knees. Great fit, great form.

She stood beside the table displaying *Company of Fools* and began to speak to the assembled guests.

"I'm going to talk slowly enough for the interpreter to pass on my little jokes to our honoured guests, Elvis and Trixi."

That drew light laughter from the crowd. Elizabeth beamed at her guests, her eyes turning left to right, taking in the whole room. The eyes passed me, then returned. Elizabeth paused, and examined my face. She frowned. She seemed to recognize the face but wasn't sure where she'd seen it before. She got back to her speech.

"What you see before you on the table," Elizabeth went on, "is one of the most precious pieces in the history of ceramic arts."

She didn't speak as slowly as she'd promised. Maybe it was the excitement of the moment. The interpreter speeded up his murmuring, matching Elizabeth's pace, directing his translation at Elvis and Trixi. The other Chinese guys were left to fend for themselves, languagewise.

"Elvis and I are engaged in a deal today that nobody else in ceramics has ever realized," Elizabeth was saying.

She sounded confident and spunky, just hitting her stride. But before she got any further, another voice invaded the room.

"Are you receiving? Come in, please, old bean. . . ."

The voice was coming from the crimson-and-gold chair over by the left wall, and it sounded just like my neighbour Charles.

"Over to you," the voice from the chair said. "Update time, old chap. . . ."

Elizabeth had stopped talking. She and everybody else in the room had eyes only for the ugly chair.

Rocky, to my left, reached his left hand under his jacket and into his belt at the back, the place where guys like him keep their pistols. Was the idiot going for his gat? What'd Rocky have in mind? Shooting the chair dead?

"Attention, old bean," the chair went on, "we're just clearing St. Clair Avenue . . ."

People in the room were whispering to one another, pointing at the chair, probably wondering how the talking piece of furniture figured into Elizabeth's presentation.

I was the only one in the room who knew what was going on. I'd left the damn iPhone on. Now my worry was how the hell I could turn it off before Charles broadcast my name to Elizabeth and Rocky and the whole crowd.

Rocky had already drawn his gun. He was holding it close to his leg. Nobody except Becky and me could see the thing. It was a lethal-looking bit of weaponry, and it had a silencer attached to the barrel. Rocky definitely had the demeanour of a guy prepared to let bullets fly.

Isabel, standing closer to the chair than anyone in the room, got herself in gear before Rocky made his move.

"I'm sorry, Elizabeth and everyone," Isabel said, her voice at the unnaturally high pitch I'd heard earlier. She hurried up to the ugly chair in quick little steps. "My young nephew was over last week. Left his toys in the oddest places. I do apologize for the interruption."

She lifted the pillow and pulled out the iPhone, the mic and the earphones. Her hands felt around for the buttons to deactivate the apparatus.

Charles's voice hadn't finished.

". . . ETA, ten minutes from now. Signing off, Crang old sport."

Isabel flicked off the buttons a second too late.

I looked over at Elizabeth. One glance told me the penny had dropped. She realized where she'd seen me before and who I was. Her eyes looked for mine and found them. For an instant, we stared at one another. What would her next move be? Summon her husband to some kind of action? Signal Rocky to polish me off? Neither Lou nor Rocky had yet registered my presence.

Elizabeth didn't turn to either guy, not her husband nor Rocky. Her eyes left mine and beamed a smile at the crowd. She seemed to have chosen to push on with the presentation. Get it over with, I guessed, secure the fourteen million bucks in her own hands. Then she'd pass on to the punishment phase. The punishing of the Nosy Parker lawyer.

"What was that all about?" Becky whispered to me.

"Nothing good where I'm concerned," I whispered back.

"Really?" Becky said. "A person here got it in for you?"

"Something like that."

"Don't worry," Becky said, the plucky little warrior. "I got your back."

Up at the front of the room, beside the table holding *Company of Fools*, Elizabeth was talking faster.

"So it's with great honour and greater privilege that I turn the renowned *Company of Fools* to the stewardship of our friends Elvis and Trixi."

Everybody clapped politely. The interpreter nudged Elvis, indicating he and Trixi should step closer to Elizabeth. Elvis moved up, leading Trixi with him. Kisses followed all round, Elvis kissing Elizabeth, Elvis kissing Trixi, the two women kissing one another, Elvis laying another big smacker on Elizabeth.

The interpreter joined Elvis who began to talk in Chinese. According to the interpreter, Elvis was inviting everyone in the room to visit *Company of Fools* at one of his houses in China. "But," the interpreter said, quoting Elvis, "you must come under cover."

The gathering chuckled in a knowing fashion.

Elvis handed Elizabeth a plain white envelope, no doubt containing the fourteen million in a cheque or some other paper form. Elizabeth smiled a very broad smile, and another round of kisses ensued.

Isabel signalled us servers to get cracking.

"Pour the champagne," Becky said to me.

Three of the Chinese guys had left the room, and returned carrying large suitcases. When they opened the suitcases, I could see rows of compartments just the right size to accommodate a ceramic figure in each compartment. The Chinese guys started packing the suitcases.

Damn, the ceremony was whipping along too fast. Charles and the Levin gang would still be six or seven minutes from reaching the house. The Chinese contingent could be pulling away with the goods by the time the Levin people arrived. I had to stall the proceedings.

I picked up a tray of full champagne glasses and limped across the library to the group that included the principal players. Elvis, Trixi, Elizabeth, Lou and the interpreter. All of them had their hands ready to reach for the champagne. But passing out the bubbly wasn't what I had in mind. Instead, I tipped the tray, sending a glass spilling down the front of Elvis's shirt and suit jacket. The glass had landed exactly as I had intended. Another glass tumbled over Elizabeth's dress. That part I hadn't intended. It was collateral damage. Collateral soakage, to be more accurate. Elizabeth let out a *yiyi* sound. She looked like a contestant in a wet T-shirt contest. The soaked fabric of her dress clung to every curve of her delicious upper body. She would have won the wet T-shirt contest by a landslide.

Elvis fired a blur of angry Chinese at the interpreter who signalled his colleagues for help. They rushed forward with handkerchiefs to mop the boss's shirtfront. Lou, who still didn't seem to have noted that I was the careless waiter, began to perform a similar mopping job on Elizabeth's dress. The commotion had brought proceedings to a general halt. That was okay by me. A delay in things until the museum people got to the house was what I had intended.

I turned around to check who was where. Isabel was looking daggers at me. Becky wasn't sure whether to laugh or show concern. Crazy Rocky was the one I worried about. I didn't need to look far for him. He was lunging across the floor, his pistol out in plain sight.

"I got you now, pal," he said. He was talking to me, the gun pointed at my chest.

"Rocky!" Lou said, his voice riding on its familiar combination of cool and authority. He'd put aside his mopping for the moment in favour of upbraiding Rocky. That meant his eyes fell on me for the first time that I was aware of. But Lou kept on addressing Rocky, the only guy in the room with a gun in his hand. "Not in here, Rocky, for god's sake."

Rocky slowed his stride. "Just a knee, boss. Lemme cap the son of a bitch. Maybe two knees."

"Rocky," Lou said in an even sharper voice than before. "Leave Crang till later. We got business first, you blockhead."

Rocky ignored his boss. He lowered his aim to knee level. My knee level. The guy was totally serious about capping me. He was nuts enough to do the job in front of all these witnesses.

He cocked the revolver. He was a fraction of a second away from making me a customer for a wheelchair.

To my left and Rocky's right, I registered a swish of movement. Rocky turned his head slightly. He'd had a glimpse of whatever I'd seen. It was Becky. She had a champagne bottle in her hand, and she was pulling it back into smacking position. She swung it around, practically at blur speed, until it made a resounding connection with Rocky's right hand. It hit square on his wounded pinky.

Rocky let out a screech of pain. Then his eyes shut, and he slid to the floor. The guy looked like he'd fainted dead away.

Lou reacted first. He snapped his fingers at Spike and one other bodyguard.

"Drag that moron out of here," he said, pointing to Rocky. Then Lou turned back to the soaked Elizabeth while the bodyguards carted Rocky away.

Elvis had taken off his sopping shirt, and a guy in his posse who had removed his own shirt handed the dry replacement to his boss. The rest of the guests were staring at the strange events, knocking back champagne and babbling noisily to one another. For the moment, nobody seemed to give a damn about me. Even Lou was ignoring me. But that would last only until he finished drying off Elizabeth.

Becky, standing beside me, looked as pleased as punch.

"Even if Isabel fires me," she said, "I'm glad I whacked that guy."

"Becky," I said, "you saved my bacon."

"You think he was actually gonna pull the trigger?"

"Haven't a doubt."

"Well," Becky said, "the least I could do was keep him from harming you. That's the main thing."

"Really? I'm very flattered."

"You're exactly like someone who means the world to me."

"Who's that?"

"My dad."

"Oh."

What kind of afternoon was I having? Almost got my knee capped. Lost the feeling in one leg. An attractive young woman said she saw me not as Crang the gallant man of action but as a second-line father figure.

And on the floor, right in front of me, Chinese guys were filling suitcases with fourteen million dollars' worth of ceramic figures they'd heisted from the rightful Canadian owners. For a moment I had too much on my mind to decide what to do next.

38

The library door, which had been half open the last time I looked, swung all the way in, banging against one of the Chinese guys with a suitcase. Through the door charged Charles and what I took to be the ladies of the Levin board.

"Grab the guy with the suitcase," I shouted at Charles.

Simultaneously, Elizabeth let out a sound somewhere between a shriek and a cry of distress.

"Melissa?" she said. "What are you doing here?!"

Charles put an arm lock on the Chinese guy with the suitcase while a tall, slender woman stepped out from the crowd of Levin ladies. She had a pronounced take-charge manner and was without question Melissa Novak. She even looked like a younger Lauren Bacall.

"Elizabeth," she said, "don't bother to resign from the board. We've already voted to kick you off."

Melissa glanced down at the two Chinese guys packing *Company of Fools* figures into their padded suitcases.

"What do you think you're doing?" Melissa said. "Who are you people?"

Lou turned his head from Elizabeth's soaked dress. "Who the hell are you, lady?" he said to Melissa, one authority figure to another.

"A representative of the museum that owns these figures," Melissa said. "Got that, buster? And who the hell are you?"

"I own the house you just trespassed into."

"Then you better watch your step," Melissa said, "or your wife'll be off to the hoosegow."

The interpreter, taking all of this in, fired a blue streak of Chinese at Elvis and Trixi. The longer the interpreter talked, the more steely Elvis seemed to get. When the interpreter finished, Elvis snapped off a bunch of sharp-sounding orders to his guys. Taking their cues from Elvis, the guys turned steely themselves. They were snappy about unloading the suitcases. They put the figures back on the display table and hurried out of the library with the empty cases.

The interpreter turned to Elizabeth.

"Mr. Wang want me to tell you, deal off," the interpreter said. "Thanking you and goodbye from Elvis and Trixi."

Elizabeth hadn't said another word since Melissa's arrival stunned her into a state close to catatonic. Lou was giving her wet white dress the final drying touches with his handkerchief and a couple more hankies his bodyguards had contributed to the operation. All the while, Elizabeth had been holding the envelope from Elvis up in the air, keeping it safe from the danger of further champagne spraying.

Elvis, Trixi, the interpreter and the last remnants of the Chinese contingent began their swift troop march toward the library door. As Trixi passed Elizabeth, she reached up and plucked the envelope from Elizabeth's hand. Elizabeth still made no sound. The Chinese kept speed marching until they disappeared down the hall, gone with empty suitcases and fourteen million bucks.

"Ladies," Melissa said to the Levin women, "prepare the *Company* figures for transport back to their rightful home."

The women got busy with their assignment while Melissa made a survey of the room. Her eyes landed on me.

"Mr. Crang?"

I nodded.

"One more service, if you please," Melissa said. "Where is Hugette Jennings?"

I'd already noted Hugette slumped on the crimson-and-gold armchair on the other side of the room. If it was possible for a six-foot woman to look forlorn, Hugette had managed the feat. She appeared even more drained of hope than Elizabeth. Tears trickled down both cheeks. She stared, unspeaking, at Melissa.

"You, young lady, are fired," Melissa said. "And when I'm finished with your reputation, you'll never work in the ceramics world again. In any capacity."

By the end of Melissa's short dressing-down, the room had fallen silent and almost empty. Lou's pals and their wives had already beat it. The Chinese were gone. Isabel now led Becky and the other catering kids in the direction of the kitchen. Melissa, the Levin ladies and Charles hiked away with the *Company of Fools* figures. Charles gave me a jaunty wave of departure, followed by the dreaded thumbs-up.

Only Lou, Elizabeth, Hugette and I were left in the library, aside from Spike and two other members of Lou's bodyguard squad. They stood, unmoving and alert, in the room's far distances.

"Crang," Lou said to me, "one thing I'll say about you, you got a lot of balls, still hanging around here."

"Some clients think it's my most winning characteristic."

A cranky expression took over Lou's face. He said, "You aren't out of this house in two minutes, I'm telling my guys to finish the job Rocky started."

"Lou," I said, "you need my help."

Lou came as close to blowing his top as I'd so far seen. "What the fuck you talking about?" he said.

"You still got a killing on your hands, and I know the only way to resolve it," I said.

Lou seemed to have nothing to say to that, at least for the moment. He was a quick thinker, and maybe he'd anticipated some of what was to come. He and I both knew his wife could soon be dealing with the law if things didn't break right for her. Lou had no doubt figured out in the last few minutes that Elizabeth had messed around with stolen ceramic figures, the figures that had until a few minutes ago been sitting in his very own library. That was one of Lou's problems, but not the only possible source of trouble.

"Grace Nguyen's the dead victim in the story," I said, "and the person who caused her death was young Hugette here."

All eyes turned to Hugette in the ugly chair. Up until then, her weeping had included no histrionic carryings-on. Now she dropped her head into her hands and let out a terrible wail.

I waited until she quieted by a decibel or two. "But I've got the inside dope to make the argument she couldn't have intended to kill Grace."

Hugette lifted her head and looked at me. "It was an accident!" she said, her voice so loud it seemed to echo off the walls.

"Where in hell are you getting the so-called inside information, Crang?" Lou said. "What makes you think the dame here didn't do a deliberate killing? You can't be dumb enough to take her word for it. Everybody caught in a murder, for crissake, everybody says they didn't do it on purpose."

"Hugette and Crang are right, sweetheart." Elizabeth spoke up for the first time, her voice not much above a whisper. "It really was an accident."

"What makes you so sure?" Lou asked his wife.

"I was there," Elizabeth said. "I was out at Highbury that night."

While the rest of us considered what Elizabeth had just said, she wore the look of someone who wasn't through with the personal revelations.

"Grace threatened us," Elizabeth said. "All we needed from her was one more of the copies she'd made of the *Company* figures, but she refused to give it to us. She had finished it, the one with the giraffe face, but she said unless we paid her another half a million dollars, she was keeping it."

Hugette spoke up. "She said she needed more money because she was pregnant. Right away, I knew she was lying."

"Afraid not, Hugette," I said. "Grace really was pregnant."

"Come on, Crang, how'd you find out a thing like that?" Lou said, clearly not enjoying any of what he was hearing.

"From one of the very few people in a position to provide intimate information about Grace," I said. "From the coroner who did her autopsy."

Hugette slumped a little in the awful chair.

"You have to understand the pressure, Lou," Elizabeth said. "We all stood to profit enormously from the deal, me, Hugette, Rocky, Grace herself, and then, out there in the Highbury driveway, Grace was saying she'd pull the plug on everything."

"Rocky, he's in this everyplace I look," Lou said. "The guy's turned into somebody way more trouble than he's worth."

"The reason I hired him, Lou," Elizabeth said, "I needed someone big and mean to protect the girls."

"Forget Rocky for a minute, you two," I said. I aimed a question at Elizabeth. "What happened out there at the house with Grace? You and she and Hugette were arguing about her demand for more money. What came next?"

"Not so much an argument," Elizabeth said. "But, anyway, what happened after that was Hugette suddenly swung her fist at Grace."

"I'd never punched anyone in my life before," Hugette said, her voice on the edge of hysteria.

"Grace fell over," Elizabeth said. "At first, I thought it was a joke. Grace was faking. I might've even laughed. But then I realized she was dead, the way she looked, her nose and eyes, the mess of her face."

"So you and Hugette dragged Grace's body into the woods?" I said.

"From the driveway, yeah," Elizabeth said. "Then we went back into the house. We found the giraffe figure right away in Grace's makeup kit. Grace had finished it. So we packed it up, and left Highbury."

"A couple more questions," I said. "Why was Hugette out there that particular night?"

"The times she came to Highbury," Elizabeth said, "they were when Grace had finished one or two figures. Hugette picked them up, usually on Mondays, and hid them in a secret place in her office at the Levin. Waiting for when we switched Grace's copies for the originals."

"A switch that took place this morning?" I said.

"Yeah," Elizabeth said. "At 4 a.m. Hugette is a very efficient person. She brought the originals down to me waiting in the Levin's parking lot."

I thought for a minute about how things might have turned out if I'd waited longer at Bartello's and intercepted Elizabeth in the parking lot. No, I thought, that was a mug's game, all the what-ifs. I was going to stick to present realities. Always a good philosophy.

I had a couple more questions for Elizabeth.

"Why did you send Isabel to pick up Grace at Highbury that night when you knew Grace was already dead?" I said.

"That damn Isabel's been talking to you," Elizabeth said. It came out like the accusation it was. Elizabeth seemed to be recovering her fighting spirit.

"Everybody's been talking to me," I said. "Including you. So answer the question."

"It was like a piece of misdirection, getting Isabel to drive out there," Elizabeth said. "So if the cops should get into it, and one of them asked me what I knew, I could say I knew nothing. I'd tell the cop I even sent my housekeeper to drive Grace long after she died."

"Cynical," I said.

"I call it smart," Lou said.

I said to Elizabeth, "It was the same thing when you and Hugette asked Rocky if he killed Grace? A piece of misdirection?"

"If you want to look at it that way," Elizabeth said.

I shrugged and turned to Hugette. I wanted to get her ready for what was to come in her life. "I'm guessing you haven't had a doctor look at your hand," I said. "Underneath the glove, your right hand's probably a mess."

"How could I have gone to a doctor?" Hugette said, her voice rising, the wail threatening to make a return. "I'd have to tell him how it happened. But I didn't mean to kill Grace. I just lost my mind for a second. I didn't know what I was doing."

"We'll get to that part," I said. "But first you'll need to get the hand examined right away. X-rays, photos of the outside of the hand, the whole deal. They'll be part of what your lawyer'll take to the Crown."

"What are you talking about, Crang?" Lou said.

"A lawyer's got to make a deal for Hugette by Monday. Promise the Crown a guilty plea in return for a reduced charge. Plead to manslaughter probably."

"Oh, I get it, smart guy," Lou said. "This is the part where you say you'll take the case, and, by the way, your fee's a million bucks."

"The fee would be a long way short of a million, Lou," I said. "But I'm not going to be the lawyer in the case anyway. I'm going to recommend someone you should hire."

"What, out of the blue, you're turning modest?"

"Lou," Elizabeth said, "we've got to look after Hugette."

I turned to Elizabeth. "You'd better look after her. Hugette's your best hope."

"Explain that part, Crang," Lou said. "Before I get more fed up than I am already."

"What you want to avoid," I said to Lou, "is the Crown taking the case against Hugette to trial. If that happens, all the crazy stuff'll come out in the testimony, Elizabeth's shenanigans at the Levin and so on. But if Hugette makes a deal ahead of time, pleads guilty to the manslaughter, there'll be no trial, no big revelations in court, nothing for the media to go nuts over. And, not the least, Hugette'll get a much lighter sentence."

Elizabeth moved over to the crimson-and-gold chair. She perched on the chair's arm and put her own arm around Hugette. I crossed the room to a desk against the far wall. There was a holder full of pens on top. I picked up a pen and got a sheet of paper out of the top drawer.

"Here's the lawyer's name," I said, writing on the sheet. I handed it to Lou.

"Phil Goldenberg," I said. "Nickname's Fox because that's what he is in court, foxy. He'll do a great job for Hugette. The other name on the paper, Wally Torgol, Fox'll know what that's about."

"Who's Torgol? Another lawyer?"

I shook my head. "Better than that. Wally's a guy who says Grace's death wasn't murder, and his opinion counts for a lot. He's the one I mentioned who did the autopsy."

Lou seemed to have made a decision in a hurry. He stood up, and looking at me, he said, "I got to make phone calls, Crang. Check with my own people about this stuff you're telling me."

When Lou finished his little announcement, he didn't leave the library right away, as I expected him to. Instead, he stood in place staring at me until his staring and his silence began to turn a little eerie.

"I get the impression I'm being dismissed," I said.

"See, you can be a bright guy when you try," Lou said.

"Not bright enough to have recognized early on what a mean son of a bitch you really are," I said. "Even by crime-kingpin standards."

"Crang, you want me to put a couple of my guys on you who won't screw up like Rocky did?"

"Not particularly," I said.

"Then don't still be here when I get back."

Lou walked out of the room, moving like a man on a mission. One of the three bodyguards, not Spike, went with him. I looked over at Elizabeth and Hugette. Elizabeth was still holding Hugette, and Hugette was still weeping.

I turned away. I could still hear the sound of the weeping behind me as I limped out of the library and down the hall to the front door. There was no sign of the caterers, nothing of Isabel. No Rocky either. I kept on limping toward the front door when Lou Janetta called my name.

"Crang, you interfering asshole," he said. He was standing in the kitchen door, a cellphone in his hand. He seemed to be waiting for someone to come on the line.

"I don't feel any warmth for you either, Lou."

"If it was left to me," Lou said, "I'd have pinned the whole thing on Hugette, no bullshitting around with Crown deals. Make her take a murder fall and another for screwing around with the ceramics."

"That's petty vicious talk, Lou," I said. "Hugette's the most vulnerable person in the whole pitiful story."

"So?" Lou said.

"You know, Lou, you're worse than what I said. Worse than mean, but I can't think of the right adjective. Nasty is part of it."

Lou laughed. "Yeah," he said, spreading his arms as if he were embracing the entire house. "But take a look what it's got me. All this and Elizabeth too. And nobody can do a fucking thing about it. Especially not you."

He turned his back and began to talk into the cell.

I opened the front door and walked out to the driveway. There was no doubt in my mind that Lou was what I'd just called him, nasty. Not to mention arrogant and all-round loathsome. As far as I was concerned, the thing he said about throwing Hugette to the wolves tipped the scales forever against him. Sure, he was a crime kingpin, which was enough by itself to rank him high on the negative scale, but crime kingpins were part of everyday business if you were a criminal lawyer. What counted for more, Lou had no decency. I could feel myself working up a high boil in my feelings about Lou. The guy was a number one creep.

In front of me, as I walked through the driveway, were seven cars still left from the party. There was the black Navigator and Elizabeth's sporty little number. The rest must have belonged to Lou's muscle guys. But one of the cars looked out of place. It had no flash about it. It was a humble sort of vehicle, an innocuous-looking grey Volvo station wagon. This, no question, was Spike's delivery car for the horse.

I stopped and inspected the Volvo, front and back, both sides. Such a plain car, a family car, a station wagon, for Pete's sake. Perfect for people who liked anonymity in their mode of transportation. After a minute or two, I'd seen enough. I walked the long block to my own car and drove away.

At home, I made a martini and sat with it in the dining room, looking out at the backyard and all its fresh earth. When I finished the drink, I mixed another and took it into my little first-floor office. I dialed Dan Tommasino's home number. Dan was the head of the Toronto drug squad, not a bad guy for a cop.

He sounded surprised I was calling him. I couldn't blame him.

"You got the Three Amigos in your sights?" I said.

"Have had for a couple of years," he said. "Not that it's done us any good."

"That's about to change," I said. "Got something to write on?"

Dan said he did, and I started. "Eleven o'clock tonight, a grey Volvo station wagon's going to deliver two kilos of heroin to Three Amigos. Car's got Ontario plates, number NAD460. The horse is under the matting in the back. Guy at the wheel, he'll be alone in the vehicle, is one Percy Colombo, better known to his pals as Spike."

There was a pause at Dan's end, a thoughtful pause if one could characterize a sound over the phone.

"Colombo is one of Lou Janetta's people," Dan said. "But I bet you knew that already. You probably realize we haven't touched Janetta since I don't know when. Probably never. Now you're handing us not just the Three Amigos but a small wedge into the Janetta mob. They may not be as untouchable as they were now that you've made this phone call."

"And you're wondering how come I phoned," I said.

"You're supposed to defend low-lifes like Janetta."

"This time, a one-time-only deal," I said, "it's personal."

"You want to expand on that?" Dan said. "Give me a little more substance?"

"That's enough for tonight, Dan."

Dan waited a few seconds, maybe hoping I'd offer him extra stuff, but when I added nothing, he said, "Okay, thanks, Crang. I gotta get my guys rolling."

Dan hung up.

I took my martini into the kitchen and made a tuna salad sandwich. I ate and drank in the living room in front of the television set. I punched the remote looking for something to take my mind off the mess I'd left on the Bridle Path. I found it, baseball on Peachtree TV, Atlanta at home to the Mets. The announcers were the part I loved about Braves home games. They were good old boys, baseball lifers. They called the Braves players by their first names. Heyward was Jason, Freeman was Freddie. The broadcast was companionable and relaxing. The play-by-play guys were everybody's friends. Everybody in Atlanta anyway. I wondered if they knew the lady on the phones at *Ceramics Monthly*. I wouldn't have been surprised.

39

The phone woke me at seven-thirty next morning. I thought, groggily, it was Annie. I would be picking her up at the airport later in the morning. It wasn't Annie. It was my pal Fox.

"Are all crime kingpins as changeable as Lou Janetta?" Fox said. "Laid-back one time I meet the guy, hot-blooded the next."

"He showed up at your place?"

"Last night," Fox said. "With his wife. Beautiful as advertised."

"What about Hugette Jennings?"

"She was along too," Fox said. "I like Hugette's chances. Crown'll be stupid not to accept a manslaughter plea."

"Wally can help you with that."

"Just got off the phone to him."

"Slick work."

"Thanks for the referral," Fox said. "And, get this, the Hugette thing isn't all. Janetta was back to me at six this morning. Dan Tommasino busted one of Janetta's guys delivering horse at the Three Amigos."

"Lou was more hot and bothered this morning?" I said.

"That's what I mean about changeable," Fox said. "Last night, he's Mr. Cool. This morning, he's screaming on the phone. Literally screaming. Way up there in the sound register. Didn't seem like the same guy as a few hours earlier."

"Nothing you can do for him or his guy at the Three Amigos until later today."

"Bail court for Janetta's guy," Fox said. "I'll take it from there."

"Going to be busy times around your office."

"Listen," Fox said, "about the lunch we were discussing the other day? At Splendido?"

"Still got it on my schedule."

"Everything's the same," Fox said, "except now I'm paying."

I thanked Fox and hung up.

Three hours later, I was on the walkway outside the Billy Bishop Airport's exit doors. It was raining, and Annie and I were hugging. We hugged for a very long time.

"We going after the Guinness World Record in the hugging category?" Annie said into my ear.

"Passed that five minutes ago," I said. "The rest has been padding."

"I'd say we could double the record, except I'm worried about this rain on my new suitcase. It's so cheap I think it's made of cardboard."

Annie had left on her trip to New York with two suitcases, but was returning with three. The new addition may have been made of cardboard, but when I picked it up, it felt like I was lugging a load of bricks. Thank god, my left leg seemed to have got on the mend overnight.

"Paper in the bag is what weighs so much," Annie said. "Isn't that old-fashioned? Paper? Most of the archival stuff about Edward Everett Horton is so ancient it still hasn't reached digital. It was a case of making Canon copies or nothing."

"In this case, I take it 'nothing' wasn't an option."

"Sweetie, the stuff in here is pure gold. Lot of personal things about Horton's gayness. What effect it had on his work and career. This man was a true pioneer in the queer world. I'm loving the guy."

I drove home and served Annie a cold lunch from dishes I'd bought at Summerhill, the world's most expensive grocery store. But worth every penny. Summerhill wasn't in the Annex. It was in Rosedale, Toronto's toniest neighbourhood. No contest between it and the Annex.

We ate, and Annie asked me how the investigation of Grace Nguyen's murder was proceeding. I said a suspect ought to be announced very soon. That seemed to satisfy her for the time being. But before long, I'd tell her the whole story. I was waiting for a signal. From whom or what, I wasn't sure.

I poured us each a cup of coffee, Sumatra blend. And the doorbell rang. Annie answered it.

She came back into the dining room, saying, "A gentleman to see you, sweetie."

A tall, lean man was right behind Annie. He was my old pal, Mr. Lachrymose. Except he was smiling. Steve Lazslo had come calling.

I introduced Steve to Annie. "Grace Nguyen's widower," I explained.

Steve was carrying a large suitcase with a lot of straps. It looked like something from an Eric Ambler novel, a bag that had made many journeys through the Balkans. Steve hoisted it on to the dining room table.

I felt pretty sure I knew what was inside, but I wanted to delay the opening of the bag just to stretch out the pleasure. I offered Steve a cup of coffee. He accepted, no milk or sugar. I filled Steve's order, and the three of us sat around the table, me trying not to stare at the suitcase.

"I do duty Grace ask me," Steve said. "Here now at your house for duty."

"That's nice, Steve," I said.

Annie gave me a look that asked, what gives anyway?

"Something in the suitcase, Steve?" I said.

"Grace say I pay fee if bad things happen her."

"The fee you're talking about is for my legal services?" I said.

Steve nodded his head with vigour. "The bad things she talk about have happen her. So I am here."

"Police told you how their investigation is proceeding? Into Grace's killing?"

Annie was trying to keep the smile off her face. She had realized what was in the suitcase, but she didn't want to start celebrating while the conversation was still on the subject of Grace's death. Celebration wouldn't be in good taste.

"I know nothing from investigation," Steve said. "Maybe police know nothing too. Me, okay, not my job to know. Police, not okay, their job is solve Grace's murder."

"Succinctly put, Steve," I said.

"Sink?"

"Just means clear, Steve. Very clear. Good English."

Steve did another of his world-class Hungarian shrugs.

"Now I pay fee," Steve said.

His hands flew over the suitcase, unbuckling its straps speedily and expertly. The suitcase fell open. All of us stared at the contents. Steve's expression made him look like a Slavic Santa Claus. Minus the beard but with the same jolly expansiveness as a real Santy.

Annie and I just stared. Her jaw had dropped. I'd kept mine in its normal position. Neither of us had ever before seen seventy-five thousand dollars in cash all in one place, but there seemed no doubt the bag must be holding that much in bills. Bills of many denominations. I could see hundreds and fifties and twenties, bundles in rows and rows, each bundle held by an elastic band. It must have taken someone hours to put all the bills together.

"Steve," I said, "I'm grateful."

"Not me," Steve said. "Grace, you should be thanking her."

Steve and I shook hands, and not long afterwards, he left. He said I could return the suitcase when I'd unloaded its contents.

"There must be a moral to this," Annie said. "Getting a fee after the client's been killed."

"'Virtue is rewarded'?"

"Something better than that, honeybun," Annie said. "Maybe something along the lines of 'Honest work deserves an honest reward.'"

"Not quite honest, considering where the seventy-five grand may have originated."

"Let's forget about the moralizing."

I thought that might be the moment to fill in Annie on the parts she didn't know about in the saga of Grace, the Janettas, Rocky, the Levin, poor Hugette, Spike and the Three Amigos. But I let the moment pass.

Annie went looking around the house for all the equipment she might need when the garden goddess and her crew arrived at our place next day. I drank another cup of coffee and listened to the sounds of Annie opening and closing doors and drawers.

A few minutes later, she arrived back in the dining room carrying her new secateurs.

"Look at this," she said, holding the lethal-looking blades out to me. "Those brown spots. You know what they look like?"

"Dried blood," I said.

"That's what I think too," Annie said. "How do you think blood would get on there?"

The moment for telling Annie the whole story had just announced its arrival. For the next half hour, I described in detail everything that had gone on. Annie listened with total concentration, and when I finished, she said there were only two parts that bothered her. One bothered her a lot, the other not too much. The lesser of the two was the matter of Elizabeth avoiding punishment.

"Yesterday," I said, "in the Janetta library, I was concentrating on helping the Levin keep its *Company of Fools* and its good name and on getting Hugette the best deal possible on the killing.

Hugette deserved it, and if Elizabeth got a free ride in the process, that was just going to be too bad. There was nothing I could do about it."

Annie seemed to accept my explanation as part of doing business, especially since I'd told her about my phone call to Dan Tommasino and the possibility that loathsome Lou Janetta now had a chink in his armour. But the thing that bothered Annie a lot was me forgetting to lock the back door on the night Rocky tried to throttle me. I said I'd remember about the lock next time.

"What next time?" Annie said.

I shrugged, not as good as a Hungarian shrug but not bad.

"One never knows," I said.